PRAISE FOR MA

"In *Mariah Is Missing*, mystery writer David Henry Nelson has crafted a classical whodunit set in the horse country of Montana in the 1970s. Nelson paints a loving tableau of the times and the people drawn to Montana's cold winters. Fans of Anne Hillerman, J.A. Jance and Nevada Barr will enjoy his cleanly paced mystery."
— Dana Haynes, author of *Sirocco* and eight other novels; managing editor of the *Portland Tribune*

"*Mariah Is Missing* is a compelling story made real by Senator David Henry Nelson, who I served with in the Oregon Legislature and who was a prosecuting attorney in Montana during the 1970s. This novel is an absolute page turner. I read it start to finish in one day."
— Vern Duncan, PhD, retired Oregon Superintendent of Public Instruction

"When Mariah, a beautiful young teacher with a heart of gold, goes missing, we're dying to know who did it. Amid the investigation we become engrossed in the other central characters, particularly the opinionated Ana and her two love interests — Rib, a married, ruggedly handsome, deep-thinking veterinarian, and Jack, a hotheaded rancher whom Ana slowly tames. Which man will she eventually choose? And of course, who killed Mariah? The author keeps us absorbed throughout."
— David Aretha, award-winning author and editor

"It's hard to believe *Mariah Is Missing* is David Henry Nelson's first novel! From the prologue through the initial chapters describing the mystery surrounding Mariah's disappearance, this is one of those books that's hard to put down without reading to the very end. Character and scenery development made me 'know' and 'feel' the people and setting in Collins County, Montana.

As subsequent chapters unfold, the suspense dramatically builds. The ending chapters are both frightening and satisfying, leaving me with a desire to return to the earlier chapters to see if I could have figured out sooner the solution to Mariah's fate. An excellent read! I hope to see the movie version someday."
— Dixie Lund, PhD, two-time interim president of Eastern Oregon University

"This story takes the reader to a small town in beautiful North Central Montana, a rural area where no major crime ever happens. Then a young school teacher disappears. Was a crime committed? As the story continues, the reader wonders which one of these characters is capable of committing a crime. The suspense continues until the end, when the story takes a surprising turn. *Mariah Is Missing* makes for great weekend reading. It has suspense, interesting characters, and a unique story. I truly enjoyed reading this novel by David Henry Nelson."
— Abel Mendoza, PhD, former industrial chemist and inventor with 28 U.S. patents

"The slice-of-life mystery kept me turning pages and constantly second-guessing every action. It had characters that were relatable and a setting that one could resonate with...I was able to immerse myself completely into the storyline..."
— Melody Chaves, Eastern Oregon University student

"My work with Dave goes back decades, first as colleagues in the senate, most recently as governor and in his service on the Eastern Oregon University Board of Trustees. He is an exemplary leader — professional, fair, balanced, open to new ideas. Dave's dedication to Eastern Oregon, the university and the region, is admirable and a model of diplomatic leadership that I hope others follow."
— Governor Kate Brown, Oregon

MARIAH IS MISSING

A NOVEL

MARIAH IS MISSING

A NOVEL

DAVID HENRY NELSON

Published by Cenatorial Publishing

ISBN (paperback): 978-1-7377174-0-9
ISBN (ebook): 978-1-7377174-1-6

Edited by David Arethra
Book design by Christy Day, Constellation Book Services

Printed in the United States of America

To Alice and the children, Eric, Steve, Cameron, and Ronda, who have supported me in this complex process of creating a story.

PROLOGUE

FRIDAY, JANUARY 9, 1976

Mariah Morgan surveyed her kingdom—if you could call a converted two-acre patch of North Central Montana a kingdom. She didn't own the land; Jack Moser did, but Mariah controlled the acreage and the ten students who attended Marias River Country School.

Her domain was a teacherage, that uniquely American adaption of education for rural learning, but to Mariah, the rectangular building with its one set of concrete steps leading to the classroom and the other set to her living quarters represented the promised land.

Mariah watched from the bottom of the concrete steps in front of her classroom as the pickups driven by her students' parents carried them away as they left the graveled parking lot. She had dismissed her students early Friday afternoon, excited by the thought of the coming weekend. Her blue eyes sparkled and her long brown hair blew in the steady north wind. She lifted her arms to the sky, saying a short prayer, thanking God. Her right ring finger shone with her silver ring gleaming in the sunlight.

At twenty-four years of age, Mariah realized she was at a crossroads in her life. She had been saved by God at a young age, thanks to her mother's faith, and while she worried about her father's commitment to God, her optimism in the power of her faith was reassuring. However, life had become more complicated since last September.

She had found love with a man, an older man, that tangled her relationship with God.

She turned back into the classroom, skipping up the steps, locking the door behind her, then entered her living quarters through the inner connecting door.

Mariah, intent on spending time with Tucker, her palomino horse, hurried to her bedroom to change from her teaching dress to her riding clothes. She donned jeans, boots, a blue work shirt, a heavy coat, fur-lined gloves, and a ski stocking cap.

She glanced into a wall mirror as she changed clothes, comfortable with the snugness of the clothing surrounding her 120-pound body, thinking she wasn't exactly a beauty queen, but men were attracted to her. With one last glance at the image in the mirror, she smiled at herself and left to attend to Tucker.

As Mariah descended her residence steps, Jack Moser drove up in his two-toned tan and white Chevy pickup.

Mariah folded her arms in front of her at the sight of this handsome man ten years older than her. If looks were all that mattered to her, she thought, Fat Jack Moser, as he was called, could have been a pick for any woman. He wasn't fat even though that was his nickname, but rather six feet tall, trim, and muscular with a mustache under his roman nose. She tried but couldn't remember the color of his eyes because they were hidden behind classic, green-tinted aviator sunglasses, or for that matter his hair, for it was always covered with a baseball-style cap with an eagle insignia.

"How's the New Year?" he asked, rolling down his window, exhaling a misty cloud of breath in the cold air.

"Rushed," said Mariah. "I'm going to ride Tucker this afternoon. What's on your mind?"

"Do you need help?" Jack rested his left arm on the open window.

"No, I can take care of him myself. What do you want?"

Jack shifted in his seat, and couldn't meet Mariah's stare.

"Would you go to dinner with me tonight? The Two Medicine has a Friday night special."

Mariah lowered her head and took a deep breath before answering.

"No. I have plans, but thank you for asking." Mariah kept her gaze directly on Jack and touched his arm.

"I've got to keep trying," offered Jack, his face turning red. "One day, you'll find time for me."

"I'm sorry, but I've got to take care of my horse, and I have plans tonight." Mariah stood her ground, being awkward in the moment. "I don't mean to hurry you off."

"Yes, you do," spat a now angry Jack. "I expected you to accept."

Silence hung heavy between them, neither willing to be the first to speak. Mariah's knees began to weaken. She hated being in this position.

Finally, Jack put his pickup in reverse, changed gears, and then roared out of the gravel parking lot.

Mariah sighed, crossing the gravel road to where Tucker was sheltered in his stall in the gambrel-roofed barn with a single cupola perched on top like a hunting hawk. Still shaking from the encounter with Jack, Mariah walked rapidly, thinking Jack didn't understand the word no. *What is wrong with men?* she thought. They all thought they were a gift to a woman.

She passed the ancient trailer house where Swede Davidson lived, but she saw no sign of him and entered the barn. Mariah conversed with Tucker as she saddled him for a ride in the frozen wheat fields that lay east of the barn.

"I've got a date tonight. Are you jealous?"

Tucker pawed the ground, gave a slight jump off his back hooves, then turned his head toward Mariah with deep, languid, pooled brown eyes.

"Are you laughing at me or giving me the go-ahead?"

Tucker whinnied and swished his majestic white tail.

"Admit you are jealous. You should be because I am in love, and guess who is coming tonight?"

Receiving no answer from the horse, Mariah considered her actions from last week.

She had sent Rib Torgerson a note asking him to meet her as he had done so many times since last September. Rib had not answered, but he had faithfully appeared every Friday since that magic night. Mariah felt sure he would come to her.

An inner warmth ran through her body as she thought about their time together; however, a frown flicked across her face as she planned to put her cards on the table without knowing how he would respond.

After finishing her ride, Mariah retired to her living area, showered, combed through her hair, and applied light makeup with a swish of perfume. She dressed in a dark-purple, long-sleeved sweater, covering a paisley-patterned shirt with a button-up front. She paired her outfit with black slacks and red tennis shoes.

Mariah tossed a Caesar salad for dinner and brewed a cup of hot chocolate. After cleaning her plate in the sink, she returned to the kitchen table, clearing space to check her students' homework from today's class assignments, while awaiting Rib's arrival.

Seven o'clock turned to eight. She anxiously arose from her chair and went to the refrigerator.

The door knock startled her as she had not heard Rib's pickup enter the gravel parking lot.

Mariah reached for the doorknob.

"Rib, is that you?"

PART ONE
THE CALL

CHAPTER 1

SATURDAY, JANUARY 10, 1976

Swede Davidson had been drinking since the day before New Year's, mostly from his stash of homemade dandelion wine. Swede did not seek alcohol every day, but two-week bouts of nonstop boozing were common. When he had to work, he could stay dry; when he didn't work, he drank.

It hadn't always been that way as Swede had taken advantage of the GI Bill after his World World II service, graduating from Eastern Washington College of Education in Cheney, Washington. He planned to be a teacher; however, his marriage to the daughter of the owner of an insurance agency in Spokane put him on the path of a career selling insurance with an established clientele.

Success was his ruin. Money flowed as the area recovered from the war. He joined the Spokane Country Club, ate at the finest restaurants, and drove a sporty Cadillac Eldorado convertible. However, the demons from his war experience held him in their grasp. By the mid-1950s, he was divorced from his wife, his golf membership had been terminated, and his Cadillac gone. The ex-father-in law booted him from the agency and Swede disappeared into the eastern slopes of the Rocky Mountains, gainfully employed as a sheepherder near the town of Dupuyer, Montana. His alcohol-fueled binges had driven his choices, ending in a train wreck.

Today, at age fifty-six, he sported a bulbous nose and circles under his eyes. However, he didn't carry a large belly, and outsized hands and muscular arms with a set of broad shoulders showed he wasn't afraid of work. He had scars above both eyes and a jagged line down his left cheek suffered during a drunken brawl on First Avenue in Great Falls. He had grown tired of herding sheep and now lived in an ancient trailer house provided by his employer, Jack Moser, doing farm labor: driving machinery, herding cows, and irrigating wheat and barley.

Swede remembered a few things since New Year's Eve, but there were periods of blackness where he didn't have a clue of what he had done. The last sober moment he had was on the 31st of December, feeding cows and helping Jack Moser prepare for the coming calving season. After that, there were flashes he couldn't tell were real or just dreams.

What the hell, he thought. *It's Saturday night and time to go to Fort Collins and have a drink of fancy whiskey.* He was tired of his horse-piss dandelion wine.

* * *

Swede drove the twenty-five miles to Fort Collins by the backroads as dusk had fallen. Interstate 15 would have been quicker, but he figured the police would be on the paved roads and ignore the graveled ones. He lived northeast of the town, across a gravel road from the country school where Mariah Morgan lived and worked. He slowly maneuvered his old Ford pickup, taking wide turns at the many crossroads, his mind scrambling to remember what he had done during this spree. One image came to his mind was helping one of his coworkers jump-start a pickup. Was it Duke or Cobey? He couldn't be sure if that was a dream or for real.

He asked himself whether he had seen Mariah yesterday or for that matter today. He remembered thinking about going over to her house, asking if she wanted a little sip of his wine. He knew she would refuse, but he liked to be around her. She was young and smart and…well, you know. It wasn't a lack of courage that stopped him, nor decency, but rather the realization that his time had passed.

Had he waved at Mariah from his window inside the trailer on Friday afternoon as she walked to the barn? He thought he had, but couldn't remember if she waved back. He continued drinking the rest of that afternoon, passing out for a time. He remembered being wakened by a knock on his door and it had turned dark outside. But what had happened after that? He couldn't come up with anything. Swede turned his attention back to his driving and the thought of a drink at Busty's bar.

These graveled backroads would take him into the east side of Fort Collins and onto paved Front Street, where he had his pick of taverns. It took a little more time, but he had to make sure no cops caught sight of him and made him walk the line. A man had to stay out of trouble to drink and reach the magic point where the clicking sound goes off in his head. *Life is good*, he thought.

Saturday night was his time to do the town. In this part of Montana, wintertime dictated that you either ice-fished, skied, snowmobiled, drank, or chased your neighbor's wife on your days off, and Jack Moser had given him two weeks' vacation.

Today's wind blew him sidesaddle to Busty's Tavern. He parked in the alley, intent on using the back door.

As he entered, staggering to the right, he collided with a man coming out of the men's room. Swede fell on his left side, tried to get up, but fell back down.

"God damn you," he hollered at the bigger man who stood over him with a half smile, a half sneer, and clenched fists. "You did that on purpose."

"Watch your language, you old drunk," came the reply. "I should beat the shit out of you."

Swede tried to get up but was pushed down again by a strong hand.

He recognized the face above him belonging to Cobey Graham, who worked with him at the Moser ranch. Cobey had not changed from his work clothes and smelled of cattle, his muscled tattooed arms visible with his sleeves rolled up. He was a tall man with snarling eyes, smashed-in nose, and curling lips.

"Just like you to kick a man when he's down," thundered Swede. "I helped jump-start your pickup last night. Is this the thanks I get?"

At that moment, Lefty Basham, the bartender, stepped between them.

"That's it, fellows," he said. "Or I'll throw you both out." His deep bass voice boomed with authority. Lefty was shorter than Cobey with a larger belly, but fearlessly looked him in the eye. His black pants were held up by suspenders matched with a white shirt and black bow tie.

Swede looked up at the two men still resting on his left elbow. He knew Lefty meant what he said and Swede wanted his drink. Swede smiled at both of them and said,

"Just a little misunderstanding. If you would help me up, I'll behave."

Lefty looked at Cobey, waiting for a response. Cobey nodded his okay.

Lefty held his right hand out to help Swede up. "Tow the line, both of you. There are women in here, so find your manners!"

As Swede started for the bar, Cobey brushed his shoulder with his elbow. "Watch your step, old man."

Swede, thirsting for a drink, ignored him as Lefty stepped between them again, saying to Cobey, "You don't listen too well. One more word and you are gone."

Lefty and Cobey stared at each other as Swede staggered to his circular bar stool, demanding that Lefty pour him a drink. Lefty gave Cobey one last look. Cobey sneered back.

Lefty arrived behind the bar, grabbed a bottle of George Dickel Tennessee Whiskey, and poured Swede a straight shot.

"Drink that up and stay away from that guy. He's trouble."

"You can say that again," snorted Swede. "You should see him out at the ranch working cattle. If he gets a chance he will bullwhip them." Swede studied his drink. "Yeah, he kicks at the dogs when they bark at him. Cobey is downright mean."

Swede gulped down the whiskey in the shot glass in one quick swallow.

"I could take him in a fight. I know some things he doesn't, and even if he is younger, I could whip him."

"Whoa down a minute," said Lefty with both hands on the bar. "You promised me there would be no more trouble. So keep your word!"

Swede cast his eyes over his right shoulder to where Cobey sat with his wife. "I'll keep my word, but I'd like to kick that bald-headed bastard right where it hurts."

"I'd be careful there," suggested Lefty. "He's taller than you and outweighs you by twenty-five pounds. He's younger, and look at his arms with those tattoos. That boy has been in prison. I wouldn't blame you for wanting to wipe off his snot-eating grin, but not in here. Understood?"

"Pour me another one," demanded Swede as he turned his head to focus on the barroom. Through rheumy eyes, he saw several tables on the large, one-room floor. At one table he recognized his boss, Jack Moser, sitting with a woman he knew to be Jack's mother and another man he didn't know. Jack's mother owned the bar.

Sitting at the next table were Cobey and Duke, along with their wives, and another couple he didn't recognize. He worked with the two men at Jack's ranch, preferring his time with Duke, who had worked for the Mosers for many years. Under his breath, he cursed at Cobey.

The jukebox played country music. Two pool tables were busy, and the noise from the drinking crowd was growing louder. One table had an arm wrestling contest. Swede prided himself on his arm strength, and he thought maybe he could goad Cobey into a match. Swede weaved his way to the table where the arm wrestling winner determined the next challenger. He passed by Cobey's table.

"Are you man enough to take me on?" Swede dared. Cobey scoffed at Swede, tossing his head about, but he didn't respond, remembering Lefty's warning.

Swede won his first match and waited for Cobey to challenge, but Cobey didn't take the bait, ignoring Swede, preferring to play pool.

Swede decided to ask Cobey's wife to dance, but she refused. Swede then asked Cora, Duke's wife, but was turned down again. Swede finally asked Jack's mother at the next table to dance, and they stumbled around the dance floor. The woman was relieved when the song finished, leading Swede back to her table.

"I don't need any trouble in here," she said. "It's time for you to go home or find another bar."

Swede started to argue, but Jack stood up next to his mother. "She's right. It's time for you to leave."

But Swede didn't leave. Instead, he wandered over to a far table where other wives were sitting, asking for a dance, which made one of the husbands walk over and face him.

"Is there a problem here?"

Swede sized up the man in front of him, deciding whether to take him on.

Lefty, watching the developing conflict, stepped out from behind the bar between the two men. "No sense in ruining a party," said Lefty. "Come on back to the bar, Swede, and I'll buy you one last drink." Lefty took Swede by the arm and led him back to the bar.

"Pour me that round you promised," Swede slurred.

Swede slid onto his stool, nearly sliding over it, feeling like a bucked-off bronc rider. But he regained control by grabbing the side rail of the bar.

With his head lowered between his arms until it was nearly on the bar, Swede shook it from side to side with exaggerated intensity. "I'm here to get drunker than seven hundred dollars. You damn well better serve me."

"There is no fool like an old fool, particularly if he has been drinking since New Year's Day," said Lefty as he grabbed a shot glass, pouring two fingers of cheap whiskey into the tumbler. "That's the end for you, old boy. You're past your seven hundred-dollar mark. Finish it and go home, and don't be asking any of those gals to dance on your way out."

After Lefty's sharp order, Swede raised his head, looking at the bartender through bloodshot eyes, making no motion to let on whether he understood. Swede lifted his hand and knocked over the glass of whiskey.

"You're out of here," snapped Lefty, grabbing for a bar towel.

Swede drifted in dreamy thought, wondering how he had ended up at Busty's with the whole damn bar ready to place a two-by-four alongside his head.

"God, help me," he murmured.

Swede stumbled off the stool and wobbled to a stop at the men's room on his way to the back door of the bar. Lefty had kicked him out. He had made the men in the bar angry by wanting to dance with their wives, and Swede couldn't remember what else he had done.

"I am free," he said to the back door as he pushed his way into the night.

The cold January air slapped him in the face as he walked toward his Ford pickup. He stumbled but righted himself in the brisk air of the winter night, sensing a presence behind him.

Then he went dark as an object smacked the right side of his head. He didn't feel the next blow to his left temple.

CHAPTER 2

MONDAY, JANUARY 12, 1976

Marias River Country School stood on the southwest corner where two graveled county roads intersected, forming a tee. If you looked to the north or east or south, you could see endless prairies and sky. However, if you looked to the west, the majestic Rocky Mountains, seventy miles away, grounded you. Mariah Morgan was the resident schoolteacher.

A closer view revealed a farmstead on the southeast corner of the intersection directly across from the school. Looking to the west with the Rockies in the background, only one farmhouse a mile down the road was visible, and Interstate 15 lay beyond.

The school appeared out of place amid the flat farmland, with white paint, a mesh wire fence boundary on all sides, and a graveled parking lot east of the building. Six swings, a long slide, and a merry-go-round were located to the south of the school, and a single basketball hoop rose above the gravel road entrance. A five hundred-gallon, silver-painted diesel fuel tank sat on a box frame next to the outer west wall where a red-bricked chimney funneled a furnace's exhaust to the sky. There were no trees.

The entrances to the schoolroom and Mariah's residence lay on the south side of the building. Two large windows had been set into the south-facing wall, one for the classroom and one for the living quarters. The east and west sides of the building had no windows, but the north side sported four smaller windows equally divided between the schoolroom and the residence. The two spaces measured equal in size and were connected with an inner door.

On that Monday morning of January 12, 1976, six dirt caked pickups and a sole Chevy sedan were scattered across the graveled parking lot. Children, bundled up against the cold wind, ran through the schoolyard, and parents, all women, were gathered in front of the schoolroom door, anxiously waiting for Mariah Morgan to open the locks to begin the school day.

That morning, Mariah had not opened the schoolroom nor made an appearance. The door to her living space was unlocked and slightly ajar. Laurel Simmons, one of the mothers, had gone into the residence side of the building to call the sheriff's office from a brown rotary telephone hanging on the wall near the kitchen table.

Deputy sheriff Jerry Severtson answered the call, duly noting the time as seventeen minutes past eight o'clock on Monday, January 12, 1976, and the caller's name.

"Something is terribly wrong. We need help," cried Laurel. "Our schoolteacher has not opened her classroom, and children and parents are freezing in the cold, not knowing what to do. Our teacher is never late, and besides, her car is still parked in the parking lot. Can you do something?"

"First, tell me where you are calling from," requested Deputy Severtson. "Are you reporting a missing person, or is someone hurt?"

"No one is hurt," stammered Laurel. "But our schoolteacher is not here. Her car is, and the windshield is frosted over; I told you that, haven't I?" Without waiting for an answer, Laurel continued, "Mariah is never late, and the door to her residence is slightly opened."

"Where are you calling from? I can't help you if I don't know your location," asked the deputy.

"I'm sorry. I'm calling from the Marias River School, north of town," said Laurel. "I know something is wrong, but I don't know what to do. Can you send someone to help us?"

"Yes, ma'am, someone will be out as soon as possible. It'll be a little bit of time because you are so far out of town, but someone will come out to check things over. The sheriff is in his office, and either he will come out or I will. Stay where you are and get those kids to a warm place. Do you know the school's phone number?"

After hanging up, Deputy Severtson walked into the open door of the sheriff's inner office. "Laurel Simmons from up north called in a missing person. The schoolteacher at Marias River didn't show up for work today."

Sheriff Wendall Wagner looked up from his chair. "Christ, what a weekend. First a fatality on the interstate and Swede Davidson getting beat up behind Busty's and now a missing schoolteacher. What's happening to us?" He slammed both open hands on the desk.

The sheriff, hoisting himself from his chair, pulled his brown uniform pants above his protruding waistline. His bushy eyebrows knitted together in disgust. "It's this marijuana trade we have in the county that is causing us all this trouble. We've got to clean it up."

"It's the new year," ventured the deputy. "My horoscope last week told me to be on the lookout for strange happenings." Deputy Severtson stood in stark contrast to his sheriff. They both wore their brown uniforms with insignia of the sheriff's office on their left shoulder. Jerry was five inches taller at six-foot-three and trim through the belly. Wagner seemed to wear a perpetual scowl while Jerry always looked like he was sharing an inside joke only to himself.

"That's nonsense," scoffed the sheriff, looking up at his deputy. "I believe in facts. Did the lady sound serious?"

The deputy nodded. "Demanding is more like it. It could be serious. Do you want me to check it out?"

The sheriff extended his arms, cracking his knuckles with his fingers interlaced.

"It's not that I don't trust you, but this might be important. Both of us should go."

Jerry muttered something incomprehensible.

"What did you say?" demanded Wagner.

"Nothing," grinned Jerry. "I think that's a great idea."

* * *

Deputy Severtson drove while the sheriff sat in the passenger seat, reading through reports on Swede's attack.

"Not much in the way of evidence. Swede was hit on his right and left temples with a hard object, but we don't know what. The bartender indicated Swede had come into the bar already tanked up, had a dispute with some guy he worked with at Moser's. Lefty breaks it up with a warning. Swede caused trouble with some of the bar folks, including guys he works with, and Lefty gives him the heave-ho. Swede leaves and is found outside the back door knocked out cold for how long no one knows. He is lucky he didn't freeze to death in this weather."

"Swede's alive," said the deputy. "But he is in a coma with skull fractures. He might not make it. The ambulance took him to Columbus Hospital in Great Falls. Evidently, there is a Doctor Powers there who is good at treating head injuries. Do you want me to go down there to check on him?"

"No, wait until we get word that he can talk. Keep checking in on the people in the bar. Someone might remember something that can help us. Talk with Moser's farmhands and see what they know. Swede has a criminal mind." The sheriff paused. "He might be selling drugs."

Deputy Severtson thought the sheriff put the entire human race into the "criminal mind" category, but he didn't express that opinion.

Instead, he asked the sheriff, "What do you think we will find out here at the school?"

"I'm coming around to the idea that something bad happened. From what you told me, this schoolteacher didn't show up in class this morning.

The door to her house had been left open, her car with frost on its windshield was parked outside, and concerned parents were on the premises. It doesn't sound natural to me."

"The teacher is a young gal," chimed in the deputy. "Maybe she got tired of this godforsaken county and took off with her boyfriend. She will show up when she is good and ready."

"We can't take that chance," said the sheriff. "There is a lot of drug dealing going on in this county with all the Air Force guys checking on their missile sites. Those fly-boys come from all over the country, stationed at the airbase in Great Falls, and who knows what they do driving their fancy blue Air Force trucks."

Again, Deputy Severtson held his tongue. He thought the sheriff came up with some weird theories without much proof, but then again, if everybody truly does have criminal intent... The deputy didn't complete his thought as the sheriff broke in.

"Could be a lot of reasons why she didn't show up for work. You might be right that she took off with a boyfriend, or she will show up, but we need to check into the possible drug connection."

Both men drifted off into silence as their vehicle turned off Interstate 15 onto the gravel roads intersecting the farm country that led to the schoolhouse. They would go east two miles, then north two miles. Both were familiar with the location.

Their vehicle climbed a slight hill before descending toward the school.

The sheriff cursed. "Damn those people. Don't they know we have a possible crime scene here?" Wagner shook his head. "Then they'll blame me if something doesn't go right. People around here think because I didn't go to college I don't have a brain."

Jerry held his tongue, looking at the schoolhouse and the milling parents and children.

Several children played in the skiffs of snow, chasing each other in front of the schoolhouse proper; six adults were standing in front of the building's residence door. Four of the pickups in the parking lot had their motors running, exhaust steaming out of their tailpipes.

"Those people are ruining any chance for us finding any evidence if this a crime scene," said the sheriff as he looked over at the deputy. "You should have told them to leave the area."

"I told them to stay put in their vehicles," said the deputy. "I couldn't control them from Fort Collins. And we don't even know what has happened, so go easy until we know the facts."

"Damn it. Wouldn't you think people have a lick of common sense? Get all these people's names and phone numbers," ordered the sheriff as they hopped out of the vehicle.

Jesus, thought the deputy. *I know how to do my job.*

As they approached the parents, the whinny of a horse floated from Swede's place across the road.

The sheriff acknowledged the parents with a nod and then asked, "Can someone tell me what is happening here?"

"Our schoolteacher is missing," answered Laurel Simmons as a cloud of condensation burst from her lips. She was dressed in a red and black checkered Mackinaw insulated coat with a black neck gator and red headband covering her long black hair. She wore blue jeans tucked into rubber galoshes, looking every bit like the working farmwife she was. She stamped her feet and moved her arms in front of her, warding off the cold as she answered the sheriff.

"I usually drop my kids off at eight, and the door to the school is opened, but this morning, Mariah didn't appear. My kids jumped out and started playing with other kids outside in the snow. I went over to Dawn's car to see what had happened. She didn't know anything more than me, so we decided to wait."

"Go on," urged the sheriff.

"Mariah always has the school open at eight. Finally, I decided to try her home door. It had been left partially opened. I knocked and yelled out Mariah's name, but no one answered. I decided to go in and call your office. Did I do something wrong?"

"No, you did everything right. Nothing to worry about, but I'm going to ask all of you to give your names and phone numbers to deputy Severtson here. I know all of you, but if this missing person report turns into something serious, you'll have to be contacted again."

The sheriff opened his notebook with pen in hand. "Tell me what you know about the teacher. Does she have family close by, is she married, and who could we contact to locate her? Those sorts of things."

"She is not married," offered Laurel. "Her parents live over by Flathead Lake, but she has an uncle, Donald Morgan, living south of Fort Collins. I don't know of anyone else. Oh, she has a lot of friends in the Episcopal Church in town. Maybe they would know where she is."

"Does she have any boyfriends?" asked the sheriff.

Laurel hesitated. "I shouldn't say if she does or doesn't. I don't know of any steady boyfriends, but I saw Jack Moser's pickup here last week. I think on Friday, but I'm not sure. I'm not into gossip, but I've heard Jack has a crush on Mariah."

"You said last Friday?" He turned to Deputy Severtson. "Did you get that down in writing?"

The deputy rolled his eyes, but the sheriff didn't notice as he turned back to Laurel.

"Any other suspicious activity around here? I know Swede Davidson lives across the road. Would he be involved with Mariah?"

Again, the sound of a horse reached their ears.

"Mariah kept her horse over at the barn next door," said Laurel. "I heard Swede had been taken to Great Falls after he got beat up. Is that true?"

"Yeah, Swede is in a coma," replied the sheriff. "You didn't answer my question."

"I don't know," admitted Laurel.

"How about Jack Moser and Mariah?"

"All I know is Jack let Mariah keep her horse in that barn trying to cozy up to her. But that's only a rumor."

"Anything else?" asked the sheriff.

Laurel shifted her feet before answering.

"I've seen the vet's truck over there many times because the horse had been sick. It seemed like every time I drove by, I saw it. I remember that fancy toolbox."

"Do you remember the name of the vet?"

"I think it was Rib Torgerson's pickup. He's been at our place several times." Laurel looked at the sky for an answer. "Yes, I know it was his."

"I'll check him out, and I'll talk to her uncle and get some phone numbers. She might have gone back to her parents for some reason. Now, why don't you folks go home? School is canceled until we can find this woman. My deputy and I need to check the area. I'll take it from here and call you when we know something."

He turned to the deputy, asking, "You got the phone numbers, didn't you?" Deputy Severtson kept his eyes down on the notebook, indicating that he had done his job with a nod, wondering why the sheriff asked these dumb questions.

The sound of a horse rang in their ears again.

As the parents and their children departed, Deputy Severtson wheeled around, starting for the barn across the road. "I'll check on that horse. If the schoolteacher hasn't been around to care for it and Swede is in the hospital, it might need feed and water. I can't stand to see an animal suffer."

The sheriff waved him off. "Go ahead, and keep your eyes out for anything suspicious, something out of the ordinary. I'll check the inside of the house." Wagner watched his deputy walk toward the barn across the road, shaking his head, thinking to himself. *I should check out the horse myself.* He tried to crack his knuckles through his leather gloves, then wiped his nose on their brown leather backing, first with his right hand then with his left.

* * *

Sheriff Wagner climbed the four concrete steps to the entrance of Mariah's living quarters.

The curtained windows of the door swayed slightly as he pushed the unlocked door wide open. Standing outside, he made a mental note of what he saw. He didn't want to contaminate the scene like those parents he had just talked to.

Cramped area, thought the sheriff. He walked lightly into the kitchen, where the refrigerator and the electric stove were pushed together on his immediate right. The kitchen sink and cabinets were on his left, leaving a narrow pathway to the teacherage's tiny living room.

The sheriff gingerly stepped over a throw rug pushed against the refrigerator. On the wall to his right hung a rotary phone above more cabinets. The kitchen table, pressed against the cabinet, had an open textbook called *Your Country and Mine,* surrounded by paper sheets with correction marks on them and a red pencil. A half-full cup of a chocolate drink and car keys rested near the book.

A curtained window framed a traveling trunk covered by a throw rug; the living room wound to his left toward the classroom door. A television and stereo system sat on the chest, with speakers to its side on the linoleum floor. A watercolor painting of the Rockies, not yet hung, rested on the bare floor alongside a wastebasket, and a small couch offered seating, its pillows set off by a framed print of waterfalls directly above the furnishing.

The bedroom was next. The sheriff took note of the bed, one side of it pressed against a wall, leaving barely enough room to walk into the room. Pictures and birthday cards sat upon a mirrored dresser with two bottom swing doors and two pull-out drawers on each side. Two suitcases sat on the floor next to the dresser with clothes and a large sun hat perched atop them. The double-wide bed had been made up, but a white, quilted blanket lay all rumpled and twisted on top of the bed.

One red tennis shoe lay askew on the floor with the sole facing the bedside wall.

The sheriff glanced into the bathroom as he slowly made his way out of the living area, making a mental note to check that more thoroughly for any possible drug use. He left the building and walked to his car, where he reached for his two-way radio and called his office.

"Send out the investigative team right away—cameras, fingerprint kits, the whole works. You know the drill."

Deputy Severtson approached the police car. "That horse hadn't been fed for a while. I found the water trough nearly empty, but all in all, the animal is in good shape. What should we do with it?"

"There is more trouble here than an old horse. Looking through the house leads me to believe a crime has been committed. We have more than a missing person. I can just feel it."

"What is going on?" asked the deputy, throwing his head toward the building.

"Nothing good," answered the sheriff. "The front door was slightly open, a throw rug is pushed up against the refrigerator, and there is an open schoolbook with graded papers and a pencil sitting on the desk along with a cold half-full cup of chocolate and car keys. The bedroom has a tossed look to it with a single red tennis shoe by the bed."

The sheriff scratched his forehead. "I think that teacher had been grading papers when some interruption occurred. I don't like the fact that the door had been left ajar. Also, her car has a heavy frost on it. Let's go check to see if there are any fresh tire tracks in those skiffs of snow."

Upon inspecting the parking lot and the frozen vehicle, the sheriff shook his head. "Let's go check on the other side of the building." The sheriff turned to the west. "But I don't expect to find anything. Those damn people have ruined any tracks."

With the sheriff leading the way, he and the deputy walked past the south front of the building to the westside, where the heating oil tank rested on a wooden frame next to the red chimney.

Deputy Severtson squinted in a northerly direction, toward the wire mesh fence and the gravel road. "Does that look like a drag trail to you?"

The ground had patches of wheatgrass poking above the windblown snow. The sheriff bent low, studying the marks. "Damn right it does. It's faint, but you can see where the snow has been pushed away. And that fence has a bow to it where something heavy could have possibly been lifted over it." The sheriff studied the slight indentations in the snow and grass, rubbing his chin with his right hand. "A car could have been parked on the gravel road. Let's check it out."

Not wanting to disturb the fence in case the sheriff's theory worked out, the two men walked back past the front of the building through the parking lot, gaining access to the east-west gravel road. As they came to a spot directly north of the faint gouge in the schoolyard, both stopped at a nearly circular red pool staining the very edge of the gravel about a foot from the grassy borrow pit running parallel to the road.

"Looks like blood to me. It could be red hydraulic oil, but I don't think so." The sheriff got down on his knees, putting his face close to the circular mass to sniff it. "If it was oil, there would be a scent, but I don't smell much of anything. Fresh blood has a secular smell, but this stain is dried and soaked into the gravel. Go get an evidence bag out of the car, along with some plastic gloves and a digging tool. If you brought a camera, bring it too."

Deputy Severtson hurried to the police car and soon returned with the requested items, including the camera.

"Take a picture of that red spot before I dig it out," ordered the sheriff. "And keep a record for the chain of evidence. If this turns out to be blood, we have a crime on our hands."

Deputy Severston took several pictures of the circular red soil, after which the sheriff carefully dug out the center of the collection, along with bits of gravel. His digging revealed that the red material had soaked an inch or more down into the loose pebbles.

"Lots of something spilled here," he commented.

Deputy Severtson sealed the bag, labeling the time, day, and year, along with his signature.

Chain of evidence, he thought. *Things have to be done by the book, and I am good at doing my job*. A glint of metal caught his eye from the road about fifteen feet away from where he stood.

"I think we have something else," called out the deputy as he walked toward the shining object, finally bending down to inspect a small wristwatch with its latch torn. "I better get another evidence bag."

After adding Deputy John Johnson and Montana State Highway Patrolman Sam Loftus to the investigation, the rest of the afternoon saw them gathering clothes from the teacherage and taking more pictures of the inside of the building and the outside, including the roadway. During the afternoon, the sheriff directed deputy Severtson to take the evidence bag full of red-stained gravel to Great Falls to the forensics lab for testing.

The sheriff, satisfied, ordered the doors to be locked, intent on leaving for his office to locate telephone numbers for the schoolteacher's parents.

The sheriff stood by the Montana highway patrolman. "I thought we might find this woman had gone home to Mommy and Daddy, but with the watch on the road and possible blood nearby, it's worse than a missing person." The sheriff nodded his head with assured movement. "I'm usually right about a crime being committed."

The patrolman nodded. "It doesn't look good. Can we hope for a better outcome?"

The sheriff looked at him with a settled gaze. "Hope is not a strategy."

CHAPTER 3

SATURDAY, AUGUST 30, 1975: LABOR DAY WEEKEND

During the Labor Day weekend four months before Mariah Morgan disappeared, Ana McGuire and Rib Torgerson met at his mountain cabin seventy miles west of Fort Collins.

Half Dome Crag, sitting in the Two-Medicine area of the Northern Montana Rockies, towered before them as they rode together on that sunshine-filled day. Montana's Big Sky lived up to its promise, contrasting its crystal-blue hue with its endless mountains' majesty.

Ana sat tall in her saddle, the picture of womanhood at age forty-five. She was fit from running three or four miles through the streets of Fort Collins each day. She didn't care if people talked about her unladylike exercise, nor the fact that she been widowed ten years ago and never remarried. After all, she thought, she had been the duly elected Collins County attorney for the past three years with the distinction of being the only woman to hold that office in any of the fifty-six Montana counties. Her two children, Marion and Carter, were attending the University of Montana in Missoula and Montana State College in Bozeman.

Ana smiled to herself, comparing her two children with the background she shared with Rib. She had attending the Missoula school and Rib had gone to Bozeman. Her hazel brown eyes shined, matching the tawny brown hair tied in a ponytail, as she thought about the time she would spend with Rib this weekend. She had ridden horses most of her life, and her infectious smile had always attracted men.

Rib Torgerson looked like the cowboy in the Marlboro Man ad, except she had never seen him smoke. His light gray stetson curved above his ears, showing flecks of gray hair. The hat set off his blue denim work shirt framed by a leather vest. His eyes matched the color of his shirt. He wore a wide leather belt fastened with a buckle he had won bulldogging at a Great Falls rodeo. His leather chaps covered faded blue jeans that slipped over tan brown cowboy boots. Spurs dangled at the heel of his boots.

Ana called out to Rib , who rode ten feet in front of her.

"Every time you bring me here, I have the best of all worlds. Riding in these mountains gives me hope. Tell me again about their history."

Rib twisted in his saddle with a sly grin showing off his perfect teeth. "Are you tired of sitting in a law office all day, filing complaints against your neighbors who are only trying to make a living? Between you and the sheriff, the whole county will get locked up. How do you live with yourself, being the only female county attorney in the state, putting the clamps on folks?"

"I'm serious. I want to know everything about the Two Medicine and the Rockies," Ana replied, ignoring his question.

"Not possible," said Rib. "They are too big and have been here too long. We don't have the time to fully educate you, except to remind you that you need your wits to survive up here. There are grizzlies, mountain lions, and wolves waiting to eat you, and then there're eagles, hawks, and buzzards to clean your bones." Rib waited for a reaction.

"Oh, you can't scare me. I'm safe with a big hunk like you, except you hit the big five-zero this year. I can tell you aren't the man you used to be." Ana jabbed at him.

"You didn't complain last night," Rib said. "And your body is as supple as it was twenty-five years ago. I haven't lost my memory."

Ana giggled. "Has it been that long?" She smiled at the thought of her time with Rib. "I love it here. I love being with you. Can you handle it?"

"I can handle it as long as you can handle me being married to Connie," answered Rib. "Didn't you want to talk about these mountains?"

Ana stopped smiling at the mention of Connie.

"I want to talk about both the mountains and Connie, but let's save her for later." They continued to climb the trail, keeping the mountains in view. Ana broke the silence.

"Half Dome doesn't look like a mountain, but you claim it is."

"It's like a reef," explained Rib. "Millions of years ago, there existed an inland sea stretching from the Gulf of Mexico to the Arctic Ocean clear to the Appalachian Mountains. Then, not so many millions of years ago, tectonic plates collided and thrust up the rock through the water, creating these arcing flat-atop monuments we call the Rockies."

"You make it sound simple, but as jagged and twisted as these mountains are, it's hard to believe they were underwater. But if you say so, I believe it."

"You can see Chief Mountain," Rib said, pointing to the north. "It sits out from the main range like a watchdog, but it's nine thousand feet tall. It doesn't have a peak. It's like the Half Dome or like Ear Mountain." Rib turned and pointed to the anvil-shaped formation seventy-five miles south of their location. "A bigger formation exists back in the Bob Marshall Wildness over in that direction." Rib pointed southwest. "It's called the Chinese Wall and stretches forty miles or so north to south. It marks the Continental Divide, but only a mountain goat could climb it."

"You love these mountains, don't you?" observed Ana. "I can see why."

"The Blackfeet Tribe considers them sacred ground, particularly Chief Mountain and a couple of mountains around Two Medicine Lake named after some lovers. Lots of history in the Two Medicine. The Tribe has names for them, but white men came along and put their own brand on them."

"Do you work with the tribes or use any of their lands?" asked Ana.

"The Tribe has their own way of looking at the Two, which I agree with most of the time. They have been here a lot longer than us, and their belief in a Great Spirit as the creator of life rings true to me. I'm not a church-goer, but roaming around these mountains convinces me of a bigger hand at work."

Ana took in the wilderness, marveling at its size and beauty. Living in Montana had its strong points, even if the wind blew every day. She might feel tiny in this setting, but somehow, it gave her comfort, and she didn't mind the constant feel of air moving against her cheek.

"How did we get here?" Ana asked.

Rib turned in his saddle with a questioning look.

"I don't mean riding here, but why you and me?"

"We've had the conversation before," Rib reminded her. "My answers aren't going to change."

"Sometimes I want more than a weekend with you," said Ana. "I'm widowed. You're married to Connie. Yet, you and I are good together. Why can't it be forever?"

"I can't give more than what we have," Rib insisted. "If we were married, I doubt we would be here enjoying ourselves. Can you accept what we have for what it is?"

"You know I love every second of our time together," said Ana. "I want that feeling every day."

Rib grunted and spurred his horse up the trail. Ana followed.

"What do you say we ride over to Badger Creek and have that picnic lunch you packed?" Rib called back to Ana.

She had an urge to gallop freely, but the steep trail and overhanging pine boughs gave her pause. She told herself to get a grip on reality; Alison Nancy Anderson McGuire, nicknamed Ana, would never become Alison

Nancy Anderson McGuire Torgerson because Rib Torgerson, riding in front of her, had a wife named Connie.

Ana spurred her horse into an open meadow following Rib. Riding up next to Rib, she gently slapped her reins on his back.

"You remember we are not married," she reminded him. "You would think you had some magical hold on me, but forget it—you don't. I could ride right out of here now. Don't think you can order me around."

Rib cast a sideways glance at Ana, but he didn't say anything.

"You could ask me If I have a better idea...," ventured Ana.

"Your ideas lead to trouble," said Rib. "You are right. I have no hold on you. I would hate to see you ride off without me on such a gorgeous day. Tell me your idea? I am your humble servant."

"You are never anyone's humble servant. Let me look closely in your eyes so I can see what you are really thinking."

Rib bent over his saddle with his eyes wide open and his mouth spread in a playful grin.

Ana kissed him full on the lips, stretching in her saddle. "If you can think of a better idea than that, let me know as soon as possible."

Rib laughed. "You have the last word. I still think we should go to Badger Creek. How does that sound to you?"

"Passable," said Ana. "But this conversation is not over yet. I'm not kidding. You live only for the moment, and I'm thinking more and more about my future."

Ana waited for a response, but Rib remained quiet. Ana kept the pressure on. "What happened to us that glorious summer before you married Connie?"

Rib shrugged, not speaking.

"You should have married me so we could live happily ever after. We still could. How's that for an idea?"

"You are a handful, aren't you?" Rib shook his head. "You never give up on a subject, particularly when it comes to matrimony. Look, men and women expect happiness in a marriage, but what they get is a corral full of horse shit. If we had gotten married, you would be more unhappy than my ever-faithful Connie, who is wondering what I am doing on Labor Day away from her. She wanted to golf this weekend." Rib waved his hand in disgust.

Ana reined her horse in, falling back and putting distance between her and Rib. She barely heard Rib say, "Being here with you is better, but I'm not going to change."

"But we are so good together," Ana called to Rib's backside. "We talk about everything: my dead husband, your wife, my law practice, your ranch, the idiocy of dealing with my sheriff and county commissioners—you name it, we talk about it, even if we disagree. The thing I love about you is you listen to me. Most men don't do that."

"You've seen through me again," admitted Rib, twisting in his saddle. "I learned long ago, maybe from my mother, that you can catch more bees with honey than with vinegar. That's my secret weapon with unpredictable women like you."

Ana spurred her horse to catch up to Rib. "What keeps us coming back to each other?"

"Beats me," said Rib. "You're smart and damned attractive, and I'm vain. Not much reason to hang out together."

"Oh, you love me only for my brain," teased Ana. "You were checking in some unusual places last night, and I think you have less than noble ideas for this afternoon at Badger Creek. I'm right about that, aren't I?"

"Again, checkmate," agreed Rib. "You know me too well. It's a good thing we aren't married because my life would be a living hell." Rib winked at Ana.

"Damn you, Rib." Ana reined in her horse. "I'm not going an inch further unless you apologize to me right now." She winked back at him.

"My deepest desire is to make you happy," confessed Rib. "I'm sorry. Now can we move on to Badger Creek?"

* * *

That evening, on the bear rug in front of a roaring fire, Ana curled up in Rib's arms with a glass of red wine.

"You never answered the question of why you didn't marry me," Ana reminded him, breaking the embrace and pointing her index finger at Rib. "You never called. I only caught wind of your marriage to Connie fourth-hand from a so-called friend who had the satisfaction of seeing me cry really big tears. I'm still mad at you. Why do you keep calling, and why do I keep answering?"

"You accept me for what I am," said Rib. "My wife knows what I do. She might know about us, but nothing is ever said. You are right that we can talk about anything. But I'm getting the idea that maybe that isn't enough anymore." Rib waited for an answer. Seconds passed.

Ana laced her hands together, looking directly into Rib's eyes. "For better or worse... Isn't that how the marriage vows go? You are my soulmate. You are right when you say that the expectations of marriage don't live up to reality, but there are times when I would like to try."

"Honestly, I don't think I could be tied down to one woman," admitted Rib. "I don't see that as bad, but other folks do. You couldn't stand to live with me on a day-to-day basis knowing how I am. You and I are better off doing what we are doing." Rib hesitated, deep in thought. "You make me happy."

Ana gritted her teeth, her smile gone. "I want to be loved with honesty and tenderness. I need you in my life."

Ana reflected on that admission for a moment. "But if I can't have what I want, I'll live with it. And you never answered my question of why you didn't marry me instead of Connie."

"If one thing on your list is love, then you have it from me," said Rib, ignoring the question. "I love you, Ana. My love isn't traditional, but it's real. Can you accept what I have to give you?"

"You live under your own rules," concluded Ana. "You go day to day, even minute to minute, changing your mind according to your own needs. Damn me too, because I love you even when you drive me crazy. I think we should be married."

"With anyone else, I might agree," Rib replied. "But you don't think like an ordinary woman, although right now, I'm starting to have doubts. Yes, you lost a husband, but you have a successful law career and, importantly, your independence. You could have ridden off today and not looked back." Rib turned thoughtful. "I'm glad you didn't."

"But can't you see how I think about things?"

"Think about it," said Rib. "All anyone has are fleeting moments of happiness, sorrow, love, hate...any number of such things, and then the next day brings something new. The sun comes up again and doesn't give a damn about you or me. I see it every day, and I choose to live how I see fit."

Ana kept quiet, thoughtfully holding her hands and the words she wanted to speak. Then, she took Rib's hands in hers, looked into his eyes, smiled, and asked, "What do you have in store for us tonight?" Barely pausing, she continued, "I mean, what's for dinner?"

Rib leaned back, grinning and shaking his head. "Torgerson's tenderest tenderloin, cooked medium rare as you ordered. Those steaks are an inch and a half thick, aged to perfection, and paired with your favorite cabernet. Dinner should take care of some of your needs." He took her in his arms. "I'm not sure if you have other ideas, but let us see what the evening brings."

"Don't get your hopes up." Ana pulled away from Rib's embrace. "You will have to bring your best game and work on your pickup lines. I've had better offers." Ana kissed Rib lightly on the lips. "Your range riders could give you some lessons."

Rib, seeing the playfulness returning between them, asked, "Since you are so worldly, what is the best pickup line you've heard since Richard died?"

Ana hesitated, deciding on an answer. "One of your rancher neighbors came right out and asked if enough time had passed that I wanted to do that thing again, but he used the 'F' word."

"I can guess who that might be," mused Rib.

"Another neighbor, using his standard line with every woman, looked sincerely in my eyes and said, 'You good-looking son of a bitch. I'd like to take a run at you.'" Ana laughed at the thought of that night. "I could have answered that I would run faster with my skirt hiked up than he could with his pants down, but I smiled and told him I had no interest."

Ana waited for a reaction from Rib, but seeing none, continued. "Most men are gentlemen and ask for a dinner or a movie, then expect something in return."

Ana paused.

"Is that what you have in mind? If it is, you had better come up with a better plan because it's my choice regarding what happens after dinner. It's always the woman's choice, and don't you forget that. Oh, hell, what am I saying? You already know that."

Rib threw his head back in laughter. "You have a way of making a man feel mighty small with only one thing on his mind." With a sideways look at Ana, Rib teased, "I think we should talk about marriage."

Ana reached over and kissed Rib. "I have a better idea," she said.

CHAPTER 4

SATURDAY, AUGUST 30, 1975: LABOR DAY WEEKEND

Mariah Morgan crossed the gravel road separating her county school from Jack Moser's barn, where she kept Tucker. The Rocky Mountains, seventy miles to the west, shimmered in the sharp Saturday morning air that Labor Day weekend. Montana's big blue sky stretched from the Rockies eastward in an arc that seemed to last forever. To the northwest rose Chief Mountain; and to the north, the three round humps of the Sweet Grass Hills; and to the east, a flat butte called the Knees; and to the southwest, the anvil shape of Ear Mountain. The morning sun, crisp and clear, made her shade her eyes.

Mariah waved to Swede Davidson, one of Jack Moser's hired hands, as Swede sat enjoying the rising sun on a makeshift porch attached to an ancient trailer house. Besides teaching ten students of various grades at the Marias River Country School, Mariah had two essential tasks: taking care of her horse and convincing Swede to give up his drinking. Mariah spoke of the Gospel to Swede, but faith in the Lord couldn't measure up to Swede's friendship with John Barleycorn. By the looks of Swede, her mission today would be to saddle up Tucker.

Swede had a jug of homemade dandelion wine in his left hand as a balance to his right-leaning lawn chair. Mariah thought a gust of wind would roll Swede off the chair onto the rickety wooden porch.

Swede waved her over. "Do you want a swig of my finest dandelion?"

"No," she shouted back. "You are an also-ran. I'm taking Tucker for a ride. You go easy on that wine. It's only nine o'clock. Besides, KSEN radio tells me there is a storm coming."

"A little nip wouldn't hurt you," slurred Swede. "It's guaranteed to make your ride even better."

Swede took a drink. "You might even forget about this religious stuff you keep throwing at me."

Mariah ignored him and continued into the barn to saddle up Tucker.

Swede made all kinds of brews, his specialty being dandelion wine because it had a strong taste similar to brandy and the alcohol content to go with it, and the dandelions grew in abundance around the homestead.

Mariah had tried the wine, but having been burned by its taste, refused to drink more.

Mariah judged Swede to be in his sixties, but Swede never revealed his age, even when asked. Swede would not talk about his past, but he appeared well-educated when sober. His politeness came across to Mariah whenever he helped her with Tucker's care when she could not do the feeding and watering. Occasionally, Swede would saddle the horse and groom it, but never did he want to ride it.

Mariah teased Swede relentlessly, but Swede would reply, "A man could get hurt riding an animal weighing a thousand pounds who kicks, snorts, and throws his head."

Mariah didn't see Tucker that way, but she had to be careful around the animal as he did raise up his hooves once in a while. Mariah thought that men treated horses much like they treated women: domineering and disrespectful. But Swede had been respectful, and Mariah trusted him not only with Tucker but with herself. Today, Swede didn't help saddle Tucker but sat lost in his dandelion wine.

Mariah stepped into the old barn and the stall where Tucker stood. She had a small apple and gave it to the horse, who chomped it down. Mariah took Tucker's short snort as a sign of satisfaction, making Mariah smile. She patted him around the neck, reaching for a curry comb to give Tucker a brushing. Tucker gave her a quiet nicker as if to entice Mariah closer to her. He tossed his head and mane, and swished his tail.

Mariah enjoyed grooming Tucker as much as riding him. Running the comb across Tucker's body in slow, circular stokes gave her as much satisfaction as Tucker received, with the added bonuses of cleaning away his unwanted hair and dust and making his golden coat shine. As she started the slow movement around his neck, Tucker swung his head around, trying to give her a playful bite, but she pushed his head away, remembering the one time he had given her a painful nip.

Mariah groomed Tucker each day even if she didn't ride him. If she rode, Tucker would get two brushings, one before the ride and one after. The closeness Mariah had with Tucker bordered on intimacy. She wondered if she could find the same thing with a man. She told herself to forget that kind of thinking. Today, Tucker would get her full attention.

A peaceful sensation settled over Mariah as she climbed into the saddle and began a slow gallop across the newly planted wheat fields. She could look down from her height and see the blades of wheat poking their heads above ground. How would the tiny plants survive the coming cold winter? Swede had told her seeded winter wheat needed a freeze, or it wouldn't head out and produce kernels; vernalization was what he called it. She had no other choice but to believe him, impressed by his use of a word she had never heard before.

Mariah rode east for two miles until she came to a fence line marking another county road, turned to the south for the seeded field's length, and then cut in a diagonal direction back to the barn. Swede did not move to help her unsaddle Tucker but continued to sip from his jug and occasionally yell out at unseen intruders.

Mariah unsaddled Tucker, wiped him down with a towel, and grabbed the curry comb, starting the process of grooming him with slow, gentle, circular strokes. The same peaceful feelings apparent when she had started the ride persisted as she mused about being a country schoolteacher.

Mariah ignored her parents' concern about being stuck in the middle of nowhere, living alone without any man around. She told them that Swede protected her and lived right across from the road. Mariah felt very much at home even though the cramped teacher's living quarters depressed her at times. Yet Mariah loved her job and the children she taught. She had oceans of respect for the farm families that entrusted their children to her. Most of the men were respectful and their wives dynamite—those women who spent their time working the fields and cattle on equal footing with their husbands, taking care of the children, being involved in the community's social life, and still maintaining a sense of humor and boatloads of common sense.

Mariah fantasied about being that kind of woman as she knew of country schoolteachers who had married ranchers and farmers.

As she finished her second grooming of Tucker, she asked him, "How would you like living in your own place with another man and me? Think you could handle it?" Mariah frowned, thinking of Jack Moser, the owner of this barn and ten thousand acres of land.

Mariah had dated men her age but had never felt comfortable with them. She preferred maturity over youthful passion. *Jack Moser is older*, she thought, but his arrogance and overall attitude didn't light her fire, and besides, she told herself that there was more to marriage than money.

Jack, a single man, had been persistent about dating Mariah, asking her to dinner on several occasions in the summer before Labor Day. Jack's persistence had not paid off because of an incident at a square dance in Fort Collins on the Fourth of July. Mariah had dressed in a green, V-neck, long-sleeve pullover, set off with a turquoise tribal necklace, short shorts showing her shapely legs, and open sandals that put her red-painted toes on full display. He had asked her to dance, and Mariah had refused.

Jack's face turned red; his neck bulged as he hurled out the words, "You don't know what you are missing. Any woman would break her neck to dance with me."

Mariah had been intrigued when asked for the dance, but instinct kicked in, and a "No" seemed best when first approached. His reaction made her think of Jack as terribly crude, rude, and therefore unacceptable. Mariah wanted something different. *He probably doesn't know how to treat a horse either*, she decided. So, Mariah continued to refuse any dates with Jack, although he had become much more agreeable to her after their first meeting as Jack kept finding ways to stop and visit Mariah at the schoolhouse.

* * *

A month earlier, on Friday, August 8, Jack had approached Mariah for a dinner date,

"Why don't you go home. I have work to do," Mariah snapped. Jack had left, not in an arrogant, angry manner but with hurt feelings.

Mariah had felt poorly about sending him away in her abrupt manner, so she decided to make amends by asking him to come to her church on Sunday, thinking that would be a safe place. The invitation would create an opportunity for her to judge Jack in a different setting as religion played an essential role in Mariah's life, and she wanted to see where a prospective mate stood, not that Jack held that position, but his age and the possibility of being a farm wife made him an option.

Religion had always been a part of Mariah's life, with her family taking her to the Nazarene church as a child. She had spent June of the last summer as a counselor at a Nazarene camp with young people from all parts of Montana. She loved that time, although she had changed her church affiliation to the Episcopal Church in Fort Collins. As she had grown older, the more conservative views of the Nazarenes gave way to the Episcopalians' openness, the latter starting to accept women as ministers. Mariah loved the weekly Episcopalian communion, and singing gave her added incentive as the Fort Collins Episcopal choir held a prominent church service role. The Episcopalian belief of one Baptism for the forgiveness of sin intrigued her as she had been raised on God-fearing preaching, and the thought of Hell scared her.

Mariah had called Jack the following day, asking him, "Will you come to my church tomorrow? I sing in the choir so I can't sit with you, but we could meet at the coffee hour after the service."

Mariah expected a turndown, but Jack surprised her by accepting.

"I would love to go to church with you," he said, thinking he had hit the jackpot. "What church and when can I pick you up?"

"You can't pick me up," Mariah replied. "I sing in the choir, and our practice is an hour before the service. This is not a date, but if it is too much for you, I understand."

Mariah regretted her decision to call Jack.

"I've not darkened the door of a church since my mother made me go back in the olden days," Jack said. "The Lord knows I've done bad things in my life. A good confession is what I need."

Jack had more interest in spending time with Mariah than visiting his sins, but he didn't say as much.

"This is not about confession," Mariah stammered. "It's about friends sharing a day at church. Are you sure you want to go? It's not too late to reconsider, and it won't hurt my feelings."

"Anytime that I can spend with you is what I want," Jack said. "I can be open with you, and you seem to say what is on your mind. What church did you say you go to?"

"The Episcopal Church," Mariah repeated. "Remember, this isn't a date. It's only two friends sharing their faith. Please don't take my invitation as something it isn't."

"Agreed," Jack said.

Silence held between them over the telephone. Mariah knew she had made a mistake, considering the gossip if she and Jack spent too much time together during the social hour. Mariah had not considered that the church members would view them as a couple. In Fort Collins, the word would spread fast that she and Jack were an item.

Jack had taken the invitation as a come-on. *Hell,* he thought, *I might even become a regular at church if it gives me time with Mariah.*

* * *

On that Sunday morning, as the sun warmed the eastern sky, Mariah woke early to feed and water Tucker, then showered and put on an ankle-length polka dot dress with a high neckline and a pair of low-heeled shoes.

Why did I think I needed to be kind to Jack? she wondered. *He would be a catch for any woman.* But she had not felt any spark between them since the first time they met at the summer dance. Yesterday's telephone call had confirmed her feelings as Jack had tried to control the church meeting, wanting to pick her up and drive her.

Couldn't she act in a Christian way without it being taken as something it would never be?

Arriving at the church, Mariah joined the choir practice, giving Ana McGuire a special hug. Mariah thought of Ana as a mother figure. During a break in the singing, Mariah had confided her concern about having Jack come to church.

"Jack is taking this all wrong," Mariah lamented. "I felt guilty about the way I treated him, asking him to leave, but he looked so hurt that I wanted to make it up to him. He thinks we have a date."

"When a woman calls up a man and asks him to church, it could be taken as a serious invitation," Ana informed her. "Men look at a woman a lot differently than we think. Jack has a thing for you, and he can't figure out why you don't return the favor. I'll be with you at coffee hour so it won't look like a relationship between you and Jack. His mother is a good friend of mine. It will turn out okay. I promise."

"Oh, thank you," sighed Mariah. "You always have the right answer. I love it when you take care of me."

"Don't give me too much credit," cautioned Ana. "I've got problems of my own." Ana did not elaborate, but she smiled and took Mariah by the arm to resume their singing. "Let's meet here after the service and go to the coffee hour together. We'll outsmart Jack and have a good time doing it."

* * *

After the service, Mariah and Ana walked into the church community hall for coffee hour. Jack stood on the other side of the room with a group of farmers and ranchers. He excused himself from the group, saying he had "a crucial date." Jack approached the two women with a smile, holding out his hand for Mariah to shake. He nodded to Ana. The group of men had watched him walk across the room to the women.

"Mariah, why don't we go to brunch at the Two?" Jack suggested. "We could make a day of it."

"Mariah and I were going to my place for a light sandwich," said Ana as she intervened into their conversation. "I don't think there is enough for three."

Mariah stayed silent.

Jack eyed Ana, then looked to Mariah. "Looks like you have two choices," Jack said. "Which one will it be?"

"I'll wait for a third offer and then decide," Mariah replied with a forced laugh.

Jack frowned. What were these two women doing? His face flushed red. No one spoke.

"Well," Jack said, drawing out the end of the word, "that doesn't leave me with any option but to go by myself." Jack had imagined a morning and maybe an afternoon with Mariah, but it didn't appear that would work out. He wondered what Ana had to do with this.

"I do have other plans," Mariah said to Jack. "Can you forgive me?"

"How about a rain check?" Jack suggested. "I'll come to church next week if you'll have brunch with me afterward."

"No, I can't do that. It's too much, and who knows where I'll be next weekend?" answered Mariah. Mariah thought that Jack's question summed up her feelings for him. She could be a friend, but his pushy style didn't please her.

"Your mother would love to see you keep going to church. Heaven knows you need help," Ana chimed in.

"Where did that come from?" Jack asked. "You're making lunch, and three is a crowd. I got the message. I didn't ask you to brunch. This is between Mariah and me. Stay out of it!"

Ana, enjoying herself, continued. "If you won't take me, how about I ask you to brunch? Will you go to the Two with me this morning?"

"Not on your life," snarled Jack as he clenched his fists. He knew he had been caught between two women who seemed suddenly intent on giving him fits. He didn't know how to respond, so he didn't, simply glaring at the two women.

"You two think you have me outnumbered," he finally grumbled. "I am not giving up on Mariah."

Jack returned to his group of men friends, asking himself, *What purpose did those two have, embarrassing me that way? I wanted to spend time with Mariah, but that lady lawyer got in the way. Damn her.*

Ana and Mariah gave each other a knowing smile but didn't gloat. Jack had an obvious interest in Mariah.

"He is a hotshot helicopter pilot," Ana pointed out. "I bet he hasn't been shot down like that before."

Mariah could only giggle. "The way he approached us is exactly why I can't find any spark with him. Jack says the strangest things in the strangest ways. He came right up to us, ignored you, and practically demanded I go on a date. I want someone more polished."

"Good luck finding Mr. Right in this town," said Ana. "Jack is used to getting his way and can't handle it when someone stands up to him." She paused before adding, "He is a handsome devil. Give him credit for his looks."

"Did you really mean for us to go to lunch at your house?" Mariah asked.

"No, but we can," decided Ana with a mischievous grin. "We could go to the Two for brunch. Wouldn't that make Jack angry?"

"Let's not press our luck," warned Mariah. "I need to go back and take care of my horse. Thank you. You have been a sweetheart, stepping in and saving me from myself."

Mariah gave Ana a hug and left the building.

* * *

Mariah returned her attention to Tucker, thinking, *I've got to look forward not backward.*

She spoke to her horse. "I guess you wouldn't like living with a man like that."

CHAPTER 5

MONDAY SEPTEMBER 1, 1975: LABOR DAY WEEKEND

That same Labor Day weekend, ten miles south of where Ana and Rib had been riding, Jack Moser looked over the mountain corral that held thirty head of his cattle, rounded up from the deep canyons and pine trees of his summertime pasture. *A perfect fall day*, he thought, bringing in the last of the animals without having to scour the trees and the draws in a foot of snow with chilling north winds to contend with. Experience had taught him a hard lesson: to be early in Montana when getting work done. He had no patience for obstacles he could not control such as the weather. He added women to his list. Jack's effort to gain a schoolteacher's affection had gone nowhere.

Jack envied the animals in the corral, spending their summer surrounded by cool, high mountain air with lush grass and fresh water in the creeks while he toiled on flat farmland, moving irrigation pipe from field to field, harvesting the grain, doing fall seeding, and having to eat a peck of dirt and swat away hordes of mosquitoes. Of course, he didn't have to dodge a charging grizzly bear, nor hungry wolves or cougars. Maybe he should count his blessings, he decided.

The Rockies held a special place in his heart. Jack had hunted elk and deer in the fall, skied in the winter, and brought his cattle to pasture in the spring and summer. The only part of this trip he had not enjoyed had been the ride up with his hired man, Cobey.

Cobey had regaled him with stories of his conquests of numerous women and his fights with many men. Of course, Cobey conquered in every instance, but Jack knew that the need to brag indicated a shallow personality. His fellow helicopter pilots from Vietnam would have never spoken that way as they were always happy to survive a mission, knowing the next one might be their last.

Cobey had been with him about a year now; the man did his work and had been the point person for the summer pasture. Jack appreciated that about him, knowing that Cobey worked better when he received compliments.

"Hey," Jack said to Cobey, "job well done. Let's finish loading them and head for home."

"Yep, and did you see me back this truck up to the chutes? A perfect job, wouldn't you say?"

Jack shook his head and rolled his eyes, not yet immune to Cobey's ego.

Jack's experiences in Vietnam haunted him. Usually, it would be a loud noise or a surprise that set him off, but Cobey's constant bragging had managed to bring Jack to a dangerous breaking point. If another vehicle had been available, Jack would have taken it back to the ranch, but there was only the semi. If Cobey had the wheel, Jack might have feigned sleep, but would it be worth the gamble that Cobey wouldn't drive off a cliff or otherwise cause damage? Jack made his decision.

"I'll drive, and you sleep," Jack said. "There will be plenty of work to do unloading these critters at the ranch. Get some rest, and the less you say, the better. I need to think about a few things, and all your talk distracts me. Do you understand?"

Cobey glared at Jack but then nodded, and both men climbed into the cab of the semi. Silence held.

Jack kept his eye on the road as he descended from the mountain with his cattle. He held two hands on the steering wheel while his mind raced over the direct command he had issued to Cobey to keep quiet. Cobey had not said a word since, but Jack had caught the angry glance. *A small victory*, he thought.

Jack's mind spun, flashing back to the forces that had led him back to the ranch after the war. He had survived Vietnam as a helicopter pilot ferrying troops into position, carrying supplies, and mostly hauling out wounded soldiers as a medevac helicopter pilot. Every mission could have been his last, but he found himself alive after several hundred flights, returning a decorated war hero with a Bronze Star.

Jack also received the Purple Heart after a mission, heading into a hostile landing zone. A bullet fired from the ground into his approaching helicopter as he sat in the pilot's seat had crashed upward through his front window near his feet, entering through his helmet above his forehead and exiting through the upper-left corner of his headgear. Two inches lower and to the left, and he would have been dead. At the time, in his early twenties, Jack had shrugged it off, but now, ten years later, he dreamed about how close he came to meeting his maker. Afterward, he would find himself sitting up in bed, sweating and taking deep breaths.

Jack had gone to the local Fort Collins doctor, who diagnosed his symptoms as indicative of an anxiety attack, prescribing valium in heavy doses. Jack had taken the drug for a while, but the after-effects had left him in la-la land. He quit taking it and didn't go back or see another doctor, preferring to tough it out on his own.

The dreams persisted, during which Jack would often be flying his helicopter, approaching a landing zone, and watching for the stretchers running the wounded to his aircraft. The *chop-chop* noise of the helicopter blades, combined with the popcorn popping sound of .50-caliber machine guns, would add to the confusion of smoke and dust and chaos of picking up the wounded. He would wake up alive, but shaken.

Jack remembered the passing of time at his base camp, sitting in a thatched hooch waiting for the whistle to blow, giving them seconds to run to their Hueys for another mission. Their helicopters had become the workhorse of the operations in Nam, replacing the jeep. The jungles and mountainous terrain dictated new warfare, where the sky was used to get from battle to battle.

"Hell," Jack yelled. "Every pilot deserved the Medal of Honor!"

"What did you say?" asked Cobey as Jack's shout had woken him.

"Never mind," said Jack as he returned to his own thoughts, and Cobey went back to sleep. In Vietnam, orders were given, and he carried them out. When the bad guys were shooting at him, Jack didn't think about politics or where he fit into the grand scheme; it became personal that someone had the intent to kill him, and by God, he did everything he could to make sure that didn't happen.

One of his fellow pilots had flown General Creighton Abrams, commander of their forces in Vietnam, to a meeting in Saigon. When the general had left the meeting, he had been mad as hell, according to the pilot, because "Those Goddamn politicians in Washington, DC, were tying his hands, not letting him win this war."

Jack had thought about what the pilot had said until his next mission; then, his job became ferrying the wounded and surviving. He followed his orders, come hell or high water.

Jack had been bothered when he came home after his tour of duty when the American public shunned him for his Vietnam service. The war had brought out protests fueled by the media's scorn of all things government, mainly when it came to the military. He had expected a hero's welcome, but there were no parades or recognition of what he had done for his country. He knew he had anger issues.

Yet Jack had not lost his love for the freedom Montana provided. When he compared it to his time in Vietnam, he couldn't understand the opposition to the war. Jack knew that some of his buddies who had made it back had not managed the adjustment to civilian life, especially after hearing how people condemned the war and the soldiers who fought in it. Jack had no remorse over serving in Vietnam, but his dreams indicated he hadn't quite come to terms with his wartime experience.

He had not had time to reflect on his future after his tour of duty had ended. He returned to Montana to find his mother, Peggy, divorcing his father—or maybe his father divorcing his mother. He didn't know which, but he abruptly found himself the boss of the Moser ranch. His mother, Peggy Moser, had not seemed that upset about her husband leaving, and his father, after taking a flight to Kauai, never returned to Montana, telling Jack, "There is a warm wind in Hawaii. I don't have to fight the cold and blowing snow from those Montana winters. I'm staying here where I can live without working my butt off every day."

I'm not like that, Jack thought, as they turned off the Valier Junction road heading for home.

* * *

Jack recognized his mother's car as he drove into the ranch. The fire engine red of her Pontiac Firebird two-door was hard to miss. Peggy Moser stood in front of the old farmhouse, with her hands on her hips, surveying something that had once been hers. Her dyed red hair, pulled back and bound up in a fiery bun, didn't quite match the color of her car, but had a more vibrant tint, and her hazel green eyes didn't miss a detail. The cleavage of her ample front and the shortness of her skirt highlighted her sensuality. She knew what she had and she flaunted it.

Jack wondered what she wanted. "Christ," he muttered. "She never shows up, unless she has some sort of scheme in mind."

Jack glanced at the sleeping Cobey, finally hollering at him to wake up. "Start to unload these cattle. I've got to take care of my mother. I'll help you in a minute." Cobey nodded his understanding.

"What's up, Mother?" asked Jack as he climbed out of the truck. "You hardly ever come out here anymore."

"Nothing," Peggy said. "I am alone today and needed company. It's a holiday—or have you forgotten? I like to come out here to the ranch. I lived here for twenty years."

"Make some coffee," requested Jack. "I'll help unload these critters and join you when we're done."

Peggy walked into the kitchen of the ranch house.

"Not much has changed," she said to the familiar painted walls. Looking around the kitchen, Peggy saw the same curtains, the same kitchen table, and the same stove but a newer refrigerator and coffeepot. A thin film of dust covered the kitchen counter. *This place needs a woman's touch*, she thought.

Peggy knew precisely where the coffee would be. She poured a generous amount of water into it and let the pot perk. Jack had been right. She did have a purpose.

Jack had confessed to Peggy that he had found the love of his life but that love had not been returned. A potential solution to her son's problem had popped into her mind, but she would have to broach the subject slowly.

Jack came through the door and threw his hat on the hall tree, revealing a bushy head of brown hair. He kept his sunglasses on.

"Thanks for the coffee. It's been a long day." Jack pulled up one of the kitchen chairs, sat down, and eyed his mother. "Don't kid me," he said after he had taken a sip of the brew, cocking his head toward his mother. "You always have a reason when you show up unannounced. Give it to me straight."

Peggy nodded, thankful she didn't have to beat around the bush. She had liked that about Jack since the day he became old enough to talk back to her.

"I'm worried about you being alone out here. This house needs a woman, and you tell me your honey won't give you the time of day. Is that right?"

"I knew it," scoffed Jack. "Your whole life has been one big effort at controlling people around you because *you know best*. Why do you think I joined the Army? I needed to get away from your constant running of my life. Best thing I ever did. I don't need your help with my love life."

"Oh, you don't need my help?" asked Peggy. "What are you doing on Labor Day riding in the cab of a semi with a hired hand? Wouldn't it have been a lot more fun with a woman by your side?"

Jack couldn't argue that point. Having the schoolteacher by his side would have been sweeter than his hired hand. He remained silent as his mother continued.

"You should have called up Margie down at the drugstore. She is cute, brilliant, and has a sense of humor. You two would be a great match." Peggy had someone else in mind but suggested Margie first, knowing Jack wouldn't consider her.

Jack replied, "Margie has a boyfriend in Shelby. I hear they are getting married. Anyway, I've told you, it's the schoolteacher I want. I am making progress, but she only wants to be friends. I can fix that. I know I can."

"When a woman makes up her mind about something, it's hard to change it," argued Peggy. "You aren't making progress so you need to change your tactics. Make her jealous, or do something besides asking her for a date! You know, I worry about you. I want you to be happy."

"I'm not giving up on Mariah," insisted Jack. "She keeps turning me down, but she is friendly to me, and I know there is a chance."

Jack walked to the coffeepot to refill his cup, then returned to the table. "What do you mean, make her jealous?"

"Tough luck for you," said Peggy, taking a different tact, thinking that Jack's ideal woman had made her choice. "I'm only trying to help. If you can't figure out a way to win that woman over, it's for the best. You should start looking someplace else."

"I see that you are trying to help me, and I appreciate what you are doing." Jack reached across the table, giving Peggy's hand a squeeze, somewhat surprised at his mother's concern. "Do you have any other hare-brained ideas? If you do, I will listen."

"You could help me out with one of my friends," suggested Peggy, seizing her opportunity. "You know Ana McGuire, don't you? Our county attorney? She is my best friend and caught up in a relationship with a married man who shall remain nameless to you. Would you ask her out?"

"God, no, I wouldn't," said Jack. "She and Mariah ganged up on me the other day in church. She is older than me, and who would go out with a lawyer? There would be a new argument by the minute."

"I didn't ask you to marry Ana, did I? If Mariah saw you with someone else, it might make a difference: Trying to win a woman's attention is a subtle affair. It's a competition. Give Mariah a challenge. Don't come off as being affected by her refusal to go out with you."

* * *

Jack thought back to his meeting with Mariah last week and all the times he had requested a dinner date at the Two. He had gone to the schoolhouse as he had so many times before. He knocked on her door and she answered, but didn't invite him in.

He stammered out the invitation, shuffling his feet. Mariah again refused a dinner date.

"I look at you as a friend, but it can't be anything more. I'm sorry."

"Why can't it be anything more?" Jack blurted out to Mariah, his temper showing. "It can if you want it to be." Jack had tightened his fists as his face turned red.

Mariah had taken two steps back from her front door. "You are scaring me," she said. "I can't change the way I feel. I truly like you, but my answer is still no. Didn't I say I was sorry?"

"Well," Jack had said, "I'm sorry too." His eyes narrowing to a spot on the ground, Jack kicked at the cement step with his boot. "Isn't there something I can do?"

Mariah had simply shaken her head.

Jack had then lifted his chin, squinted, returned to his pickup without a word, slammed the door shut, jammed the transmission into its lowest gear, and sped out of the schoolyard. The tires threw gravel as he made the turn toward his ranch.

Mariah walked down the steps with her arms crossed, shaking her head back and forth. How many times had Jack left her in anger? This time he had frightened her.

Jack, as he fishtailed out of the schoolyard, vowed not to give up on Mariah. But he didn't have a plan at that point. He had entered into a no-man's-land with Mariah, confused and with no direction.

* * *

Jack returned to the present, sitting in the ranch kitchen with his mother. He rubbed his chin with his left hand, lowering it to pinch his Adam's apple. His mind whirled as he decided...any landing zone in the jungle.

Jack turned to Peggy. "What do you have in mind?"

CHAPTER 6

THURSDAY, SEPTEMBER 4, 1975

Mariah had shoveled snow from her front steps and those leading to the classroom door on Wednesday morning after the quick-hitting storm on Tuesday night. This afternoon, she swept them with her broom. The wind had blown, the temperature dropping from the mid-sixties to the low twenties as the storm had raged. Today, the sun shone brightly in a blue sky, but the weather had barely reached the low forties, with a slight southerly breeze. The snow melted slowly, with patches of brown grass showing above the whiteness of windblown drifts.

Mariah had dismissed her class at three o'clock, straightened up the classroom, and changed into her work clothes to take care of her horse.

School had started on Tuesday with a class size of ten students ranging in grades from kindergarten to sixth. These children belonged to the farmers and ranchers living in the area; they sent their kids to her school rather than other options in the Fort Collins, Shelby, Chester, or Conrad districts due to the school's location—which saved the parents miles and hours of commuting each day.

Mariah watched weekly episodes of *Little House on the Prairie* on her small television in her cramped living room. Many episodes concerned the growing pains of the second daughter of the family, Laura. Mariah identified with that character as she recognized that her life was changing day to day, becoming more complicated. Michael Landon as the father and the farmer had particular appeal as she thought of him as handsome and the type of man she would like to marry.

Mariah envied the hard-working ranch mothers of her school children. Those women were smart, friendly, and humble with keen senses of humor. Nothing seemed to bother them, or if anything did, somehow, a solution could be found. *Did they think of me in the same way?* she asked herself.

At that moment, Swede Davidson came running across the gravel road that separated the school building from Jack's land where Swede lived in his tiny, ancient trailer house.

"Come quick," Swede yelled, waving his arm. "Tucker is sick."

Mariah heard Swede's voice from within her quarters but couldn't make out what he said. She went to her front door as Swede banged on the door of the school. Mariah returned to the classroom through the inner door as Swede ran to the other entrance. Mariah opened her school door, wondering what could be so wrong that Swede had lost his cool. Finally, Swede came back to the school door, meeting Mariah.

"You got to come," said Swede, catching his breath while leaning his hands on his knees. "I'm all done in. Tucker is sick, and I can't help him. He doesn't like me anyway, and now he won't even let me in his stall."

Mariah returned to her front door and reached for her coat hanging near the door entrance.

"What is wrong with Tucker? Haven't you been feeding him and giving him water?" Swede's urgency alarmed her.

"I've been taking good care of him," insisted Swede. "That horse doesn't like men. I bet someone has taken a club to him, and he remembers."

They hurried, crossing over the gravel road and reaching the entrance to the barn.

Mariah kept her horse on the east side of the building sectioned into stalls. The floor consisted of old, tar-type pavement, soft enough to leave marks from shod horses. A dairy had been its original purpose, and there were individual hay troughs attached to the walls, along with rusted metal stanchions used in the old days to hold cows in place when milking.

Tucker sported a white mane and tail, accentuating his golden color, set off by white stocking hooves up to his ankles' fetlock. A Palomino's temperament was determined by its species and how it was treated. Mariah thought Tucker to be gentle, but Swede disagreed.

Tucker stood with his head down near his front legs, pawing the ground, then kicking his hind legs to his stomach and arching his back as if to urinate.

"He won't let me come near him, and he's acting real strange," said Swede. "This idea of taking care of your horse is not for me. Horses are unpredictable. You never know what they might do." Swede paced the center of the barn, not coming any closer to the horse. "But I hate to see any animal suffer, and your horse is sick."

Mariah approached Tucker in his stall as the horse pawed at the ground and whinnied, tossing his head. Mariah backed away.

"Do you have a phone in your trailer?" Mariah asked.

"No, I don't need one."

"Go over to my place," instructed Mariah. "The phone is on the wall above the kitchen table. Call the veterinarian. Tucker is sick."

"Who should I call?" asked Swede. "I don't know any vets."

"There is one in Fort Collins," Mariah told him. "He has a ranch west of town. I don't know him, but Jack tells me he is the best. Hurry! There is a phone book in the top right-hand drawer next to the table."

Swede half-walked, half-ran to the teacherage, still out of breath from his first trip. Swede fumbled through several drawers before he found the phone book but had trouble finding the veterinarian's number. Finally, he made the call.

In the meantime, Mariah approached Tucker, who was still nipping at his hindquarters. She found a bucket and filled it with water. At first, Tucker refused to drink, but Mariah persisted, talking slowly and calmly.

"Swede is calling the vet. You are going to be fine," she reassured the animal. Tucker would not take a drink but kept pawing the ground and swinging his head to bite his backside. Time passed with no sign of Swede.

"Where is that Swede?" Mariah asked her horse. Tucker continued pawing the ground.

Mariah decided to go find the man. She closed the door to the barn, dashing back to her house, only to find Swede sitting on the kitchen chair eating the remains of a cinnamon roll.

"What are you doing?" Mariah demanded. "Did you call the vet? What did he say?" Tears came to her eyes. "What if Tucker dies? Then what will I do? How can you just sit there?"

"I called the vet," said Swede. "But his secretary answered. She told me her boss is at Jack Moser's place pregnancy-testing cows. The secretary is going to radio him, and she will get back to me as soon as possible. So, I am waiting for her call."

Swede ate the last of the roll.

"Tucker needs help right away," Mariah insisted as she stood with her hands on the back of a chair. "Do something, will you?"

"The secretary said she would call back as soon as possible," repeated Swede. "I couldn't leave this phone till I got word back from her. What else could I do? I can call her back, but you can't rub a jug and expect a genie to appear. We have to wait for her call."

The ringing of the phone jarred the silence of the room. Mariah jumped up to grab it, but Swede was closer and casually answered, "Hello?" A few moments of silence followed, with Swede nodding his head in agreement or shaking it in disagreement.

"Thank you. I will pass the word along to Mariah."

"What did she say? How soon can the vet get here?" Mariah grabbed Swede's coat sleeve.

Swede put his hands up, signaling for Mariah to settle down.

"That secretary gal talked to the vet on the radio, and he will drop by as soon as he gets his work done. She told me not to worry, that horses had a mind of their own, and as long as they aren't down on the ground not breathing, they will survive."

Mariah's tears streamed down her face. "What did I do wrong? I don't want Tucker to suffer."

"That gal said not to worry—the vet will be here as quick as he can. He's only a couple miles down the road from here. I told her what the symptoms were, and I didn't get the impression they were life-threatening." Swede gave Mariah a smug look. "You need to have some faith!"

"How can you talk about faith when someone needs to look after Tucker? Tucker could die, and no one cares except me. Where is that vet? Doesn't he know this is serious? I hate him for not coming right now!"

"He'll be here in good time," said Swede. "You tell me all the time that things happen for a reason. So, trust the vet to show up. You aren't practicing what you preach."

Mariah hesitated, tears still on her cheeks. "Oh, Swede... You are right. I will put my belief in God that Tucker will be fine. You have been such a gentle person...so good to Tucker and me. I don't know how to repay you."

Swede thought if he were younger, he could suggest something. Swede grudgingly admitted to himself that he sometimes thought of Mariah in those terms.

Mariah contemplated calling another vet. Shelby, Conrad, and Brady had vet's offices, but her wristwatch showed almost four in the afternoon, which lessened the chances of getting one today. Swede had made the call and confirmed the Fort Collins vet would show up. It occurred to her that she was not practicing her faith and that she needed to have patience and trust that Tucker would be okay.

Still, Mariah simmered as the minutes passed slowly, not knowing if and when the vet would show up. She wanted action right now. How would she react to some male-driven horse doctor? Would he be arrogant and condescending like her father, making her feel tiny? He might come wandering in, tell her to give Tucker the horse equivalent of two aspirin, and be on his way. She vowed that she wouldn't let that happen.

Mariah could remember seeing the vet once or twice around town, although not at her church. She wondered if he was a Christian man. The picture in her mind made her recoil. He would be close to her father's age, which worried her. Her father was a dominant "Do it my way or hit the highway" guy with a drinking problem. This vet could be the same type of person.

At ten after five, Rib Torgerson, rancher and doctor of veterinary medicine, drove into the schoolyard in his white, sixth-generation Ford 150 pickup. A white, custom-made toolbox covered the pickup's entire bed, where he carried veterinary supplies and medicines with pull drawers on both sides, and beneath them, long drawers accessible from the end gate.

He climbed out of the driver's side door in a graceful, straightforward manner that Mariah took note of.

"Howdy," he said. "I understand there is a sick horse around here. Where is this animal?"

"Tucker is inside the barn across the road," Mariah explained. "You need to hurry because he is sick. He is droopy, paws the ground, and keeps biting at his flank. He's across the road. Come this way."

Mariah, Rib, and Swede made their way across the road to the barn, with Rib driving his pickup and Mariah and Swede running to Tucker's stall. Tucker's head drooped close to the ground while he pawed at the straw scattered about the floor. Sorrowful described only a portion of the horse's appearance; distracted and uncomfortable completed it.

Rib reached out and gently patted Tucker's neck, smoothly moving to Tucker's left shoulder and cradling the horse's neck in his left arm. Rib spoke softly into Tucker's ear. "Whoa, boy. We are going to take a look at you to see what's up." Rib's voice was gentle and soothing as he took a pinch of Tucker's shoulder and released it. The skin kept its peak shape for several seconds. Then, Rib pried open Tucker's mouth, inspecting his teeth, gums, and tongue while talking in the same quiet, smooth voice.

"Looks like a case of colic caused by dehydration," said Rib. "That's only an educated guess. The pinch on his shoulder should have disappeared immediately, but it didn't, and his mouth is too dry. Let me do some other tests to make sure. Here, pretty lady, hold on to these reins. What did you say your name is?"

"I didn't say my name," said Mariah, recoiling at being called a pretty lady. "It's Mariah Morgan, and Tucker is the horse."

Rib, ignoring her comment, went to his toolbox bringing back a stethoscope, moving to the left side of the animal.

"I'm going to listen to his insides," declared Rib. "I'll be able to tell if his gut is still moving. If I don't hear anything we have a twisted intestine and that is trouble."

Mariah put her right hand to her mouth biting her knuckles as she watched him place the stethoscope on Tucker's belly in different places. He stood up looking intensely at Mariah. She stepped back expecting the worst.

Rib smiled. "Your horse is grumbling. He has a blockage but nothing twisted that I can tell. I'll fix a brew of mineral oil and water and tube it into his stomach. He'll be just fine if we can soften the blockage so he can pass it."

Mariah sighed in relief slumping her shoulders forward saying a quick thankful prayer. Suddenly she rushed to Rib and gave him a hug. "Thank you, thank you, thank you. This means so much to me"

Rib, at first taken aback from the close physical contact, recovered and smiled, and he reluctantly broke the embrace. "Mariah…That is your name…right?"

Mariah nodded yes, embarrassed by her spontaneous display. Swede looked on, shocked by the suddenness of her actions.

Rib continued, "You have a horse with colic. Good thing you called because we caught Tucker's condition early. This horse is dehydrated and impacted. He can't poop, but I have medicine for him. It's going to take him a while to get him hydrated, and we will have to check his feed and get him to pass the blockage. Are you okay with that?"

"Yes, do what you have to do. I want my horse to get well." Mariah was surprised by Rib's concern and let her emotions surface. "I can't stand to see him suffer. How long will this take?"

"You can't rush Mother Nature," Rib replied. "Some will depend on his overall health, which looks to be pretty good. The rest is to going to be up to him, but he will do fine." Rib paused, looking first at Mariah and then at Swede. "I might make some suggestions for his future care. Are you up to it?"

"What do you suggest?" asked Mariah.

"You need to provide this animal with enough clean water," said Rib. "Not too hot, nor too cold. Part of his problem might be the cold snap we've had the past week. Do you have a water heater for his watering trough? He is like a human. He won't drink water that doesn't fit his taste."

"Tucker drinks out of that bucket over by the wall. We fill it twice a day since the cold weather hit us," explained Swede.

"You need to change that," Rib instructed. "Buy a water trough, keep it full, and put in a water heater. Horses need up to ten gallons a day. That little bucket won't do the job. Where does Tucker get his water in the summertime?"

Swede spoke up. "There is a concrete trough out in the corral, but we shut the water off last week because of the weather. Mariah and I take turns filling his water inside the barn."

"You two figure out how to get water in here," said Rib. "I'll get on with treating Tucker."

Rib tended to the horse while Mariah and Swede exchanged ideas on how to get clean, suitable water to Tucker, finally deciding to get a watering trough, a water heater, and two five-gallon plastic jugs to carry water. Rib did his examinations, administered medicine, and then gave Tucker a shot with sedatives to ease the pain and antibiotics to ward off any possible infections.

Rib faced Mariah with a smile. "Your horse is going to be fine. You might want to walk him now and again each day for the next week. He is a lot like us. If we move around a bit, we feel better—it helps the plumbing. I'll be out at Jack's for a few days this week, so I'll stop by tomorrow morning and evening to see if there are any complications. How does that sound to you?"

Mariah, touched by the offer, smiled back at Rib. "Thank you so much for taking care of Tucker. Yes, having you stop by would be a relief to me." She reached out to shake his hand, and Rib returned the shake. Their eyes met. Rib turned to his pickup and left the barnyard. Mariah grabbed a rope to attach to Tucker's halter for a slow walk. Swede returned to his jug of wine.

* * *

At 7 a.m. the following day, Rib drove into the barnyard to check on Tucker, finding the horse improved. Returning to the pickup, he steered across the county road, knocking on Mariah's door. Mariah answered, not ready for the school day, which started at eight. She wore loose-fitting sweats, no shoes, and no makeup. Her hair was a tangled rat's nest.

She smiled.

"Mr. Veterinarian, you are up early, and I look a fright. Have you checked out Tucker? Is he okay?"

Rib smiled back, taking in the picture of this attractive young woman at her worst moment.

"Sorry to bother you, but my day starts early. I should have told you last night that I would be here before dawn."

Mariah stared into Rib's blue eyes.

Rib broke the spell, answering Mariah's question. "Yes, your horse is fine. Maybe he isn't out of the woods yet, but he is recovering. Remember to check that list I made for you, get a decent water trough for the barn, and keep the water temperature reasonable. Ice in the bucket is a sure-fire recipe for colic."

Mariah, not embarrassed in the least, laughed. "Swede and I will follow your instructions. I don't want Tucker sick. Will you stop by again this afternoon?"

Rib nodded; he would. "See you later," he said, turning to his pickup. "Jack's cows are waiting."

Rib did come back that afternoon and every morning and afternoon for several days. Mariah loved the attention. The morning visits were short as Mariah had to prepare for her classes. However, after Mariah's last class and after Rib had worked the cows, the afternoons lasted into the evenings.

After tending to Tucker one afternoon, Mariah stood in front of Rib. "Are you a Christian?"

Rib smiled. "I'm a sinner so I must be a Christian."

"What does that mean?" Mariah asked with a look of puzzlement.

Rib paused, carefully choosing his words. "I believe, like my Blackfoot friends, in a Great Spirit controlling our world. I don't know if I call him God, but I do believe in a supreme being. Does that make me a Christian? Not sure about that, but I do believe in a greater power."

Mariah, confused by the idea of a greater power being different than her God, became curious. "I believe in one God, the Father Almighty, Maker of Heaven and Earth. I don't know if I can accept the idea of a Great Spirit. Is that really how the tribe thinks?"

"Yep," Rib replied. "They have lived in this country a lot longer than we have. When you think about it, tribes have lived on this land for many thousands of years, and white men came along and changed everything, except the weather, the seasons, and Mother Nature. Modern technology has made a difference, but Mother Nature is still Mother Nature."

Mariah looked perplexed. "Yes, I see that, but what about faith in God? Doesn't that mean something? I've centered my whole life on His word and His way."

"You don't have to change," said Rib. "Everybody has different beliefs, even this horse of yours."

"How so? How can a horse have beliefs?"

Rib gave her a sideways look and continued. "One of my clients thought himself a horse trainer. He used a rawhide strap to command obedience. He ended up being stomped to death by a horse he supposedly trained. I think he turned his back on the horse, and the horse got him down and paid him back in spades and hooves."

"You mean, the horse killed him?" Mariah recoiled at the thought of a man dying that way.

"Yep, that horse had a belief that getting whipped needed to be corrected. It's only a guess, but working on Tucker tells me your horse worships the ground you walk on. Tucker is gentle and loving, and you, Mariah, have a lot to do with how your horse acts."

Mariah smiled coyly at the compliment. "Thank you," she said. "Tucker has become more than a horse. I tell him everything I do like we are a married couple. I think he understands." She met Rib's eyes with her own.

"Getting back to your religion," Rib said, changing the subject. "Love your neighbor like yourself, do unto others, judge ye not, and who amongst us can throw the first stone.... These are words of forgiveness and compassion and humility in beliefs. Live those words with Tucker, and he will treat you right."

Mariah, impressed by Rib's reasoning and surprised he had quoted some scripture, responded, "I see your point. I'm not sure I can get to where you are as it is strange to me, but I respect your view of religion."

Rib wondered how he had gotten into the religion conversation.

"God has saved me," said Mariah. "I won't back away from Him."

"Nobody's perfect," said Rib. "But I try to help my neighbor."

With a teasing smile, Mariah said, "Maybe I can save you. I'm working on Swede, but he drinks too much. His dandelion wine overpowers all reason. I tried with Jack Moser too, and he did go to church, but he is not a believer in anything except himself. You might be my last hope to save someone."

"Well, Mariah," Rib said with a laugh. "Don't be getting your hopes up. I am a sinner through and through. I live for the moment, not caring about going to heaven or to the devil." Rib had almost said "hell" but caught himself in her presence. Mariah was having an effect on him.

Rib's smile showed his pleasure at the lightness of the conversation. "Sometimes, I think I am the devil, but I try to treat people by the Golden Rule. So far, I do right, and I do wrong, but at least I try."

"But down deep, you are a good person," concluded Mariah. "I can see it when you treat Tucker. You genuinely care. You have spent more time with him than needed."

Mariah blushed through her smile, thinking Rib to be a man who would treat her with respect and kindness, the same way he treated Tucker.

Their conversations during the afternoons all through that week covered not only religion but also politics, local gossip, the Two Medicine and the Rocky Mountain Front, and a short course on Tucker's care and feeding. On Friday afternoon, as the daylight faded, while taking care of Tucker, Mariah turned to Rib. "Would you like to have a cup of hot chocolate?"

Rib nodded, and they walked across the gravel road to Mariah's home. As they walked, she placed her left arm through Rib's right arm.

CHAPTER 7

MONDAY, SEPTEMBER 8, 1975

Peggy Moser drove her red Firebird car into the alley leading to the back door of the Montana state liquor store that she managed as an agent of Montana. She loved her car and flaunted the fact she was no longer one of those dedicated, common-sense farm housewives who doted on their husbands. Her ex-husband had jetted off to Hawaii and never came back. It had been time as their marriage was in shambles, even though it had produced one son, Jack, who had become a Vietnam War hero with a chestful of medals.

She asked herself, how did she survive those lonely days on the farm before the divorce? By being tough and a survivor, she answered. The divorce hurt to the extent the marriage had been a failure, but that was ten years ago and since then she had taken advantage of every opportunity to better herself by supporting local and state politicians, and when a Democratic governor had been elected, she found herself the manager of the Fort Collins liquor store. It didn't hurt that as part of the ranch settlement in the divorce, while not receiving land, the money payout allowed her to buy a local tavern, which she remodeled to her likeness and renamed Busty's. She made it a success.

Peggy unraveled herself from the front seat of the Firebird, not quite as limber as she had once been, but, she thought, *For an older broad I move well enough.* Music and dancing filled her life, and today she hummed her favorite tune: "He can't run his own life. I'll be damned if he'll run mine." That tune was her anthem and applied to all of her relationships whether romantic or not. She had financial independence and she loved it.

Upon entering the back door, she moved to the safe to remove the money for making change when the store opened at ten and the sales would start. Handing the money made her feel powerful. "I love my liquor store," she shouted to the walls.

Peggy had her life in order, except the problem of marrying her son off to the right woman.

* * *

The liquor store had a front room with an entrance opening into impressive shelves of hard liquor filled with pints, and fifths, and half-gallon jugs. However, the real action took place in the back room as it had become the meeting place for a select group of locals.

Peggy ran the Fort Collins liquor store under a contract with Montana. Under state rules, she had to be open Monday through Saturday from ten in the morning to six at night. The state had a complex set of regulations, but as long as she stayed...more or less...within the guidelines of Montana's rules, she could run the store as she saw fit.

Peggy drank gin, sometimes with a tonic, but more often straight, but never to excess because she liked to be in control of her body and mind and to control what other people did. Peggy had come upon the idea to make her store a social gathering place, governed by her rules. She had fixed up the back room with two comfortable reclining chairs, two folding chairs, a table, and music to go along with the plumbing fixtures already in place. Two Oriental rugs graced the floors, along with a refrigerator/freezer unit. Peggy limited who came in and went out of her back room.

While running for the county attorney's office, Ana McGuire became a regular in the back room after developing a kinship with Peggy. Both women were Democrats in a robust Republican county. Ana had run in the last election and won with Peggy's support. It didn't hurt that one of the Republican candidates, after losing the primary, started fighting with his fellow Republican and ran as an Independent. They forgot about Ana, and after splitting the Republican votes in the general election, Ana won with 45 percent. Next year, Ana would face a much different election, as rumor had it that a new young lawyer, Dan Jacobson, was running as a Republican.

It was the Monday following Labor Day in 1975, and Ana looked forward to going to Peggy's lair, sitting in a recliner chair with a glass of gin, and talking.

Ana closed her office in the stately old Fort Collins courthouse at five o'clock, going directly to the liquor store. Ana walked down the alley to the store's back door, letting herself in with a key Peggy had given her. Peggy occasionally allowed Ana to serve customers, justifying the door key Ana had in her possession. Ana sometimes opened the store on Saturday mornings when Peggy left town or was otherwise detained, usually with a new man.

Ana could barely make out voices from the front of the store as Peggy waited on the rush-hour customers coming off work, stopping by for the fixings to spike their evening cocktails. Ana poured herself a gin and tonic, getting ice from the freezer. She sat in her favorite recliner with her shoes off and sipped on her drink, savoring the juniper taste of the gin.

These past two weekends had been tranquil as far as her job was concerned. Ana had met with Sheriff Wendall Wagner to discuss any criminal complaints arising over Labor Day, and despite it being a holiday, there had been only three DUIs and a few fights. No car wrecks or deaths; all in all, pretty mild.

The sheriff had not found any marijuana-related issues, which surprised her, as he had made it his priority to clear the county of that dreaded gateway drug. The sheriff had accused Ana of being soft on crime when she had to curtail some of his searches. Probable cause did not exist in this county—at least as far as Sheriff Wagner was concerned. Ana believed the sheriff would not support her in next year's elections.

Last Wednesday, she had her regular meeting with the three male county commissioners. The chair, George Daniels, had a fine sense of humor that she adored, plus a realistic view of his duties. Commissioner Sam Johnson brought a different perspective to the table. Around the courthouse and in many parts of the county, Sam went by the nickname of Jesus Johnson. The third commissioner, Joe Perone, quietly went about his business and said very little. The meeting had gone smoothly, with the main topic being the county building a hospital with federal Hill-Burton funds. Ana looked forward to the evening with Peggy.

Ana poured herself another drink and filled another glass, ready for Peggy. She guessed that Peggy, after closing the store and needing to balance the scales for the day, would be ripe for a cocktail.

Finally, Peggy came into the back room.

"You trying to get a job as a bartender?" asked Peggy as she grabbed her drink, lit a cigarette, and settled into the other recliner. "Everyone, plus all the bars, decided to restock their shelves. Folks are still celebrating Labor Day or looking forward to the Stampede."

Peggy took a strong pull on the drink. "And how did your Labor Day weekend go with that married man?"

"Fine, as if you really cared," said Ana, in a disgusted tone. "You don't approve, so don't beat that dead horse."

"I don't disapprove," said Peggy with a smile. "But you will get hurt eventually, and I'll have to pick up the pieces. It's only a matter of time. You know it as well as I do. You don't have a future with Rib."

"I can't give him up," alibied Ana defensively. "If what I am doing is wrong, I don't care. I have to put up with being a woman in a man's world.

I'm widowed, forty-five years old, and my two children are on their own. I'm entitled to happiness."

"Yes, you are," agreed Peggy. "But life is seldom aware of your needs. You can have whatever pushes your buttons, enjoy the moment, do your thing...but there is a price to pay in the end."

Peggy looked directly at Ana. "Are you willing to pay it?"

Ana and Peggy each sipped their drinks, deep in thought: Ana about her relationship with Rib and Peggy about the considerable favor she was planning to spring on Ana.

"Are you going to the Stampede?" Peggy asked.

The official title of the Fort Collins rodeo was the Blue Ox Stampede, which celebrated Paul Bunyan and the fall equinox at the same time. But the locals had shortened the name to the Stampede, and the original name had faded from use. A rodeo and a dance were two main attractions, along with house parties that started the week after Labor Day. The Stampede signaled the beginning of fall, a celebration of the harvest farmers had stored in the bins and the winter wheat seeded in the ground. Harvest combines and winter wheat planting drills were idle for the winter, some in sheds and others parked on the prairie, marking the end of another growing season.

"I can't stand rodeos," said Ana. "There are too many macho men drinking, chewing tobacco, spitting, and otherwise being obnoxious. I'm not interested."

"How about the dance?" Peggy asked. "Good music, enough food, and you are a dancer. Remember that time we went to the Black and White Ball? You danced the heels off every man there."

"But that was then, and this is now," Ana pointed out.

"Now is the time to think about your future. I'm your campaign manager, and I'm advising you to get out and act like a politician with an election coming up: Go out in public to let people know you are still alive. Voters will get the impression that you are better than they are if you don't mingle with them, especially in this town."

"I don't think I am better than anybody," argued Ana. "I'm not desperate either. It's such a bother to get dressed and smile when I don't want to be social. People don't respect your privacy. They won't take the time to call my office or some other lawyer's office, but it's okay to come up to me at a dance and ask a legal question. My satisfaction is that they are getting what they pay for. I'd love to send them a bill but never do."

"You've made your point." Peggy took another sip of gin. Ana lolled back in the recliner with her eyes closed.

"You are desperate," said Peggy. "Look at what's on your plate. A doomed relationship with Rib, an election coming up where the powers in the courthouse will oppose you, and you waste your time drinking with me in this hell hole of a back room. What kind of life is that?"

Ana smiled with her eyes closed.

Peggy leaned forward in her chair and took another stiff swallow of gin. "I'm going to level with you. I need your help with Jack, and I think I could help you at the same time. Does that make sense?"

"You know I would do anything for you," said Ana, sitting up straight in her recliner, opening her eyes wide. "You are my dearest friend. What do you have up your sleeve that can help both Jack and me?" Ana sighed. "I need help? No, I don't need help."

"I'm having a small party this coming weekend at my house," Peggy explained. "It's Sunday night, and I want you to come and spend some time with Jack. He has this thing for a schoolteacher who won't give him the time of day. Jack thinks he can handle the situation, but he is naive. Mariah Morgan is her name, and she teaches at the country school near Jack's ranch. Do you know her?"

"Yes, I do," said Ana. "I sing with her in the church choir. She claims to be a born-again Christian. She is intelligent and pretty, with an excellent soprano voice."

"That's right," Peggy confirmed. "But Jack is lost in the woods when he is around her."

"I know," Ana said. "Mariah and I raked your son over the coals a while back at church. Mariah is too much for Fat Jack." Ana covered her mouth with her right palm. "Oh, I'm sorry. You don't want Jack to be called by his nickname. Everybody in town calls him Fat jack, and it slipped out."

Peggy, sensing Ana's guilt, found it convenient to give her a stare that showed disappointment. "I don't care what Jack's nickname is. I want to know what else you know about this woman."

"Mariah looks to me as a mother figure," said Ana, still embarrassed. "We sing in the choir and have coffee. Mariah has a belief about God that might not suit Jack's lifestyle. I would describe her as a reformed fundamentalist searching for a church home. Mariah likes the Episcopalian approach to religion, but she was raised stricter. I think she graduated from a Nazarene college in Idaho."

Ana paused, waiting for a response from Peggy. Peggy studied her drink.

"Mariah has the church bug," continued Ana. "Would you ever confide in being a born-again Christian? I can't imagine saying something like that, but Mariah makes no bones telling anyone who will listen. I think she is too religious for Jack. He would have to go to church regularly. I can't see him doing that."

"For this woman, he would jump off a cliff, and he has been going to church," countered Peggy. "I am worried about him, but he won't listen to me. Jack thinks I'm hare-brained. But you, Ana...you could set him straight on how to treat a woman. He needs direction, and you are the person to help him."

Ana sat up straight in her chair, drawing back from Peggy. Peggy leaned forward with her hands held in prayer.

"Please help. Please!"

"It sounds like you want me to take up with Jack." Ana shook her head. "Not on your life, and not even on your death. I can't be a nursemaid and a lover at the same time. Remember, I'm ten years older than Jack! Can you imagine the talk around town? I thought you wanted me to run for reelection next year!" Ana shook her head with emphasis. "No, I won't do it."

Peggy looked at Ana with hound-dog eyes, imploring her to help. Her folded hands still together.

"You have a way about you that commands attention. Jack is heartbroken. He needs someone like you to get him through this."

Ana continued to shake her head, getting up from the recliner.

Peggy tilted her head to the right, narrowing her eyes. "Do you remember that time we went to Great Falls to see Ray Charles? That Air Force guy took to you, not taking no for an answer. I had to come to your rescue. You were too polite and didn't want to be cruel. I got right in his face and told him to buzz off, and he did."

Ana stopped shaking her head but crossed her arms in front, standing with her weight on her left leg.

Peggy continued. "Do you remember after Richard died and every married guy in town wanted to satisfy your needs? Who helped you? I did. The only time you didn't listen to me, you ended up with Rib. How has that worked out? I had your back every time, and now I need your help with Jack. Will you come to my party?"

"Leave Rib out of this." Ana paced the floor. "Okay, I'll come to your party, but it's against my better judgment. I'm only doing this because you made me feel guilty." Ana finished her drink in one swallow. "You are my best friend, and I am thankful for all you have done for me. I'll do what I can with Jack, but I need ground rules."

"There are no ground rules," said Peggy. "Except to show up at my party. I will serve drinks and snacks. Play it by ear to see what comes next. That can't be too difficult for a lawyer, even if you are a woman."

"Oh, goddamn it," said Ana, pretending to be hurt. "If you keep saying mean things, I might back out on you. Already I'm sorry that I agreed to this...this...whatever you call it."

Peggy could only smile. Mission accomplished. "Will I see you before Sunday?" she asked.

"Probably," said Ana. "Gin might be the only thing that can get me through this charade."

* * *

The next evening, after six o'clock, Ana returned to Peggy's lair, where Peggy had closed up the store waiting for Ana. Ana had called Peggy during the afternoon to set up the meeting.

"I can't go through with this Jack thing," Ana blurted out. "I thought about it all night, not getting any sleep, and your idea to help Jack is terrible. I can't help you or him."

Ana stood with her hands on her hips, chin lowered, eyes narrowed in front of Peggy, who reclined in one of the chairs.

"No, no, and a big no," continued Ana. "I'm the county attorney, not a romance counselor. Your idea to help Jack is too much for me."

Peggy shrugged.

Ana started to pace the room, frustration twisting her face. "I can't do this. I know you have helped me many times, but it's too much to ask."

"Sit down and have a drink," said Peggy.

"A drink won't help. You'll try to change my mind, and I won't do what you are asking." Ana sat in the other recliner, taking deep breaths, steeling herself for Peggy's response. But Peggy changed the subject.

"This hasn't been my best day either, with a state liquor inspector inventorying the store. That damn man asking questions is a newbie that I need to train to my way of running this place. He wanted to know what these two easy chairs were doing here, and the refrigerator, and the ice bucket, and that half-full bottle of gin. He mentioned the rules didn't allow for the consumption of liquor in the store. I agreed and offered him a drink. He refused, ignoring my attempt at humor. Anyway, I agreed to clean up my act." Peggy smiled. "Are you sure you don't want a drink?"

"No, I don't need a drink, and I don't need to go along with helping Jack either," said Ana.

"I'm not asking you to seduce Jack," assured Peggy. "Spend some time with him. Teach him skills and manners so he does right by a woman. Jack has opportunities to find the right one, but he screws up somehow. He is stuck on this schoolteacher: She doesn't see it the same way, but she is friendly to him."

Peggy stood up from her chair, dashed her cigarette into the empty bottle of gin, and pointed her index finger at Ana. "For Christ sakes, Jack is thirty-three years old, single without any prospects for a good woman, and he doesn't have a clue about how to get one. My fault, I understand, so you don't need to remind me of my mothering skills during my gruesome marriage. It's a wonder he isn't queer."

"Don't be so hard on yourself," consoled Ana. "God knows every mother has that thought at some time. Jack seems like a good guy."

"Oh, Jack has good qualities," said Peggy. "But he needs to find a wife, stop drinking, and take an interest in what is happening in Fort Collins. He isn't clumsy on his feet. You should dance with him."

Peggy stared at Ana, who sat silently with a twisted look of disbelief. "Well, you should dance with him," she continued to insist. "You might have a different opinion. A man who can dance is good in bed."

Ana added a shake of her head to her distorted face, but she could see tears forming in Peggy's eyes.

"Come on," Ana said. "Jack is just like you, except he is a man. You are stuck in your own ways, opinionated, stubborn, and you don't give a damn what you say or who you say it to. I'm guessing Jack doesn't have a filter, and you have spoiled him. He's your only child."

Peggy lifted her face to Ana, her eyes still shining wet. "He won't listen to me. I'm his mother, and he brushes me off. But Jack might listen to you. He needs a woman of the world with experience, and, honey, you have a boat full."

Peggy laughed through her tears. "I didn't mean that in a bad way. I suppose now, you will not even give me the time of day. I'm sorry, but I'm desperate. I need your help with Jack. Please!"

"Damn you," retorted Ana. "I came here convinced your idea wouldn't work, and I still feel that way." Ana hesitated and sighed. "But you are making me feel guilty again, and I will consider it. There are a few days before your Sunday night party. I'll sleep on it and give you an answer tomorrow."

"Jack needs a woman like you," pressed Peggy. "And it wouldn't hurt you to get out of that current hiccup with Rib." As the two women eyed each other, Peggy spoke bluntly. "Rib is a dead-end for you."

"Rib and I are none of your business. Shut up about us. You are impossible, trying to fix Jack and me at the same time. That won't happen, and if that is a part of this whole scheme, I am out right now."

"This is not about you and Rib," defended Peggy. "Jack thinks going to the Shelby whorehouse is a date. He has no concept of what goes into a relationship. Margie down at the drugstore would be a good match for him, but expecting her to lay down and spread her legs for no reason doesn't cut the mustard. He never thinks about a woman's view. I don't think he has any idea of foreplay and afterglow."

"I don't expect to have a physical relationship with Jack," Ana declared.

Ana counted all the pitfalls she could think of, including her being older than Jack and the fact that Jack would surely make a pass at her, making it uncomfortable when she had to refuse him.

"This is insane," grumbled Ana. "I can't see it working. Jack is a grown man, and like you, he is no dummy. How can I pull the wool over his eyes without him thinking I am some sort of weirdo? An older woman taking after a younger man... We have nothing in common. I could tell him I could help him, but if he has any sense at all, he will walk away."

The two women faced each other, neither speaking. Ana giggled, and Peggy grinned. They both relaxed.

"I could use young blood in my life," sighed Ana. "It would give me a new perspective on men. I can imagine a roll in the hay with Jack. He is damn good-looking, but it will never happen."

Peggy beamed. "Then, you will help?"

Ana grunted that she would. "I have concerns because I have enough to deal with staying ahead of the commissioners and the sheriff, and I'm not going to stop seeing Rib. How can I juggle all that and do justice to Jack? I'm not a magician pulling a rabbit out of the hat."

"That's true," said Peggy. "But you are a woman and a damn good one. You'll find the time and think of the right thing to do. You can make this challenging, and besides me, who gives a damn if anything comes out of it? If necessary, I'll work my magic on the commissioners and the sheriff. None of them are the brightest bulbs in the room. Do we have a deal?"

"God, how are you able to talk me into these schemes?" asked Ana. "I should nix this idea, but I gave you my word." Ana shook her head. "I'm not sure of my next move."

Peggy, seeing an opening, cocked her head to one side and said with a grin, "Don't worry, I have a plan. You can't expect to coach Jack in one evening, so why don't you and I go to the dance at the VFW hall this Friday night with Jack? I will invite my man too. Jack can dance. I taught him all the good moves, and he does have a natural rhythm."

Ana rolled her eyes. "You call that a plan? I call it trickery. First, it was just Sunday night, and now you're asking me to join him Friday night too? Next, you will have me telling Jack that I am here to seduce him and ask him to spread his legs."

"That is a possibility," exclaimed Peggy. "I hear it is a chic French custom that mothers farm their sons out to their friends to teach them the facts of life. If you came and asked me to educate your son, I would do it."

Ana stuck her tongue out at Peggy. "Unladylike is how that comes off. I don't believe a mother would do that."

"It's true," insisted Peggy. "I read it in *Playboy*. This is the '70s. Haven't you heard about free love and the pill? Women are creating a revolution in this country, and we are part of it. Exciting, isn't it?"

Chagrined, Ana changed the subject. "Let's get back to the plan. I dance with Jack...and then what? Put it all on the line and tell him what I am doing and that you are the brains behind it all? Or I could flirt with him and be the dumb blonde waiting breathlessly for his next word or laugh outrageously at his stupid jokes. Or I could be a sexy slut with only one thing on my mind. Do you have any ideas?"

"I don't have a clue about how you should act," admitted Peggy. "You'll have to play it as it goes. Jack is headstrong, and I can't predict how he will react. He is more serious after Vietnam and sometimes shows a temper. Get him talking about the war. He never says anything to me, but you could jog his memory. Use your acting skills, be subtle and sophisticated, like you do with all the men you work with. I'm desperate for Jack to find someone to marry."

Ana let her shoulders slump. She turned to Peggy.

"Truthfully, what are we doing? You and I are drinking in the back room of your liquor store, breaking rules right and left and plotting to marry off your son. Don't we have something better to do? You know, save womankind from childish men? Win a Nobel Peace Prize?" Ana gave Peggy a resigned look. "I better go before I change my mind again."

Peggy hugged Ana, whispering in her ear, "See you Friday night."

Peggy watched Ana leave through the back door, lighting another cigarette and pouring half a glass of gin for herself. The gin gave her a warm feeling as it trickled down her throat.

"This is going to be grand," she said as she sat back in her recliner. "Ana is true blue, and Jack is going to get schooling he won't forget. And maybe a woman to marry."

CHAPTER 8

FRIDAY, SEPTEMBER 12, 1975

Ana drove to the VFW hall. The evening would feature drinks at half-price, folding chairs placed around tables, and room to dance to a jukebox featuring the latest pop songs along with country-western.

The moment had arrived. Ana parked her car and entered the veteran's hall. The time was five after seven as Ana did not want to appear too early or too late. She walked in and noticed the building was jumping with activity and that no one cared when she arrived. Peggy had claimed a table for four people as she had brought her latest beau, Rod Carlson, the project manager, for the road repair of Interstate 15.

Peggy waved her over to her table, where Rod and Jack were in deep conversation. As Ana approached the table, neither man acknowledged her nor offered to seat her.

"Hello? Anyone home?" Ana asked.

Both men ignored her, but Peggy returned her greeting.

"Pull up a chair and sit down. The music is just right for dancing."

Ana pulled the chair from the table and sat down, doing a mental roll of her eyes, thinking this would be a long evening unless she directed traffic.

"Gentlemen, which one of us is buying the first drink?" she inquired.

Both men turned to her. Rod immediately apologized. "Ana, I'm sorry. Bad manners don't make friends. I'll buy the first drink."

Jack sat silently. Ana replied to Rod. "Thank you. What is so important that you two can ignore your manners? Some football game?" Ana smiled her best smile. She knew how to distract a man's attention as she determined that the conversation needed to be changed.

"Jack, what do you think about drilling for oil in the Rocky Mountain Front?" Ana wanted to see if Jack could form an opinion and express it.

Jack, caught off guard by the direct question, took a moment, then answered. "There are two sides to that story, but I don't think it is a good idea. I know our country has an oil crisis and is getting robbed by the Arabs, but to me, the Rockies are sacred, particularly the Two Medicine country. I'm not Blackfoot, but I'd hate to see all that beauty destroyed by a bunch of oil rigs." He paused. "The Tribe should have some say in how their land is used."

Ana, taken back by the passion of Jack's stance, couldn't think of a response. She did make a mental note of how Jack had formed his opinion. Ana secretly agreed with Jack.

"All of us would be better off if we left the Front as it is. Have you spent any time in the Two Medicine?" Jack asked.

Ana ignored the question. She didn't want to reveal her special weekend with Rib. But Jack's response had given her a new perspective on the evening. Jack could articulate a firmly held belief. He was intelligent, but was he a jerk? He always wore those damn aviator sunglasses even at night. She would have to find out more about him.

"Your mother tells me you like to dance," said Ana. "Would you care to dance with me?"

The jukebox had started playing "Proud Mary" with Tina Turner singing. The beat had started out slow but was now at the fast swing of the song. Jack stood up and turned toward the dance floor. Ana pushed her chair back and followed him, casting a doubtful look at Peggy and pointing at her chair as she got up to dance. Rod and Peggy followed them to the dance floor.

"Tina has an edge to her voice, doesn't she?" Ana commented as Jack turned around to face her.

Jack didn't respond as he grasped Ana's hands in his, starting a jitterbug where their bodies were separated from each other. He twirled Ana around in a graceful motion, pulling her into his body, challenging her, then spinning her out, bringing her back under his arm, their footsteps in perfect sync. The music ended with Jack spinning Ana around into his arms.

"Not bad for a farmer," remarked Ana as she pushed him away.

"What do you mean? I'm a damn good dancer. You could hardly keep up with me."

"Oh, I can keep up with you," assured Ana with a sly look and grin. "You are just beginning to learn that." Ana had changed her mind during the song. Jack was bright, and he could dance.

"Why are you called Fat Jack?" She had felt his firm body when he had pulled her into his arms during the dance.

Ana saw Jack look embarrassed before he answered. "When I see something that I like, I say, 'That's fat.' My pilot buddies stuck me with Fat Jack."

"I wouldn't like to be called fat if you ever came to like me," teased Ana.

Jack looked into Ana's eyes. "I could come to like you," he decided. "But, it would be a cold day in hell. I haven't forgotten that Sunday in church with Mariah. I still can't figure out what you two were trying to prove."

Ana saw her opening. "Mariah was not comfortable with the two of you looking like a couple. She asked me to stay with her during coffee hour."

"What do you mean, looking like a couple?"

"Mariah felt bad about something and invited you to church as a gesture of friendship. She hadn't thought through the picture it might paint that you two were dating. You have to try and understand how a woman thinks about those things."

"Why would that make a difference?" questioned Jack. "I want to be with Mariah."

"But what have you done to make her want to be with you?"

Jack looked at Ana but didn't have an answer.

"You need to be concerned about those things," explained Ana. "A woman has a choice. So, what have you done for Mariah lately that would make her sit up and take notice?"

"I don't like where this conversation is going," grumbled Jack. "It's none of your business."

"You're right. It is not my business, but the question is how to get closer to Mariah, isn't it? I can help you."

"I don't want your help. I can take care of myself. I'm not impressed with your ideas."

"You should be concerned about how a woman thinks. We have a point of view and feelings. Surely, you are aware of Mariah's needs, or have you even thought about it?" Jack stared back at Ana without answering.

They ended their dance. Jack walked in front of Ana and back to his seat, not holding out Ana's chair for her as she sat down, silence engulfing them. Peggy and Rod kept dancing.

Ana confronted Jack again across the table. "You never answered my question. Tina Turner has an angry edge to her voice. Do you think that is because she is black or because she is a woman?"

"Hell, I don't know, and I don't care," said Jack. "I like the way she sings. You can dance to her music." Jack shifted uneasily in his chair, thinking back to his Sunday morning grilling by Ana and Mariah. "Why are you asking me these questions? Women and men are attracted to each other. So what? The color of skin might make a difference, but I don't worry about those things."

Peggy and Rod returned to the table where Ana and Jack were glaring at each other. An awkward stillness hung over the table.

Jack's face turned red as he faced Ana across the table.

"Why are you so upset?" asked Ana. "We can agree to disagree. I like what you said about the Two Medicine. No drilling on the Rocky Mountain Front suits me. We haven't agreed on everything, but that is unrealistic, isn't it? Don't give up on dancing with me, even if I called you a farmer."

Jack, pouting, replied, "Well, someone might ask you to dance, but it won't be me."

"Oh, you think you are the only game in town? Watch this!" Ana stood up and confidently walked to a table four spaces over near the dance floor's center and asked the man sitting there to dance. He readily accepted, joining Ana on the floor. They danced to Issac Hayes' slow, soulful song, "Walk On By." Ana allowed the man to pull her into his body as they slowly settled into each other's arms. Fat Jack pretended not to see but glanced out of the corner of his eye.

Peggy, now dancing with Rod, watched from the dance floor, smiling on the inside but serious on the outside, trying not to show her interest, but Ana already had Jack stammering, confused, and angry, and now she was dancing with another man. Peggy ended her dance with Rod by asking him to get her another drink. She started back to the table where Jack sat alone.

Jack waited for his mother to sit down. He looked at her for sympathy. "You told me Ana would be my date tonight. What is this all about? What is she doing dancing with that fellow?"

Peggy shrugged. "You better talk with Ana about your problems. I can't help you." Peggy could hardly keep her grin from showing as she awaited Ana's next move.

The Isaac Hayes song ended with Ana smiling at her partner, who happened to be an attorney in town. Daniel Jacobson could be Ana's competition for the county attorney's job in the next election, but Ana sang with his wife in their church choir, and Ana had great respect for Daniel's work as a lawyer.

Daniel's wife returned to the table as the music stopped. She and Ana hugged, exchanging a warm embrace, and Ana whispered, "Thank you. I'll fill you in later."

Ana returned to Peggy's table, where Jack pouted. Ana didn't miss a beat, speaking directly to Jack.

"Don't ever forget a woman has a choice. What is special enough about you for me to waste my affections if you don't treat me right? There are a dozen men here who would love to make a pass at me. Give me a reason to like you."

Rod returned with drinks for the foursome. Peggy lifted her glass, mouthing a silent "Hallelujah" as Ana played her role perfectly, talking tough to Jack. The tug of war and exchange of words delighting her. Peggy wanted to give Ana an Oscar for her performance.

Jack, on the other hand, sputtered out, "Aren't we on a date? You are supposed to stay with me."

"Give me a reason why," Ana pressed.

Jack was silent.

"I sit at your table, and you ignore me. You don't stand and hold my chair or offer to buy me a drink. How could you expect me to worship the ground you stand on if you don't care. As I said, there are cowboys in here who would treat me like a woman. This is not a date. Other men will dance with me. I brought my own car to leave when I want to. I'm not dependent on you."

Jack, flummoxed by Ana's directness, could not manage an answer.

"The dance with you is nothing compared to the heights I've experienced in my life," Ana continued. "What else do you have to offer?"

Jack regained his composure, seeing the slight grin on Ana's face. "All right, I'm getting the drift here. Why don't we dance?" Jack liked the challenge Ana had directed at him.

Jack stood and walked behind Ana, helping her with her chair. They moved to the dance floor with Ana leading the way as Charley Pride's "Kiss

An Angel Good Morning" played on the jukebox. Jack tried to hold Ana tight, but Ana pushed him away with her brightest smile.

"Keep your distance, Mr. Fat Jack Moser. A woman needs time. You men are all the same, with fast hands and rough touches. Slow down and treat a woman with respect."

The song ended and Jack and Ana returned to the table where Peggy and Rod had just seated themselves after their dance.

Jack gave Ana a deep appraisal with interest in his eyes. Her words came across to him as a promise for the future. He smiled and kept his distance as he spoke.

"I apologize for my rudeness. I don't mean to push the envelope. I will do better in the future." After a moment of silence, Jack asked, "Is there a future?" Jack now enjoyed the game being played. Ana had bewitched Jack, just as she planned.

"There is no need to apologize," said Ana, "but can you accept the idea of taking your time to build a relationship? Rushing is not in my nature. A woman will make the decision anyway, so why don't you sit back and enjoy?"

Jack didn't have an answer to that question either. Ana let the silence between them linger. She guessed that Jack's mind was absorbing her directness. She had purposely put him on the spot to see his reaction. In her mind, Jack could be salvaged. He had passed her test with his response to the Two Medicine with a reasoned answer. He danced gracefully. And Jack was handsome. Ana smiled at Peggy sitting across the table. Peggy returned it.

Peggy broke the silence with a laugh. "Isn't this fun? Why don't we all come to my house on Sunday night for a small party? I'll invite a couple more people to make a night of it with a cocktail hour and some snacks. How about it?"

Ana, intrigued by the conversation with Jack, agreed on Sunday night. *What could it hurt?* she thought. Jack had become more than a project. Ana's curiosity had grown.

"It's time for me to go home. I wouldn't want to ruin a perfect night," Ana said, looking at Jack. "In the old days, I'd stay until the bar closed, but not tonight. See everybody Sunday night."

Jack thought about walking Ana out but decided against it. The idea to slow down stuck with him. He could play the game too, and surprisingly, he was attracted to Ana. He had never had a woman speak so directly to him about his manners.

Jack wondered if Sunday night might hold a surprise for him.

CHAPTER 9

SUNDAY, SEPTEMBER 14, 1975

Ana drove into Peggy's driveway at 6:30 Sunday evening, prepared to have an early cocktail, some food, and then go home. She nearly turned around as she identified Rib Torgerson's distinct veterinarian pickup parked in front of Peggy's house. She groaned, saying out loud, "Damn you, Peggy Moser. What is Rib doing here?"

She slammed her car into reverse and would have left had it not been for the arrival of Jack's pickup blocking her path. She muttered more profanities under her breath. "I'm damned if I do and damned if I don't." But her promise to Peggy prevailed, and Jack had struck a chord with her on Friday night. She sighed, accepting the situation.

Peggy had set up the Friday night dance hall meeting with Jack, followed by the Sunday night social hour, and now Rib had entered the picture. A sit-down face-to-face with Peggy was now on Ana's agenda.

On second thought, Ana began to see possibilities this evening: Both Jack and Rib would be in the same room. Ana decided to walk in arm in arm with Jack and see what Rib's reaction would be. After all, Ana had enjoyed Friday night dancing with Jack, and Rib had not called since the

Labor Day weekend. And hadn't she told Rib that she could walk away from him at any time?

Ana turned off her car's ignition, hopped out, and greeted Jack with a smile and a hug.

"What is the occasion?" Jack asked, grinning to himself about his lucky day.

"Let's enjoy the evening," said Ana. "We had a great time Friday night, didn't we?"

Jack agreed, and Ana was forming other possibilities about this evening. This party might give her direction and move her forward with her promise to Peggy. And, *Jack could be helpful*, Ana thought, *if only to make Rib jealous.*

Ana put her arm in Jack's as they turned toward the house. Jack didn't knock; he just walked in. There were three couples with drinks in hand.

Peggy and Rod, Rib and Connie, and the other couple lifted their cocktail glasses to the newcomers.

"It's about time you two showed up," said Peggy. "What will you have to drink? We need to toast the evening."

Ana indicated a gin and tonic, and Jack, a whiskey straight up. Ana glanced at Rib, expecting a greeting, but he avoided her eyes. Connie stood close to Rib and gave Ana a slight nod, not speaking to her directly.

"What fun to see everyone together," Ana said sarcastically.

Peggy, catching the sharpness of Ana's voice, avoided eye contact.

"Yes, we are one big happy family, aren't we?" Peggy turned to Jack and asked, "Did you pick Ana up?"

"No, why would I do that?" Jack glared at his mother.

Ana chimed in loud enough for Rib to hear. "Jack offered, but I thought it better to bring my own car." Ana changed the subject. "Jack has promised to show me his ranch some weekend, haven't you, Jack?"

Somewhat bewildered and ignoring Ana's question, Jack turned to Rib. "I've brought all my cows back from the mountains. Is there anything else I need to do with them?" Rib had spent the last week at Jack's ranch pregnancy-testing, getting Jack's herd ready for the winter.

"A few more days should do it," mumbled Rib as he avoided Ana's glare. Connie caught the look Ana gave Rib.

"Let's have some food," interrupted Peggy.

Ana suggested a bridge game, trying to engage Jack.

"But I don't think this is the right time for cards," said Jack, but getting a look from Peggy, caught on. "However, since you asked, I would play some bridge."

Not finding two more players, Ana gave up on the card game, but another question had been answered by Jack. He did play bridge. *Another check in the positive column for Fat Jack*, Ana thought.

She settled into a comfortable chair, deep in her own thoughts. After her husband Richard had died, she had been true blue to his memory, except for her time with Rib. Why continue this charade with Rib? She knew the answer had its roots in a long-ago relationship with him when she was young and naive. Ana's love for Rib would always exist because he gave her something no one else could, not even her late husband. What was that something? She couldn't explain it; it lived in her heart.

Why not take up with Jack? Ana pondered the question.

Peggy often said to Ana, "Live a little.... In fifty years—heck, in ten years or maybe five—no one is going to judge you for what you have done. Hell, doing something out of the ordinary would be your legacy if you are interested in that sort of thing. But remember, do it with style without hurting anyone."

Ana thought that someone always got hurt, but the argument of "Who really cares?" appealed to her tonight. At this point, she didn't give a damn about her friendship with Peggy or her relationship with Rib.

The immediate problem, she thought, *is figuring out how to end this evening*. She could leave right now or stay and play out the game with Jack while hopefully managing to affect Rib.

Ana sighed, took a long breath, and turned to the gaggle of people. She would suffer this evening, playing Jack against Rib with Peggy and Connie as spectators. She perked up her head, thinking, *I can do this dance of love better than anyone here.*

Ana slid over toward the couch where Jack sat. Rib and Connie were sitting across from Jack in their individual chairs. Ana sat on the floor, putting her arm on Jack's knees and casting a radiant smile at Rib. Again, Connie returned Ana's smile with a dagger look.

"This is such a beautiful evening," commented Ana. "It's so nice to see people I haven't seen in a long time." The conversation died down; nobody could think of anything to say.

Jack spoke first. "Does anyone know when Monday Night Football starts?"

Rib answered. "The Monday after the Stampede is the first game. Does anyone know what day that is?"

"It's the twenty-second," Ana replied, looking at Peggy. "Are you going to start up your Monday night dinners again? Those butterfly tenderloins are to die for."

"I am going to have those dinners. It's almost too soon after the Stampede, but we might need to kick back and recharge after the rodeo," decided Peggy.

Ana looked at Rib, then checked her empty glass. "I think I'll have another drink," she announced, as she stood up and strolled to the kitchen to mix a gin and tonic.

As Ana prepared the mix, Rib walked in, grabbing the ice bucket and a Black Velvet bottle of whiskey.

"What the hell are you doing?" he asked Ana in a hushed voice. "You are making everyone in the room uncomfortable with the nice talk. Connie knows about us."

"I'm trying to make everyone fidget," Ana said, returning Rib's low whisper. "It's about time I find out where I stand. I haven't seen or heard from you since Labor Day. I can't go on meeting on weekends you select."

Rib gave his attention to pouring his drink. "We've had this conversation. What you are doing now isn't helping."

"You've told me that before, but maybe I'm the one who is changing," said Ana.

Peggy walked into the kitchen, and Ana, after mixing the gin drink, added two olives.

"How nice to have the old gang together," Ana said to Peggy. "I can't imagine having a more amusing evening." Ana looked first to Rib and then to Peggy. "*Monday Night Football* should be a blast." Ana raised her glass. "I've got to get back to Jack."

Peggy showed a forced smile, and Rib grumbled and frowned as Ana left the room and returned to her seat on the floor at Jack's knees. Peggy and Rib followed her into the living room, with Rib asking Peggy in his hushed voice, "Who put her tail in the ringer?"

Peggy continued to smile, ignoring him as she sat down.

Ana gazed into Jack's eyes. "When are you going to show me around your ranch?" she asked. "You promised you would find the time, and I would love to spend the day with you."

Jack replied, "Any time would be fine, except next weekend is the Stampede. How about dinner Friday night instead?"

"Friday night dinner suits me. You'll pick me up at six?" asked Ana. "But don't think that you will be able to get out of taking me to your ranch because it's Stampede weekend."

"I'll pick you up at six," agreed Jack, beaming.

As Ana had planned, the conversation took place within Rib's hearing range, though the veterinarian pretended not to listen. Sitting next to Rib, Connie gave Ana another icy stare.

Ana stood up from the rug with help from Jack, who gave her his hand. "Walk me to my car?" she requested.

Ana left the house and headed toward her vehicle, letting Jack hold her arm. At the car door, she turned, giving Jack a quick brush of her lips against his cheek. "See you Friday at six."

Ana closed the car door, leaving a grinning Jack Moser standing in the cool autumn Montana evening breeze.

CHAPTER 10

MONDAY, SEPTEMBER 15, 1975

A burgeoning glow could be seen in the east as dawn broke, the light from a rising sun detected on the far horizon. Rib Torgerson drove his pickup, heading toward Fort Collins, five miles east of his ranch. Rib loved this time of year; the fall equinox lent itself to warm days and cool nights, and last week's snow brought an extra crispness to the air, hinting at the coming of winter. Rib loved the changes in the seasons

"Goddamn," he said. "It's good to be alive." Immediately, he silently reminded himself to not say *goddamn* around Mariah. The weekend had been full of pleasure and surprise. With Mariah, it had been Friday night delight; though dinner that following Sunday held a surprise as Ana had shown up on the arm of Jack Moser.

However, Rib had sized up the situation immediately upon seeing Ana enter with Jack. He had to hand it to Peggy; she was a smart cookie with a penchant for mixing people together. Rib wondered why she got her kicks from creating drama. *Well, different strokes,* he thought. It wouldn't worry him; he and Peggy had a history and an understanding, but that had been years ago. *Nothing to worry about,* Rib thought.

He had been careful when Ana appeared. Connie knew about their relationship and even the beginnings of their romance nearly thirty years ago. Rib cared deeply about Ana and would have married her then but for his father's pressure. His dad's insistence on marrying Connie had been a mystery the man had carried to his grave.

Rib had often told Ana that she had gotten the best deal because he couldn't be tied to one woman. His relationship with Ana, born out of passion at a young age, had matured, leading to a frank conversation about each other's strengths and weaknesses. He openly admitted to Ana that his marriage to Connie had become one of convenience.

The challenge of a new woman in his life was what Rib lived for each day. As much as he adored Ana, he never would have been faithful had they married.

Mariah, the schoolteacher, had become his new focus. The woman reminded him of Ana. There were many parallels, all leading to Rib's fascination with the schoolmarm. Ana held a special place in Rib's heart, but the prospect of developing a relationship with Mariah overpowered any misgivings. Besides, Ana would be available any time he called.

Mariah had asked him point-blank, "Do you believe in God?" His answer about the Blackfeet and the Great Spirit had evidently satisfied her curiosity; Mariah had made her choice as women do. Rib didn't argue but used his experience and guile to further gain her trust.

Rib had learned to listen to women, respect their ideas, encourage their actions, value their opinion, and await their decision to get involved with him. Rib never pressured a woman to take him for her lover, always having patience; sometimes it worked, and sometimes it didn't. He justified his extramarital behavior that way, reasoning that someone else made the choice for him.

Rib passed through Fort Collins onto Interstate 15 heading north. He didn't stop at the Home Cafe for breakfast as he usually did. This morning he had scrambled some eggs, fried four pieces of bacon, and ate two slices of whole-wheat toast. Connie had long ago stopped making breakfast or lunch or dinner for him, claiming his veterinary hours made it impossible to plan any meals. Rib suspected other reasons, but he had cooked for himself in the past, and the restaurants in Fort Collins filled in for the missed home cooking.

On the smooth, paved interstate highway, he planned his day. He would stop by Mariah's to check on Tucker, then head to Jack Moser's for a day of pregnancy-testing the rancher's cattle, and then back to Mariah's to see what the evening promised. Checking each animal at Jack's place would take only a few more days. He would have to figure out another excuse to stop by Mariah's when his work ended at Jack's.

Rib steered his pickup to the right, rolling off the interstate and onto the gravel road going east. If not for his planned visit to Mariah's, he would have taken the first left turn to Jack's ranch, but he passed that turnoff and traveled to the next crossroad leading to the school.

Arriving at the barn across from the teacherage, Rib encountered Swede, who was tending to Tucker.

Swede stood with his feet wide apart as he faced Rib.

"Don't hurt that young woman. She is a sweetheart," warned Swede.

Rib eyed Swede before speaking.

"Mariah is a grown woman who knows what she wants. There is no way I would hurt her. You sound like you're jealous."

"You take care," replied Swede. "Or you will have me to answer to. I know the ways of men like you. Nothing good comes from it. Mariah is young enough to be your daughter." Swede blew his nose on the ground in contempt.

"Don't you worry," said Rib. Silently, Rib cursed, thinking that Swede should mind his own business.

"How is Tucker doing?" Rib asked, trying to change the conversation.

"If that was what you were concerned about, I might answer your question. But by the looks of it, you are more interested in Mariah. The horse is doing fine. Tucker doesn't need your help two times a day. I don't like what you are doing."

Rib, seeing no easy way to end this attack on his motives, simply nodded.

"Glad the horse is doing fine. I'll go over to see Mariah and give her your expert diagnosis." Rib turned and drove his pickup across the road to the teacherage, leaving Swede shaking his head and staring hard at Rib's departure.

Mariah answered Rib's knock on the door with a smile and an offer to come in. Once inside, Mariah gave Rib a quick kiss on the lips.

"How is Tucker doing?" she asked.

"Swede thinks Tucker is fine," said Rib. "And doesn't need a broken-down vet coming around twice a day for checkups."

Mariah cocked her head with a questioned look.

Rib continued. "Swede is right. I am spending too much time here, but you are the reason, not Tucker. Mind you, I will keep checking up on that horse of yours." Rib paused with a twinkle in his eye. "With your permission."

"You have my permission, Mr. Veterinarian. I want Tucker examined every day, regardless of what Swede says. Go work Jack's cattle and think about stopping to see Tucker this afternoon. I've got to get ready for school." Mariah had a twinkle in her eyes as well.

Rib returned the look, then gave her a light kiss. "I'll be back," he promised.

CHAPTER 11

MONDAY, SEPTEMBER 15, 1975

Peggy reflected on last night's party as she stacked bottles in the store on Monday.

As Ana had left the party, she had given Peggy a fake smile, an icy "Thank you for the nice evening," and then added harshly, "Let's talk after work tomorrow."

Jack had been befuddled by Ana's directness in asking to visit his ranch on the weekend, Rib had been perplexed, and his wife, Connie, more icy silent than usual. A perfect evening from Peggy's viewpoint; everyone had been off-balance! Peggy awaited Ana's expected after-hours tempest.

Ana stormed into the liquor store's back room at 6 p.m. sharp, ready for battle, but Peggy surprised her with the question: "What's the scariest movie you've ever seen?"

"I don't want to talk about scary movies," snapped Ana. "I want to know what last evening accomplished. You put me in the same room with Rib and Connie for some purpose that I can't imagine. What a horrible night."

"That's why we should talk about scary movies," said Peggy. "The scariest movie I ever saw was *Psycho*—the part where Janet Leigh gets stabbed by the kook. After that movie, I couldn't take a shower without locking the front and back doors, drawing all the blinds, and putting a chair against the doorknob in the bathroom. No sense in taking any chances."

"What does that have to do with last night?" demanded Ana. "A shower stabbing happening in sleepy Fort Collins is not possible. Our lives aren't at risk. Why would you worry about it?"

"You never know what could happen here in this sleepy town," said Peggy. "Running the bar and selling booze in this store gives me a view of the world that you don't have."

"You think what I do doesn't bring me into contact with real characters?" Ana shot back. "And some of them aren't criminals, but they don't make me feel unsafe."

"Me neither," agreed Peggy. "Except I still put a chair on the doorknob when I shower."

Ana put her hands on her hips. "You are changing the subject! Oh, Peggy, if you weren't my dearest friend, and if I hadn't made this insane promise to help your son, I'd walk out and leave you."

After receiving no response from Peggy, she sighed and shook her head. "I don't understand why you had to bring everyone together."

Peggy still didn't answer, letting Ana vent.

"The whole evening was a disaster. You don't think so, but I do. I don't know how else to describe it. Rib ignored me, and Connie made faces all evening. Can't you see why I'm a little pissed?" The two women exchanged glances. "The only good thing was Jack wants to have dinner with me and then take a tour of his ranch."

A satisfied smile of accomplishment came over Peggy's face. "You haven't answered my question. What is the scariest movie you've ever seen? *Psycho* haunts me. What haunts you?"

"*You* are starting to haunt me," replied Ana. "You say you want me to give Jack some direction, but what you really want is for me to stop seeing Rib."

The two women kept staring each other down.

Finally, Peggy couldn't hold back a huge grin. "Since you put it that way, I can't deny it, but it isn't my sole reason for putting all of you in the same room. Jack's future with a woman is *numero uno* with me. Humor me!" directed Peggy.

"Humor you? That's becoming my sole purpose in life. You don't need to worry about me. I can take care of myself. And I don't need a man to pick up after. I've been there, and it's not all that it's cracked up to be." Ana paused. "Did you know that Richard and I were having our issues before he got sick? He might have been chasing some local honey. I'm not sure of it, but he spent a lot of evenings away, coming home smelling like a perfumed brewery."

"Yeah, I thought as much." Peggy nodded. "I'm sorry you had to go through that and then find out about Richard's cancer. I hear things in this store and at Busty's. My guess is the daughter of the beer distributor. Their delivery man bitched about his time being beat by some married guy in town. There are not many secrets in Fort Collins that I don't hear about."

Several moments of silence passed before Peggy spoke again. "People in town know about you and Rib. As long as your affair doesn't affect them, nothing will be said, but Rib might come back to haunt your next election. You have to consider that possibility."

Ana nodded. "I love my job. I'm going to fight to keep it, but I love Rib, and I don't want to lose what we have—even if it is just a weekend here and there. Oh, God, what am I going to do? Can you help me?"

"I'm trying my damnedest," said Peggy. "But meet me halfway. I know what is going through your mind. Rib and I had a fling fifteen years ago. He's a hard man to back away from. Remember that he treats women fairly. You can't help but love him, but you aren't going to change him. Look around and make the tough decision to leave him. Rib will not ride off into the sunset with you, and your fascination with him could cost you the next election."

"You never told me about you and Rib," Ana shot back with a flash of anger in her voice. "I'm not sure I can handle any more secrets from you. Give it to me straight. What happened?"

"Sit down. We need a drink to cool off," said Peggy as she reached for the gin bottle. "It happened a long time ago, and nothing came of it. I was unhappy at the time, and there wasn't much to do in the winter except screw around. This handsome, rich guy paid me attention, and I craved the excitement. I was stuck out there on the ranch by myself. Rib provided the opportunity, and then he moved on, just like he will with you." Peggy wanted to end this conversation. "Don't be mad at me."

"I'm not mad at you," assured Ana. "I have no illusions about Rib and his wandering eye. Did Connie know about it?"

"I don't know," said Peggy. "I'm guessing she did because trying to hide an affair from a wife is hard. On the other hand, I don't think my husband had a clue what I did."

"I'm not sure I can break it off with Rib," sighed Ana. "When push comes to shove, I'll choose Rib over the job, but as you say, Rib is not going to change. Damn him!"

Peggy saw her opening. "Give your time and attention to Jack. What do you have to lose? Rib will always be at your beck and call. He can't stay away from you for too long, so give him something to think about by taking up with Jack."

The silence between the two friends stretched on as each dwelled on their thoughts. Peggy broke the quiet again. "You were magnificent at the dance hall. Jack couldn't find his way with you. Dancing with that other fellow gave him a look from the other side of the fence. I should award you whatever Hollywood gives to their best actresses."

Ana smiled. "I did it right, didn't I?" Ana had been pleased with her spur-of-the-moment plan to be direct with Jack.

Peggy pushed on. "That's only half of it. Last night, you got to Rib by coming in with Jack and getting dinner and a weekend at the ranch. Rib tried to ignore it, but I caught his eye, and if he wasn't angry, he was at least jealous. You scored points on lover boy."

Again, Ana went silent for several moments, then looked sternly into Peggy's eyes. "Are you making that up? Did I really get to Rib? That would be a first. I guess I intended to give him a jab or two because he ignored me the whole evening. Having Connie there made it awkward, but he could have at least talked to me. Connie is no dummy. She knows about Rib and me. Rib tells me she doesn't care, but Connie gave me dagger stares all night. Connie does care, and that bothers me."

Peggy, thinking she shouldn't have said anything about Rib being jealous, changed the conversation back to Jack. "Take a step back—you know, like a time-out, with Rib. What you are doing with Jack involves the promise you made to me. Go to dinner with him and see his ranch. Go with the flow. I don't expect you two to get married and live happily ever after. But I want you to give Jack direction in treating a woman. He needs to get married and have a family."

"Peggy, you aren't pushing for grandchildren, are you?" inquired Ana. "You know I'm too old to get pregnant, and I can't imagine asking you to babysit for me."

"No, I'm not worried about grandchildren," lied Peggy, hesitating before she continued. "I wouldn't mind carrying on the family to have someone running the ranch, but only for the ranch. I can't see myself herding a bunch of rug rats, even if they were my own flesh and blood."

Ana did not believe a word Peggy had just said. "I'm tired," said Ana with a yawn. "Fighting with you is exhausting. I want to go home, have a glass of wine, take a shower, and go to bed."

Peggy's advice to step back from Rib had struck a chord. Maybe time off from Rib was the answer.

Should I take up with Jack? she asked herself.

Ana hugged Peggy and left the back room.

CHAPTER 12

FRIDAY, SEPTEMBER 19, 1975

Ana fretted about the coming time with Jack. First, a dinner tonight, and then a visit to his ranch in eight days. She toyed with canceling, but her promise to Peggy needed to be kept, so that option was off the table. As she did with her law practice, Ana visualized how the date would go. She thought of it as a jury trial; who knew what the outcome would be? She certainly didn't.

Would dinner happen in Great Falls, Shelby, or right here in Fort Collins? A Great Falls trip meant an hour down and an hour back. What would they talk about? Ana worried it would all prove to be too much, especially if the dinner did not go well. Shelby did not have a decent restaurant and would be a forty-minute drive up and back. Not a good option.

Fort Collins appeared to be the best choice, but the gossip hounds would be barking over their supposed romance. Could Ana handle the busybodies? Yes, she could, but to lessen the burden, she would ask Jack for a five-thirty dinner and not change out of her office clothes, making it appear as a business dinner. Of course, most people wouldn't buy that story, but in Ana's mind, she could better justify her appearance with Jack.

Ana anticipated Friday night all throughout that week. She had meetings with the three county commissioners on Wednesday morning and Thursday afternoon, working out the details on the proposed building of a county hospital. Hill-Burton funds from the federal government were available, though the application process included several hoops they would need to jump through. Ana had told them it would be a three- or four-month process at a minimum, putting the proposed end date at the spring of 1976.

She met with Sheriff Wendell Wagner on Wednesday afternoon in her office. It was her turn, after all.

Alternating their meeting place had become symbolic of their relationship. The sheriff wanted all the meetings to take place in his office, declaring evidence shouldn't be removed from his evidence room. Ana thought it a power play and had disagreed. They had compromised, deciding that their discussions would occur on an alternating schedule, with each party taking turns. This Wednesday meeting landed on Ana's day in her office.

Ana and the sheriff had clashed on their first case three years ago, with the sheriff making an arrest for possession of marijuana. Sheriff Wagner had climbed a fence onto Gus Winslow's private property without a warrant, mounted a trash can to peer into Gus' garage, found a marijuana-growing operation, and seized the growing plants. Wagner had insisted he acted with cause to make the arrest before the plants could be destroyed, and Ana had gone to trial.

Gus's defense attorney moved to have the evidence suppressed on the grounds of an illegal search without a warrant. Wagner should have come to her first and then to a judge, who would either grant or deny the affidavit-based application. Ana had argued with the sheriff before filing the case, knowing what would happen.

The sheriff had said to her, "File the case. It will send a message to all the druggies and argue that the evidence would have been destroyed if I hadn't seized the plants immediately. I didn't need a warrant."

Ana had pointed out, "You climbed a fence and entered Gus' private property without permission, all based on an informant's word. A judge has to decide whether you could even legally enter the property. You definitely needed more evidence to make the arrest." The sheriff thought Ana naive when they lost the trial, setting Gus Winslow free.

Ana had chalked that trial up to her inexperience. But she did not file the next case Sheriff Wendall Wagner proposed, despite his objection. The sheriff had arrested a juvenile for possession of marijuana, promising the young boy immunity in exchange for help in getting the goods on the drug dealer. Wagner had concealed himself in the trunk of the young man's car, hopping out at the moment of the sale to make the arrest.

Ana later said to Wagner, "We have an issue with entrapment here. You coerced a juvenile to set up a crime where you hid in the trunk of a car to make an arrest. It is too much of a stretch."

The sheriff had retorted, "You don't have courage. You are soft on crime. This marijuana business has to be stopped, and you aren't helping. I know how to run my office, but you need to be on my side. Let me do my job!"

Ana didn't back down and didn't file the case. Subsequent criminal cases became a constant battle between them. Ana followed the law, and the sheriff continued to make his arrests. Wagner would come into her office with declarations and taunts such as, "I've got a good case here. Do you have the guts to file it? Or are you going to let some criminal walk?"

"I'll follow the laws, Mr. Sheriff, and you should too," Ana often retorted. "Do your homework, get a search warrant, and don't try to set up a crime scene. Stop trying to make everyone a criminal. You have to use discretion and common sense before bringing someone in front of a judge."

Ana did file some cases, but she made sure she could use sound legal arguments that the sheriff either didn't know or didn't want to follow. Ana judged Sheriff Wendall Wagner as a crusading man with a desperate need for power.

* * *

After Ana's Wednesday meeting with the sheriff and the county commissioners, she went to Peggy's after work, relaying the day's events. Peggy didn't have much advice in dealing with Wagner or the commissioners, but she had a mouthful regarding Ana's concerns with her upcoming date with Jack.

Peggy, with both hands on her hips lectured Ana, who reclined in the easy chair.

"Women have the final say in a relationship. I judge men by whether I could go to bed with them. I may never do such a thing, but then again, I might. There is nothing spontaneous: It's my body and my choice. A man has little to say on how a relationship develops."

Peggy bent down to Ana and gave her a hug, then held her at arm's length. "Your date with Jack will be fine. Remember that you control what happens, not him. If Jack is any kind of man, he will make a pass at you because he is a man. You have to anticipate what he will do and then decide how far you want to go."

"But hopping into bed with Jack is not on my mind," said Ana. "I don't have a plan."

"Make a plan" Peggy replied. "Remember, you control the evening. Show Jack how to slow down when he is with you. Wherever it goes from there is up to you."

Those words had stayed with Ana. Would she kiss Jack good night, or would he expect something more? Ana vowed there would be no one-night stand on this date. She decided to challenge Jack to see if he had a sense of humor or whether his ego would trip him up. Talking to Peggy gave Ana a calmness that made her feel ready to handle any advances by Jack.

Ana looked forward to her Friday night dinner.

CHAPTER 13

SATURDAY, SEPTEMBER 27, 1975

Eight days later, Ana reflected on all the surprising developments regarding her dinner date. Jack had called late on Friday afternoon, begging off, saying he had an emergency with one of his cows and the veterinarian had arrived to deal with the sick animal. Ana had been disappointed; Jack intrigued her in a way she could not explain. Ana had looked forward to the evening. Now as she prepared to drive to Jack's ranch, anticipation energized her.

That September morning, with its slight wind and bright sunshine, promised a new adventure. Ana had spent time on Rib's ranch when she was younger, working with the horses and cattle. She could pitchfork hay with the best of them and lift hundred-pound bales. All that may have happened a while back, but Ana still kept her body in shape with daily runs.

Approaching the turnoff to Jack's ranch from the south, she noticed an older pickup about a quarter of a mile away being driven at high speed and coming toward her. Ana pulled over to the side of the gravel road to wait for its passing, but the vehicle turned off on the road leading to Jack's place. She followed.

Jack's ranch lay a quarter-mile west of the gravel road. The house was an old-style, white-framed structure surrounded by a hedged lawn. Farther back, a windbreak consisting of Russian olives, pine trees, and tall, sweeping cottonwoods protected the house and several outbuildings, including a shop, a bunkhouse, a huge red barn, and several massive corrals.

The pickup Ana followed was an older black Dodge, now parked in front of the bunkhouse. Ana did not recognize the driver as he jumped out of the vehicle and ran to the barn where Jack and two other men were unloading bales of hay from a flatbed truck. Besides Jack, Ana recognized Swede Davidson; the other man was Duke, who had worked at the Moser ranch for years.

Ana parked her car and followed the driver of the Dodge pickup to the group rolling down bales of hay from a ten-foot-tall stack. She shook Jack's hand.

"Here I am, ready to work. What do you want me to do?"

"Can you throw these bales of hay down to us?" asked Jack. "It's a little climb, and you can roll them down if you can't lift them. They are heavy."

Jack's challenge brought a smile to Ana's face. "I guess no one told you that I worked a summer on the Torgerson ranch, and we had to throw bales up for stacking, not down for feeding. I can handle it."

Ana started to climb the stack of bales but turned first to Swede, giving him a gentle hug.

Swede returned the hug and flashed Ana a big smile. "I can't forget my favorite lawyer. You did me a good turn way back then, before you went to the county, when that sheriff jailed me on those trumped-up charges. We gave him hell, didn't we?"

Ana smiled again. "Yes, we did."

Ana nodded to the other men as she turned to the stack of hay.

One of them, the driver of the Dodge pickup, moved toward her.

"When do I get *my* hug?" His wolfish grin wiped the smile from Ana's face.

"I don't know you so keep your distance," Ana fired back.

Cobey Graham, the driver of the Dodge pickup, startled Ana with his directness. He was a big man with broad shoulders, a thick neck, and a pug face like it had been hit with a frying pan. And he had an eerie smile, looking at her like she was food for his imagination. Her skin prickled on her back, her neck hair rising straight up, her body muscles tensing.

"If you can give an old man like Swede a hug, think about what you could do with me."

Ignoring the comment, Ana climbed the haystack, but Cobey floated more comments up to her.

"Looks like you could use my help. I'll be right there."

Jack cut him off.

"Cobey! There's work to be done in the barn mucking out stalls. You are late to work so you get the hind tit. Grab a shovel and clean up those stalls...and don't argue. You know the rules."

Cobey hesitated, looked up at Ana on the stack, leered at her, and then addressed Jack. "Right away, boss man." He walked to the barn, grabbing a scoop shovel and slinging it over his shoulder.

Jack gave Ana a shrug. "Start rolling those bales down. Duke has cattle to feed."

When the bales had been tossed down, Jack called up to Ana, "Come on. We'll take my pickup and drive the fence line around the pasture over by the road. You can drive, and I'll do the fixing."

Jack had set aside two of his many section of land for pasture. Ana looked at the field and the seemingly endless fence row going north, south, east, and west and began to wonder if this job would take her into the new year.

"We'll only take the morning to drive as far as we can," said Jack, reading her mind. "The fences are in good shape, but I need to check them for loose wires and missing staples. You idle this vehicle down that fence line, and I'll walk beside you. Try not to go too fast, or I won't be able to keep up." Jack grinned, happy to have a good-looking woman on his ranch helping him.

As Ana slowly drove the pickup, Jack would check the wires and posts of the fence. Every now and then, Jack called out for her to stop while he got a hammer or wire stretcher out of the truck's bed to repair a wire or post.

The sun made its way to the center of the sky, meaning lunchtime. Ana had driven only a mile due to all the stops and repairs that had to be made. Jack came over to the pickup's window.

"Let's go in for lunch. Cora, Duke's wife, does the cooking. You are in for a treat at her table."

As Jack climbed into the pickup's passenger side, he apologized to Ana for missing the dinner last week.

"Sometimes, these cattle do the damnedest things. One of those critters got bogged down in a pond. We had a hell of a time pulling her out, and when we did, she needed some serious medical attention after nearly drowning. At times like that, I wonder what I am doing in the cattle business. The work is dawn to dusk, and sometimes dawn to dawn. I guess that is why my father took off for Hawaii and never came back."

Ana had heard the other side of the story from Peggy. She changed the subject. "Do you ever take any time off?"

"Not often. These cows become family. It's every day, every hour. You feed, shelter, give medical care, and handle them with love. They have personalities like people. See that bull over there?" Ana nodded yes, and Jack continued. "He is nearly 1,800 pounds of romping, stomping animal that you don't want to make mad. He looks good with that straight-line red back and white face, but don't turn your back on him. Look at his mouth and the flare of his nose. When he breathes, it's done with purpose and strength and there is always a little slobber like he doesn't care about his manners. You can see his toughness and that he really doesn't worry if you like him or not."

Ana studied the animal as he stood defying anything or anybody to come too close.

"You don't want to get into the corral with him," Jack continued. "He'd just as soon run you over as eat grass. Last week, he chased dumb old Cobey over the fence. You got to use a little common sense around an animal that mean. Cobey doesn't have much sense and he tried to use a cattle prod on him, and the results weren't good for Cobey." Jack had a look of amusement on his face remembering the sight of Cobey scurrying over the corral and tumbling to the ground. "That bull is a good judge of character."

Jack laughed at his joke at Cobey's expense. "You know better than me that if you poke someone in the eye, the urge to poke back is overpowering."

"Sounds like you and Cobey don't see the world the same way," mentioned Ana. "He is a strange man. I was uncomfortable this morning when he asked for a hug."

"Don't pay him any attention," said Jack dismissively. "He thinks he is God's gift to woman. Cobey has a good wife and two young boys, but he seems to need constant attention."

"Don't all men think that way?" asked Ana, thinking this might lead to Jack revealing something about himself. "Take you, for instance. Do you need constant attention?"

Not waiting for an answer, Ana asked another question. "How do you treat women? Are you a macho man, or is there some tenderness underneath that manliness of yours?"

"What concern is that of yours?" asked Jack. "Is that mother of mine sticking her nose in my business again?"

"Just checking on your progress with Mariah," deferred Ana.

Jack's temper showed, but he regained control, remembering he had asked Peggy for help. He smiled at Ana, happy to have her on his ranch. "Yeah, I have a thing for Mariah Morgan. She doesn't give me the time of day because of her religion."

"Matters of the heart are complicated," responded Ana. "And so is a woman. Mariah might have more reasons than just her religion. Can I give you some advice?"

Jack scoffed. "You can give me advice, but I'm damn sure I won't take it. Hell, Ana, you are a lawyer, not a shrink." Jack laughed at his own good-natured response. He liked the banter between them.

"True," agreed Ana. "But I could give you some insight into the mysteries of my world. Wouldn't that interest you if it might help your time with Mariah?"

Jack took a few moments to think about that. "Yeah, Mariah has pushed a lot of my buttons. I would do almost anything to get her attention or prevent her from pushing me completely out of her life. Mariah tells me we can be friends but nothing more." Jack shook his head in disbelief. He paused a moment, looking at Ana and then out at the prairie.

"She invited me to her church one time, and I keep going back so I can spend time with her." He glanced at Ana and said, "You know that already because you and Mariah ganged up on me that Sunday. Why am I telling you all this? You and my mother have cooked something up."

Ana touched Jack's arm. "Your mother loves you and only wants the best for you. I am getting to know you better and like what I see. I could help you with Mariah."

"Why would you do that? Aren't you friends with Mariah?" Jack asked. "You sing in the choir with her."

"Not friends, more like a mother-daughter relationship," explained Ana. "We talk mostly about religion and what Mariah wants with her life. I tell her to keep her faith, and things will work out the way they are supposed to. She is looking for a good man and you fit the bill."

"Has Mariah told you about me?" Jack asked anxiously.

"She did mention something," admitted Ana. "I got the impression you were coming on too strong."

"Goddamn it. Yes, I've come on too strong. I can see Mariah and me together. Why can't she see it? But I don't know another way."

Ana, with all the patience she could muster, answered, "Don't be so sure. Let's give it a try. I like you, but you have rough edges. You have an ego the size of the Rocky Mountains. Let's fine-tune your manner and give you a chance with Mariah."

By then, the pickup was approaching the ranch house. The crew members gathered about the front porch, waiting for the boss to show his face. Jack paused as he opened the pickup door to get out.

"Against my better judgment, I might try something. You are pushing me pretty hard, but your help today is appreciated."

"We take this slow," began Ana. "I'm going to beg off lunch with you and your crew, but how about trying next Friday night and letting me come back out to your ranch on Saturday? I've enjoyed this day more than you can imagine."

"It's a deal," said Jack. "Do we shake on it?"

Ana gave his hand a squeeze that lingered longer than it should have. "Will I see you in church tomorrow?"

Jack, touched by the softness of her hand, nodded yes and left the truck.

As Ana left the pickup for her own car, she heard Cobey laughing. "Hey, come back and stay for lunch with a real man."

Ana didn't turn around. She jumped into her car and drove to Fort Collins.

CHAPTER 14

SATURDAY, SEPTEMBER 27, 1975

Rib Torgerson, venerable veterinarian, successful rancher, community pillar, and unfaithful husband, traveled to his mountain cabin in the Two Medicine the same morning that Ana drove to Jack's ranch.

"The best medicine is the Two Medicine," he said as he steered his pickup through Fort Collins and onto the interstate. Rib had to drive an hour to reach the East Glacier café, and then it was another half hour to his cabin.

He turned north onto Interstate 15 just before six in the morning. The Rockies to the left of his pickup window were taking shape in the early half light of the coming dawn. There were no cars on the road, and his thoughts festered.

Mariah had been his latest conquest...by her choice. Still, he kept thinking about their age difference, along with her strong religious beliefs. They were not a match according to his standards as Mariah seemed to want to save everyone. Swede's drinking had been Mariah's project before he came along. He felt a jab of guilt remembering Swede's accusations, and then the thought hit him that he had become Mariah's next project.

He grabbed his steering wheel tighter at the thought of being controlled by Mariah.

However, Rib's immediate concern had to do with age creeping up on him, not that he doubted his lifestyle. However, days of working cattle for other ranchers had caught up to him, and while he could manage the work without anyone noticing his decline, he knew better. Could he keep pace with his ranch, the vet work, and his women? And hadn't Ana reminded him he had reached the big five-zero?

This last week, he had worked cattle for Jack Moser, then spent time with Mariah and her horse. He had been a tired old man at the end of the day.

Calling Ana had crossed his mind, but he never got around to it. He needed a day alone at his mountain cabin to rest and reflect on Mariah's place in his life. Rib had promised to see Mariah at her school sometime today after dark. What would transpire next would be up to her—if he had the stamina.

He didn't have to keep looking after Tucker, but the horse had been his catalyst with Mariah. Rib had the premonition that Mariah's strong religious bent would cause trouble. He weighed the burdens with the benefits and decided the latter was worth it.

At some point it would end, but he would deal with that when the time came. He'd been at that rodeo before, and he could predict the end of a relationship. Somehow, it always worked out. Anger followed by tears had been the reactions the majority of the time, but women were survivors, and life continued. He admired women for their toughness and vulnerability; he didn't understand them, but he enjoyed their complexity. A woman's nature kept him meeting new challenges. He thought the sex came second to unraveling the woman behind her motives.

After arriving at his cabin, he surveyed the needed tasks to close it down for the winter. He fastened the wooden window screens, checked to see if the rat and mouse bait had been placed out, took down the American flag, filled the toilet basins with antifreeze, and set the temperature at fifty-five degrees. He would save turning off the water until he left.

After doing his chores, he lay down on the couch and tried to nap. Sleep didn't come easy for him as sensations of guilt cascaded through his mind. When he started a relationship, he didn't look back or think it might be wrong. But his troubling thoughts about Mariah wouldn't go away. Mariah didn't deserve to be treated the way he would treat her in the end.

He finally fell into a restless sleep, waking at 3:15. Daylight might last another hour or two, so he had to get a move on to turn off the water and close the outer doors. Rib couldn't predict the winter snow depth, only that there would be drifts, thanks to the wind.

It was 4:30 before he left the mountain cabin in his rearview mirror. The day had refreshed him despite the nagging guilt he felt. Again, he talked out loud to himself.

"Damn you, Rib Torgerson. Get a grip on yourself. Mariah is a woman who made her choice. Live with it and enjoy the moment. That's your style, you rotten son of a bitch."

The drive back to Mariah's passed, and he turned into the barn to check on Tucker in his stall. Mariah, grooming Tucker, greeted him with a shy smile and a light kiss. Rib went to the horse, putting his left shoulder under Tucker's neck, and whispered in the horse's ear. "You sure are lucky to have Mariah taking care of you."

Rib turned to Mariah. "I don't see anything wrong with your horse. He is receiving top-notch care from you." Rib smiled at Mariah. "Your touch is magic. It must be your strong faith in humans and animals."

Mariah blushed at the compliment.

"Yes, I do have a strong faith." Silence settled between them.

"You have confused my thinking," admitted Mariah. "I am doing things that are a reach for me."

"How do you want to handle it?" Rib asked warily.

"I don't know," shrugged Mariah.

"I can stay or I can go," suggested Rib. "I don't want you to be uncomfortable."

"I don't want you to leave," she said. "I love you."

It was not the first time that one of Rib's lovers had told him that. He remained silent, but took Mariah into his arms and held her for a long time. Rib could feel the tension leaving her body.

They broke their embrace. Mariah looked deeply into Rib's eyes.

"Do you want to go over to my place?"

Rib nodded that he did, still not saying a word. He put his arm around her and started walking toward her house.

"I care for you, Rib. You are kind and gentle. I made a choice to be with you, but you can walk away right now if you want."

Rib considered walking away. Mariah had seen right through him with whatever sixth sense that all women seem to have. He could smell trouble brewing, but Mariah had tempted him, and he couldn't turn his back on her. Her hold on him challenged his senses.

Rib held the door open to her house.

CHAPTER 15

SUNDAY, SEPTEMBER 28, 1975

The next day the Sunday morning church service at Redeemer Episcopal Church in Fort Collins started at nine o'clock. The dawn had brought clear skies and wind. There was a crispness in the air, with the temperature in the mid-twenties.

Ana walked the five blocks to the church, leaving her house to be sure she made the choir gathering at eight.

A little earlier, Mariah drove her car out of the teacherage parking lot, calculating it would take her twenty minutes to arrive at the church. Ana had on her choir robe when Mariah walked in. Mariah found her robe, put it on, then turned to Ana, smiling, and the two women hugged.

After the choir practice, Ana held Mariah at arm's length. "You have a sparkle in your eyes. Is there something new in your life?" Ana had started taking note of people's facial expressions, especially the eyes, trying to read moods.

Men were relatively easy, but Peggy had given her the biggest clue to women by saying, "When a woman is happy, her eyes shine and sparkle. If you don't believe me, start looking in the mirror when you feel on top of the world. I've seen that special look in your eyes after your weekends with Rib."

Ana kept her attention on Mariah.

"How did you know?" Mariah asked.

"Just a wild guess," answered Ana. "Actually, you have a shine in your eyes and a bounce in your step. I'm happy for you. Do you want to talk about it?"

"Not right now," said Mariah. "Maybe after church?"

The two women entered the church, staying seated as the service began. Ana noted that Jack sat in the back row. Ana wondered if Mariah's newfound energy had anything to do with Jack. Ana thought about it for a moment, then decided there had been no time for Jack and Mariah to meet this weekend. *Something else is going on with Mariah*, Ana thought. *She reminds me so much of myself at that age.*

After the service, Ana and Mariah placed their choir robes in the proper closet, then walked through to the great hall for coffee hour. Ana enjoyed this part of the morning church gathering as she could mingle freely among the churchgoers, feeling good about herself, her town, her church, and her friends. Ana usually left the church with a sparkle in her eyes.

Ana maneuvered Mariah close to Jack, interrupting ranch and farm talk with two other men.

"I've enjoyed your company the past few days," she said to Jack. "I liked fixing the fence from the pickup cab while you did the work." Ana's eyes took in both Jack's and Mariah's reactions.

Mariah tilted her head, surprised by Ana's familiarity with Jack, considering she and Ana had taken Jack to the woodshed in August.

Jack smiled. "The time passes a lot quicker when you help me. Too bad you didn't stay for lunch. We harassed Cobey to death for his *invitation to be with a real man* comment to you. What a loser that guy is. He should be in church today, counting his blessings."

Jack turned his attention to Mariah. "Did I ever thank you for inviting me to church? If not, thank you from the bottom of my heart. I didn't think I would like it, but it does make me feel at ease with myself."

"You're welcome," replied Mariah. "I thought your view of religion a bit more harsh than what you just said. You surprise me."

Ana suppressed her smile, also surprised at Jack's response. Either he was a fast learner and had absorbed a lot from their conversations, or Peggy had been talking to him. *Not a bad comeback, Fat Jack. There is hope for you.*

Mariah abruptly cut off the conversation. "Ana, let's get a cup of coffee and sit over at that table by the fireplace. I need some warmth."

Jack, visibly disappointed by not being invited to join them, could only shrug, and he wandered off to the group of men he had been talking with before Ana interrupted them.

Taking her cue from Mariah, Ana started for the coffee table, getting herself a cinnamon roll to go along with her coffee. Mariah joined her at the far table, away from the scattered groups making conversation.

"Jack is a good person," offered Ana. "He needs polish, but the right woman couldn't go wrong with him. He still has an interest in you."

"Yes, and he has made no bones about it," said Mariah. "He isn't used to having someone refuse him. But I've seen the anger in his eyes when I've told him there isn't anything between us except friendship.... To his credit, he keeps trying."

"Are you saying there is no chance for you and Jack as a couple?"

"I don't think there is a spark between us, at least not from me. Jack might have other ideas, but no, I don't see a future with him."

"Enough worrying about Jack," Ana hurried on. "Why are you looking so full of life? I don't think I have ever seen you as bright as you are. I can see that in your eyes. Is it something you want to talk about?"

Mariah put her clasped hands on the table, hesitating before she spoke. "You know me as a Christian woman. What if I did an un-Christian-like thing? Would you think less of me?"

Ana chuckled. "Mariah, I am a successful failure if you know what

I mean. I'm educated, work hard at my job, married well, raised two children, and yet here I am at age forty-five, widowed and not quite sure of where I am going. I'm in love with a man I can never have. He's married, and he will never leave his wife. I would have married him twenty-five years ago if he had asked, but he didn't. My problem is I can't get him out of my heart. That's not your concern. I'm telling you about it because I have no high ground to judge you or anyone else."

"I look up to you so much," Mariah said. "You are smart and confident and handle people and make decisions without seeming to be bothered by anything. Do you pray to God for answers like I do?"

Ana took a bite of her roll while waiting for Mariah to continue.

Mariah looked about the room, searching for words. "I look to God, but sometimes He is too busy to be worried about me. Last night, I prayed to Him to forgive me for what I have done, but nothing let me know that He had heard. Is it because I didn't want Him to give me an answer I couldn't accept?" Then Mariah blurted out, "I have fallen in love with an older man."

Mariah became lost in her own thoughts. Ana, shocked by Mariah's admission, respected the silence, finally breaking it. "I can't give you answers. You have to work those out yourself. I can listen, but don't expect me to solve anything so personal and private. Sometimes it helps to talk to someone, particularly if you don't see an answer. So, I'm here for you."

Mariah had tears shining in her eyes. "Thank you. I don't expect you to fix my life. I could call my mother, who is the dearest thing, but I'm not sure she would understand."

Ana had several questions in mind that she didn't dare ask, such as *Who is this mystery man? What else has he done? Are you pregnant? Is marriage in the picture? How did you meet this person?*

Mariah continued. "He listens to me and values what I have to say. There is a spark between us that I've never felt before. I become lost in the moment with him, and things happened."

Mariah paused. Ana listened.

"I wanted them to happen, and that bothers me. I am a Christian woman who wanted to save herself for marriage, but I lost control, and I feel guilty because I encouraged the next steps. I can't describe the tenderness between us."

"I understand your feeling," comforted Ana. "I've had the same thoughts myself."

"That's not the worst of it," said Mariah. "He is also married. How is it possible to feel so good about a person yet feel so uncertain? I know what I've done is wrong, but it feels so right."

"What are your options?" asked Ana, with a feeling of impending dread coming over her.

Ana could see Mariah had hit a high but now was experiencing the low. How many times had Ana been in that same situation? Too many to count in her law practice, and several times with Rib.

"It all started over my horse getting sick with colic," admitted Mariah. "I had to call the vet, and he came as soon as he could. He said we had caught the attack soon enough. His name is Rib Torgerson. I suppose you know him."

Ana went silent, hiding her emotions, facing her worst nightmare.

Goddamn him, thought Ana. *What's Rib doing with this young woman? Doesn't he know he's old and past his prime?* Outwardly, Ana smiled, but her insides churned with anger combined with sadness.

Ana took Mariah's hands in hers, giving them a slight squeeze. "You do have a problem, but it is not one I can help you with right now or maybe ever. You have to look at your options to make your decisions. Right off hand, I would say you are looking at a dead-end street with a married, older man. But I'm no expert and could find myself in a similar fix one day."

Ana's shoulder slumped as she grasped the irony of that statement. She seethed inside, wanting to scream out that Rib would break Mariah's heart.

What does that man have that makes him irresistible to women, and why does he continue to play the field? Silently, she asked, *Why do I love him so?*

Ana could tell Mariah that Rib would leave her at some point. However, maybe, just maybe, Rib had changed and wanted a younger woman. The more Ana thought about that possibility, the more ready she was to dismiss it out of hand. Rib was being Rib; no more, no less. Ana fought the urge to expose her relationship with Rib. She fought the anger building in her body.

Suddenly, Ana had an idea. Why not take the other side of Mariah's dilemma and turn it against Rib? Rib had chosen a younger woman; why shouldn't Ana choose a younger man? Fat Jack. Yes, Fat Jack. *Two can dance to this tune*, thought Ana.

Ana stood up from the table. "Go home and think about your problem. Get outdoors if you can. Look around you and find something good to focus on. You have a serious decision to make, and I'm always here to help you, so call if you need me."

Ana paused, not wanting to end the conversation too soon, but she had a plan. "Sleep on your decision. There is no hurry."

Mariah shook her head no. "Thank you, you have helped me already. I still don't know what I will do."

"I've got an errand to run," Ana announced. "I'm sorry to have to leave you feeling like you do."

Ana's eyes had a hard look to them, startling Mariah. "Have I said something to upset you?" Mariah asked.

"No," said Ana. "You have made things crystal clear for me. I would love to give you my advice, but you must make the decision and live with it. Whatever happens might be good for you, or it might be bad. I can't predict the future."

Mariah smiled and stood up, and hugged Ana. "Thank you for listening. You don't know what it means to have someone to talk with that won't make judgments. I'm going home to ride my horse and think."

Ana returned the squeeze, smiled wanly at Mariah, and then walked toward Jack, who sat talking with a group of men.

"Jack," Ana announced as she broke into their conversation and sat down. "We missed a nice dinner while you were playing rancher. We can make up for it this weekend, can't we?"

Jack looked up at Ana, seeing the determination in her face.

"Are you this direct in the courtroom?" he asked. "It's no wonder you win your cases."

"I don't win all my cases, and this isn't a courtroom," said Ana. "I had such an enjoyable morning with you at your ranch yesterday that I want to fix fence with you again, or whatever work you have to do. I need to get outside in the fresh air and be physical."

Jack, enjoying the attention and looks from his table-mates, grinned. "I could take you to dinner on Friday and show you around the ranch again on Saturday. If you can stand my crew, I know they can stand you. You made everyone jealous, including me, when you gave Swede that big hug. How did you get to know him that well?"

"Swede and I go back a long way," explained Ana. "Maybe I could tell you that story over a glass of wine." Jack smiled, so Ana continued. "It's a date then. I'll meet you at The Two Bar and Grill at six."

"I could pick you up at six," volunteered Jack.

Ana considered the option, then answered with a flirtatious smile. "No, I think it best to meet you. I wouldn't want you or anyone to get the wrong idea."

Jack, recognizing that Ana had outmaneuvered him on this point, smiled back. "But it's still a date, isn't it?"

"Yes, a date," confirmed Ana. "I'm looking forward to the endless possibilities for our conversations. I'm very much interested in your opinions."

"Whoa, slow down a bit," Jack said. "Can't we have a quiet evening where we aren't solving the problems of the world? There are lots of things out of my control, like blizzards, grain prices, government regulations..."

"Oh, but you can influence events by getting involved," said Ana. "Haven't you heard of staying local and making a difference?"

The interchange between Ana and Jack brought looks of amusement to the men sitting silently at the table, exchanging glances amongst themselves.

"Well, we might have some deep things to talk about over dinner," said Jack. "Can we leave it at that?"

Ana shifted directions. "Can I come out to your ranch on Saturday and help you again? I got a kick out of watching you do all the work."

"Yeah, I guess so. There is always something to do on the ranch. I won't be fixing any fence lines, but winter is coming, and those critters need to be ready."

"Fine, I'll plan on it. See you Friday night." Ana turned and left, satisfied with the results.

She had two dates this weekend with Jack.

CHAPTER 16

FRIDAY, OCTOBER 3, 1975

The Two Medicine Bar and Grill drew diners to Fort Collins from north-central Montana and Canada. The restaurant, tucked between the Fort Collins Hotel and the Toggery Clothing Store, had a recessed entry of double doors leading to the narrow front room with a full-length bar, supposedly bought from a closed-down tavern in Butte, Montana. The mahogany bar, carved into shape through years of use by the miners of the Anaconda Copper Company, would have been the centerpiece of conversation if not for the show-stealing, Victorian-flocked velvet wallpaper of burgundy on red and gray that sheathed the walls. The ornate interior reminded some patrons of royalty and French courts of old, while others thought it a high-priced bordello from Nevada. The wallpaper covered both the front room and the spacious back room, both of which were accented by black, cushioned booths. Anybody who wanted to be seen went to the Two Medicine Bar and Grill.

Ana had planned it that way. She needed to be seen with Jack.

The wallpaper had been hung by Paul Chalmers, a retired champion bareback rider, who ended up in Fort Collins. Paul had competed in all the big rodeos in his career, including Pendleton, Calgary, Cheyenne, and even the National Rodeo Finals in Oklahoma City.

Ana took her time preparing for the Friday night dinner with Jack at the Two Medicine. She told herself to remember what she represented—the legal community of Fort Collins and the state of Montana—but she was also mindful of the need to be alluring enough to keep Jack's attention. Ana decided on a V-neck blouse with a slight show of skin and a cardigan sweater matching an ankle-length, leather-fringed skirt paired with medium-height heels. Ana applied a light touch of makeup and lipstick, followed by a dash of perfume. The blowing wind reminded her to wear a full-length winter coat.

Ana arrived at the restaurant at five to six, pleasantly surprised that Jack sat at the classic bar waiting for her. Jack stood up, waved her over, and led her to a reserved table for two opposite the side of the room where he had just been enjoying a whiskey ditch, Montana's iconic drink.

Jack set his glass down on the table, then helped Ana off with her coat, holding her right arm steady as she slid into the curved, cushioned half booth.

Ana smiled. "Where did you learn all these manners? At the VFW hall, you wouldn't hold a chair for me or even say hello. Why this new graciousness?"

"My mother taught me all those things, and you are demanding them. I'm not the clod you think I am."

"Well, I'm impressed," admitted Ana. "You are a challenge but a charming one when you slow down." Ana reached over and placed her hand on his. "I don't think you are a clod, but you are rough around the edges. There is hope for you."

They smiled at each other.

Ana raised her glass of wine and clinked it against Jack's whiskey glass. Jack laughed and raised his glass. Silence ensued as Ana and Jack's smiling eyes locked together.

Ana finally took a sip of wine. "You surprised me by saying you disagreed with drilling for oil on the Front. How did you come to that point? You are a landowner who doesn't want the government to tell you anything. You know, keep Uncle Sam out of your business."

"Yeah, it doesn't make sense, does it?" Jack admitted. "Keeping the government out of my business is my hope, but the reality is that I rely on government payments for my grain operation, government sales to foreign countries, and government regulations to ship everything I grow. I could give you a whole day's worth of government, but I have to be practical."

"Sounds like game playing," agreed Ana.

Jack tilted his head from side to side, deciding on an answer. "Since I have never been married, I can only guess that dealing with the government is like dealing with a wife. Is that close to right?"

Jack gave Ana a sideways peek, waiting for her reaction.

Ana didn't disappoint Jack, returning his sly look with one of her own. "Marriage is on a whole other planet, so don't go comparing it to the government. Nice try, but that doesn't fly with me."

"What does fly with you?" he volleyed back with a devilish grin. "You know I'm a pilot. Do you want to join the mile-high club?"

"I'm already a member. My late husband learned to fly and gave me a few flying lessons if you can read between the lines."

Actually, her late husband had not been a pilot, but Ana knew about the mile-high club, and what Jack didn't know wouldn't hurt him.

"Okay, you have me there. I didn't know your husband had his own plane," Jack replied.

"Yes, but that's not what I asked you," reminded Ana. "Why don't you think drilling in the Front is a good idea?"

"It is hard to put into words," said Jack as he hesitated, gathering his thoughts. "Those Rockies have a special place in my life. I've spent a lot of time growing up with them. My dad hunted with me in the Bob Marshall Wilderness. I killed my first elk there, learned how to take care of myself in the woods, which is a lot like taking care of yourself in a war. I credit my life being saved many times in Nam because I had to take care of myself in the Rockies. Critters living there are looking for their next meal, so you have to be alert to survive, and you have to keep an eye on the weather and the terrain. If you break a leg or an arm, you are a long way from help."

Ana wondered at exactly what point Jack had changed the subject...or had he? She guessed his survival in Vietnam still meant something to him.

She compared Rib's remarks about the Front to Jack's. Rib's concern regarded his ability to turn a profit; Jack's opinion came from a different place.

The contrast of the two landowners' approaches based on how they could benefit financially versus how much they respected the land placed both of them in a light Ana had not considered before. Personally, Ana did not want the drilling to occur. *Interesting*, she thought, *lining up with Jack on that topic.*

Ana persisted. "Did you know that this whole part of Montana had been covered with an inland sea connecting the Gulf of Mexico with the Arctic Ocean and stretching clear to the Appalachians? Of course, seventy-five million years later, we can't imagine such a thing."

Jack nodded in agreement.

"Do you know how oil is formed?" she asked.

"Kind of, I guess, but I have to admit I don't really know. How do you know all this stuff?"

"My late husband had a knack for anticipating things," Ana lied. "As the rainmaker in our firm, Richard continually watched trends. Oil came close to the top of his list. As always, I ended up doing the research. There is oil under this high prairie because it was once underwater. Oil is formed by living plants and organisms that have died and fallen to the bottom of the sea or ocean, or whatever, and have been buried by silt and subject to intense heat and pressure. Who knows how much oil is stored underneath us right now?"

Jack could not answer the question and felt overmatched by Ana's knowledge and enthusiasm. He didn't care how much oil lay beneath him.

But Ana continued. "This happened seventy-five to one hundred million years ago. Think about that. Then the sea receded, and the ground began to rise thirty-five to fifty million years ago, and the Rockies thrust up. God, can you believe all that happened on this very spot we are sitting on?"

Jack could only shake his head, not wanting to get too far into this conversation. Ana had thrown him totally off balance. *This isn't my kind of date*, he thought.

"Hell," he said, "I'm more worried about an early winter and feeding a thousand head of cattle. That gets damn expensive, plus all the hard work involved. I can't worry about what happened millions of years ago. I fear a cold, hard winter, not only for myself but for my animals. Those critters go through a lot of stress."

Ana realized she had been boring Jack with trivia.

"I'm sorry," Ana said. "Boring you with ancient history is my mistake." They both took a drink, grappling with their strained conversation.

After several moments of silence, with a forced smile, Ana took another tack. "Does all the traffic from the Air Force vehicles checking on the missile sites bother you? If the Soviets ever decide to launch their arsenal, Fort Collins and northern Montana are dead in their wheelhouses. Those blue, double-cabbed Air Force pickups ruin the whole countryside for me. It's not natural for them to be out on our gravel roads doing who knows what. The sheriff thinks they are dealing in drugs."

Jack relaxed, relieved at talking about something other than oil. "No, I don't worry about that either. No rational person or country would deliberately shoot off missiles that would destroy the world. There are enough missiles pointed at the Ruskies to give them pause. I don't see either country making the mistake of starting a nuclear war."

"For heaven's sake, you served, fighting for our country. How can you not think about some crazy guy who might fire off a missile or two right at us? I think about it all the time and worry for my children."

"I have too many ranch jobs to worry about foreign countries," Jack replied. "If I spent my day second-guessing politicians and their decisions, I'd never get any work done. I can't do much about what they do. I can only control my cattle and grow my wheat." The terseness of his voice was not lost on Ana as she changed the subject.

"Your mother is totally involved in the National Organization for Women. What do you think of women's rights?"

Jack, aware of the traps in this conversation, took his time before answering. "Peggy is usually right about those things. I haven't given it much thought, so I would agree with my mother." Jack hoped the talk about this issue would end, but Ana had other ideas. Ana's questions came on too quick for Jack to change the conversation.

"Well, if you expect to make any headway with Mariah, you better start giving some thought to how a woman looks at the world," Ana advised. "This country is changing its views. Look at me. I am one of the few women lawyers in Montana, but there is going to be more women doing man's work, and you men need to change with the times."

Jack squirmed in his seat, again feeling outmatched and ignorant. What did he care about women's rights? Jack had a ranch to run and wanted a woman at his side.

"Can't we enjoy our evening without solving these big issues?" he asked. "You have just cross-examined me on some touchy subjects. I can see why you are challenging in court. You have no mercy, going right for the jugular. You tell me to go slow with women, so I'm telling you to slow down with me."

Ana sheepishly paused, lowering her head and putting her hand to her mouth. "You are so right. I am sorry. It's a fact that a woman in my position has to be a little pushy. Going out on a date is not my usual habit. I have forgotten how to be civil. Can you forgive me?"

"It's not for me to forgive you," said Jack. "But you are making me angry. You've put me in a corral, running me in circles with a rope around my neck, trying to break me. I get the point about treating women differently."

They stared at each other, Ana with a pensive look on her face and Jack with his jaw clenched.

"It takes all kinds." Ana carefully chose her words, sensing Jack's tension. Ana noted Jack's red face, thinking that she had pushed too hard. "Let's forget all those questions I asked and concentrate on this evening," she offered. "I wanted to know how you look at the world. I appreciate having this time with you. Your mother is my best friend, and she is worried about you." Ana immediately realized her mistake in bringing Peggy into the conversation.

"I don't need either of you to shepherd me," Jack tersely replied. "What the hell is she worried about? I survived Nam, and I am running the ranch. Life is good."

Ana noted the flaring of Jack's nostrils.

"Tell me what she is worried about!" he insisted.

Ana regretted her bluntness. She had to lighten the mood and defuse Jack's angst or tell the truth. But she also thought about the insights Jack had revealed and particularly his show of temper.

"I'll be straight with you," began Ana. "Your mother wants you married with children. She is aware of your desire for that schoolteacher, but Mariah doesn't want anything to do with you except church."

"What is my mother doing telling you all that crap? That is my business, not yours," he snarled, then pushed his chair back, wanting to stand up.

Ana touched his arm. "Peggy is concerned about you. She asked for my help. Don't leave. I'm sorry we have gotten to this point. Can I make it better?"

Ana's right arm rested on Jack's left arm. He responded to Ana's soft touch and settled back into his chair. Their eyes locked again. Ana could sense the anger easing in his body. The moment of crisis had passed. She kept her hand on his forearm.

"Thank you," she said. "I don't mean to make you mad. I am here to listen. Let's be friends and talk about how you feel about anything and everything. I will not judge anything you say."

Jack did not respond right away. He picked up a menu and handed it to Ana.

"Let's order some food," Jack grunted into the silence.

Ana took the menu. "I would like the chowder bisque and a Caesar salad. What is your favorite?"

"The rib eye is the tastiest. I am going to have one with a baked potato and a salad. I need another drink too."

Ana sighed a breath of relief as Jack regained control. She realized Peggy had roped her into a labyrinth of unexpected turns. Ana's greatest surprise came when she admitted to herself that Jack held her interest. She wanted to keep seeing him.

Their meal orders were taken, cooked, and presented to them at their table. They ate in silence. The emotion of Jack's outburst lingered between them.

"I need to apologize to you," offered Jack, finally looking into Ana's eyes. "You hit a nerve, having talked to my mother about personal things. Why should it be any of your business?"

"Because your mother is concerned about you, and I'm fond of you," admitted Ana. "From what I know, Mariah has another interest. I can't get specific, but you need to stay away from her."

"I don't think I can do that," argued Jack.

"You have to step back. Mariah will likely end up disappointed in the path she is taking now, but it's going to have to play out, and you have to be patient. If you press too hard, Mariah will turn her back on you."

Jack hung his head, not wanting to hear Ana's advice.

An inspiration hit Ana as she realized their conversation had peaked. "I have an idea. Let's go dancing right now. We didn't plan on doing it, but we both need to kick off our shoes."

Ana touched Jack's cheek, guiding him toward her and nodding, imploring him to say yes with her touch. Ana resisted the impulse to hug the man. "Come on," she urged. "How can dancing hurt? You dance wonderfully, and we need to lighten up. I'm so sorry I bugged you to death with my silly questions. Come dance with me right now."

Jack, with his head tilted toward Ana, snorted and grunted. "Okay, let's go dancing and show this town how to have a good time. This will be a first for me. Usually, I get hammered and go home alone."

"You'll go home alone tonight too," reminded Ana. "And go easy on the drinks. Dancing and laughter are better medicines, don't you think?"

Jack nodded with a smile but still finished his whiskey. "Let's go," he said. "I'll pay the bill and drive you over and bring you back when the time is right."

"Oh, no, you won't, you smooth operator. If we go together, I'm driving. You've had a couple too many, and I would hate to prosecute you on Monday."

Ana and Jack exchanged looks before they broke into laughter, thinking of Jack sitting in jail through the weekend waiting for Ana to throw the book at him.

Ana drove Jack in her car to the VFW hall, where the dance floor awaited them.

CHAPTER 17

MONDAY, OCTOBER 6, 1975

Ana left the courthouse at five, making her way to the liquor store and another round with Peggy. She passed through the front door, waving at Peggy as she made her way to the inner door leading to the sanctuary of her best friend's back room. A gin and tonic would ease the pressures of the last few days. Ana poured the drink and sat back in the recliner, waiting for Peggy to finish her work. As the time passed slowly, Ana fell asleep, the half-empty glass on the table next to her. Ana had no awareness of the muted serenade of clinking bottles being sold, casual conversations, and ringing of the cash register that emanated from the front room. Peggy startled her awake a little after six by grabbing her left shoe and giving it a tug.

"Hooray, hooray, no more work today. I wish outdoor screwing would start right away," sang Peggy. "What's new?"

Ana, shaking off her drowsiness, pulled the recliner to a sitting position. "Purple rain," she said. "Purple rain. Do you know what it means? I'm dreaming about it hitting my face, and I don't like it."

"There is something in the Bible," ventured Peggy. "Doom and the end of the world, but I'm not sure I care. What are you talking about purple rain for?" Peggy poured herself a gin over ice without the tonic, then settled into the other recliner with a sigh.

"I don't know. That is why I asked you." Now fully awake, a twinkle formed in Ana's eyes. "You have been around the block more than I have. You know things that stun me."

"I read a lot of newspapers. What's it to you?" Peggy paused. "Is having been around the block a bad thing?" Peggy warmed up to the prospect of examining someone's life, maybe even her own.

"Are you trying to make up a new problem," demanded Peggy. "You have enough on your mind running around with a married man. You need to settle down as a respectable woman and get married."

"No," argued Ana. "It's just that last Friday night, Jack and I had dinner at the Two. We got into an argument, not exactly kissing and making up in the end, but we finally did go dancing at the VFW hall."

Peggy sat, enjoying her drink as she listened to Ana's story.

"That son of yours can dance. The evening turned out to be more than exciting. Anyway, some drunk kept playing this song about riding on a California highway, seeing flying alligator lizards in the sky, and getting hit by purple rain." Ana looked at Peggy with a pained expression. "Have you ever been hit by purple rain?"

"How would I know?" Peggy shrugged her shoulders.

"Purple rain keeps playing in my mind," muttered Ana. "I dream I'm paddling in this vast pond and being hit in the face with this icky wet stuff while there is no dock in sight."

"Are things that bad?" Peggy wore a look of concern. "I've seen you in some pretty tough situations, but you are a survivor, picking yourself off the ground when you get knocked down. This sounds serious. Is It?"

Ana ignored the question. "I don't think I have ever been in that kind of storm. I could understand if, instead of being hit in the face, the rain caressed me. But getting hit makes me think of getting hurt, and that's not for me."

"Tell me what's on your mind," sighed Peggy. "We are in for a long evening of feeling sorry for Ana. Am I right?"

Peggy remained in her chair and Ana stood up.

Ana took a full swallow of her drink, finishing it and pouring another. Ana had confided in Peggy before, and Peggy had always listened and given her opinion whether Ana wanted it or not.

"I deserve to be happy some of the time, don't I?" pleaded Ana.

Peggy only nodded and kept silent.

"I can't help it," hedged Ana. "There is more, and it affects what I am doing or about to do with Jack." Ana sat up in the recliner, hands spread out with her palms up, and looked at Peggy.

"I have promised to help Jack be more appealing to women. He doesn't need much work. Jack and I haven't kissed yet, and yes, he does have a quick temper as I found out this weekend, but he gets over his mad quickly. I have to admit, I am attracted to him. Do you see my problem now?"

"What's wrong with that?" asked Peggy. "Bringing a different person into your life might be exactly what you need."

"Easy for you to say, but have you thought about unintended results? It could ruin my chances for reelection."

"That is too dramatic," Peggy replied. "You won't know until you try, and how can it ruin your life? Don't exaggerate your problems."

"There is more to this than Jack." Ana turned away from Peggy and walked to the back door.

"Tell me," commanded Peggy, as she stood up and followed Ana.

"Rib has become Mariah's lover."

Peggy shook her head no and shrank back from Ana.

Ana gazed sadly at Peggy. "Mariah reminds me of me: totally in love with a man with no future." Ana then confessed, "I am jealous of her. So, I went directly to Jack, hitting him up for a date. I was hurt and angry and sad at the same time. I never react that way to anyone but Rib. Who knows what I will do next?"

"My advice is to not freak out about it," advised Peggy. "Nothing comes easy. Every day is a new one. Take these new challenges and work through them. Why don't you take a different direction and take up with Jack?"

Peggy smiled to herself and thought that Jack might benefit from Ana's turmoil.

Both were silent, mulling over the conversation for many seconds.

Peggy broke the silence. "A woman has power. Go use it. Take care of yourself by putting your interest first. A man doesn't understand a woman's needs unless she guides him."

"I understand that," agreed Ana. "I have another date with Jack this weekend. Maybe we will go dancing again or to the ranch. Right now, I don't care." Ana walked over to the table where the bottle of gin sat. She considered pouring another drink but decided against it. She turned back to Peggy with her arms out in frustration.

"I tried to call Rib but he isn't answering. Being the other woman makes it difficult. I usually wait for his calls, but sometimes I call his office. I can't do that too many times without causing more gossip. His secretary is no dummy, and she is on to us. She always asks if my cat is having problems, knowing I don't have a cat." Ana laughed. "Who am I kidding? I am so dumb."

Peggy continued her silence, letting Ana pace the floor and pour out her heart.

"I don't want to talk about it anymore. It's happened and I have to live with it."

Peggy put her arm around Ana and walked her back to the recliner. Peggy poured them both another drink.

"Do you have any good news?" asked Peggy.

Ana shook her head no, tears forming in her eyes.

"Nothing is good in my life," lamented Ana. "Between the county commissioners and the sheriff and an election coming up in a year, I'm swamped and frustrated. I'm not sure I want to run again for this damn county attorney's office."

Peggy nodded, waiting for Ana to go on.

"Do you give a rat's elbow? No, I don't think you care."

"I'm listening to your sad tale," said Peggy. "Keep hammering away."

"The sheriff told me in no uncertain terms that he is the law in this county, and as such, can do what he damn well pleases. Can you believe the arrogance of that man?"

Peggy continued her silence.

"That sheriff is going to clean up this town, no matter what. Does Collins County have a crime problem? Oh, once in a while, we have a cattle-rustling case, a burglary, or shoplifting, but I've never felt in danger here—have you?"

Peggy shook her head no.

"Driving under the influence is the biggest problem," continued Ana. "Up and coming is marijuana, and that damn sheriff is determined to eradicate drugs from here to the Canadian border. Have you ever used it?"

"Used what?" Peggy asked, looking at the ceiling.

"Marijuana, you idiot." Ana shrewdly judged Peggy's insistence on looking upward. "Are you hiding something a county attorney should know?"

Peggy, still looking at the ceiling, confessed. "Yes, I've used it and will use it again. It relaxes me, taking me to the land of make-believe. The sex isn't bad either."

"Oh, God," groaned Ana. "Am I going to have to call the sheriff and have you arrested? Why would you ever use that stuff? It'll damage your brain, your body, and your whole life if you get addicted."

"Nah, none of that will happen to me," said Peggy. "I don't use it often, and it's not the hard stuff like LSD or heroin. Have you ever smoked the weed?"

"No, and I don't plan on doing it," asserted Ana. "Can you imagine the county attorney lighting up and getting caught? That sheriff would laugh for months if he could arrest me. Sometimes I think either he or one of his deputies follows me after work to see where I go and what I do. I bet the sheriff knows I'm sitting here with you right now. Damn, I would like another drink, but with the thought of him hanging around waiting to embarrass me with an arrest, I better start drinking water."

"You got your troubles. That, I can see," said Peggy. "But aren't you overdoing it a bit? I think you need to smoke a little magic Mary Jane to take the edge off."

There was another period of silence between them before Peggy continued. "If I walked in your shoes, I would ask myself if Rib is good or bad for me. If good, then keep on doing what you are doing. If he is terrible for you, take up with my Jack. How could it hurt?"

The silence between them dragged on. Ana finally broke it.

"Did I tell you that I have a date with Jack this Saturday to go to his ranch? Do you have any advice for me? I'm not sure I will see you again this week."

"Yes, I do have some advice for you."

"This had better be good," said Ana.

"It is, so listen. I don't know if you and Jack can ever get to having sex, but if you do, you had better have it planned. Personally, I can't see anything wrong if you two developed a thing. You are a little older, but he needs someone like you. Why not give it a try? A little roll in the hay could cure a lot of your aches and pains. You have my blessing."

Ana didn't respond, but got up from the recliner to wash out her glass, gathering her coat and purse. "Wish me luck on not getting arrested for drunk driving on my way home and for making some kind of decision about Jack. Rib hasn't talked to me since Sunday night in your kitchen. He is on to other things with Mariah, so why do I sit around counting my fingers while staying unhappy? It's time to live my life, and who cares except you and me? I need to cheer myself up and dance—and do whatever else may come along."

Peggy was pleased. Clearly, Ana had taken her words to heart.

"That's my girl," cheered Peggy. "Show Rib he's not the only man who finds you attractive. I've seen you take on greater challenges than this. Now go home and have another drink. It improves your sweet-ass personality."

Ana smiled, enjoying Peggy's teasing. "I'll see you when I see you. Thanks for the talk. Why shouldn't I live in the moment like Rib? Oh, God. I'll have to tear up all my lists, throw out the old clothes, and start a new life. Sounds exciting...doesn't it?"

CHAPTER 18

SATURDAY, OCTOBER 25, 1975

Three weeks later, Ana was brewing a pot of coffee in Jack's farm kitchen for their Saturday afternoon work break. The earlier part of the day had been spent working cattle in preparation for the winter calving season. The warm wind blowing from the downslopes of the Rockies warmed the temperature to the mid-fifties. The outside work, while physically intense, had been comfortable.

Ana beamed, thinking about how much she had thrived spending the last two weekends on Jack's ranch.

Ana reflected on her relationship with Jack and the events in the month of October, starting when Jack had called late one Friday afternoon.

"Do you want to go dancing tonight?" Jack had asked. "I'm calling at the last minute, so if you have other plans, we can look at another time. I would throw in dinner if you wanted."

"I'd love to go dancing with you tonight," said Ana. "A last-minute invitation is better than none at all. I had planned to stop by the liquor store, but dancing would be great. I'm in the mood to cut loose. I don't have time to change for dinner, but let's meet at the VFW hall at seven. Okay with you?"

"Hell, yes," agreed Jack. "I've been thinking back on our last go-around dancing. I can't remember when I felt so free. I want to do that again. I could pick you up around seven."

"No, I'll meet you at the VFW at seven. It's too soon to have you driving me around, and I need the independence of my own car."

"Good with me," said Jack, a little disappointed "See you in a few hours."

Ana arrived at the appointed time, and she and Jack danced, laughed, and drank a moderate amount of liquor.

"No serious questions from me," Ana had immediately promised. "I don't care what you think about drilling for oil, or women's rights, or the Cold War. I want to dance with you."

"Good," said Jack. "You wore my brain out with all your questions. Let's dance."

They got up from the table with Jack holding Ana's chair, turning to the dance floor.

"Are you going to invite me to your ranch tomorrow?" Ana asked. "You promised, and I am going to hold you to your word."

"Yes, I want you to help with my cattle. I've got to get them ready for winter. Halloween is next week, and it seems to be a cut-off when the days get colder and the nights longer." Jack hesitated before continuing. "Do you think ghosts cause the change?"

Ana laughed at the question, then turned serious. "I'll be at your place by eight tomorrow," she promised. "Make sure you have work for me to do."

"We don't do banker hours, so show up at seven if you want to get the full flavor of the day."

Ana nodded, realizing that Jack was a step ahead of her, and she willingly snuggled into his arms for the dance. The music ended but they remained holding each other close. Finally, Ana broke the embrace, telling Jack, "It's time for me to go home."

Jack held her hand. "By myself," she added.

Ana drove to her house, basking in the night of dancing with Jack. As she undressed and found her pajamas, she thought, *I'm going to warm things up with Jack.*

* * *

The next day, Ana and Jack sat at the kitchen table having coffee and rolls. "How much more hay do we have to move this afternoon?" Ana inquired.

"Another truckload," replied Jack. "The guys could handle it if you are tired or need to go back to town. You've been a great help today. Did you enjoy yourself?"

"Yes," said Ana. "It's been a long time since I could get out in the fresh air doing honest work. Most days, I sit behind a desk wanting to kick off my high heels because my feet hurt. Now my arms and back are hurting, but it's a good hurt if you know what I mean."

"Yeah, I know what you mean. I cuss when it is windy and miserable, but I wouldn't trade it for anything." Jack half-snorted and half-laughed. "My dad got to the point where he had enough of cows and wind and constant work, but I'm still getting out of bed every morning looking forward to the day. A guy like me has to know a lot of things, so every day is different."

"How so?"

"Well, to start with," began Jack, "raising wheat and cattle take twenty-fours a day, and sometimes it seems longer. Even when I pasture in the summer, someone has to be around them, except we don't feed them hay when they graze on mountain grass. But then I have to tend the growing crops down here on the prairie, working the summer fallow, irrigating, spraying weeds, putting on fertilizer, harvesting, seeding, and starting the process for next year."

They sipped more coffee.

"I don't plan a vacation," continued Jack. "But if I do go someplace, it's usually in the summer. Oh, I take a day off on holidays once in a while, but there is work to be done every day, especially when you raise cattle. Some ranchers are becoming farmers, selling their animals and only raising wheat or barley. I've thought about doing it, but I love to work with those animals."

Ana poured more coffee, contemplating her next move. Jack continued.

"If I raised grain with no cattle, my work would be cut in half because the ground is frozen for six months. Pretty hard to plow snow and ice. I could spend my winters in Arizona, but that's not me."

"Spending time down south in the winter sounds more appealing," admitted Ana. "Golfing, laying by a pool in the sun… That's a nice picture."

Jack stood up from the table, walking to the window. "Looks like the guys have the truck loaded," he noted. "You can take the rest of the afternoon off if you want."

"Do you have to go back and help them?" Ana asked as she stood up.

"Maybe," replied Jack. "Like I said, there is always work to do on a ranch."

Ana walked closer to Jack. "I have a better idea. Come here and kiss me."

Jack hesitated, then stepped to her side, grabbed her roughly by her arms, pulled her to his body, and planted a hard kiss on Ana's lips, pushing his tongue into her mouth.

Ana broke away, wiping her mouth with the back of her hand, catching her breath. "That is not the kind of kiss I hoped for. I didn't ask for an assault."

Ana folded her arms, not angry, casting her eyes over the man in front of her. "Jack, you have curbside appeal, but your interior needs work. Do you have the man-guts to change your ways? I want to help you."

"What do you mean, teach me? What do I have to learn? You asked for a kiss, and I gave you one. What didn't you like?"

Ana laughed. "I didn't like any of it. First, you bruised my arms, then gave me a forced kiss, sticking your tongue in my mouth. There might be a time and place for that, but not with me. Men are in a rush. I want romance, a soft touch, some indication that there is more than a physical act. There is a difference between making love and having sex. A 'slam-bam, thank you, ma'am' approach won't work for me. But you do have potential. Let me show you another possibility."

Jack took a step back, not sure of the meaning and directness coming from Ana. "Where are you going with this."

Ana took Jack's hand and led him to the front room. She sat him down on the couch, sitting next to him on his right side, taking off his sunglasses.

"Sit quietly and don't move." Ana gently took Jack's right hand in her two hands with his palm facing upward. She put her left hand under his hand and, with her right hand, gently traced the flesh of his upper palm near the base of his fingers, going to the left and toward the bottom of his thumb, then to his lifeline mark where his wrist met his hand. Ana placed three fingers on his palm, lightly moving up his lifeline with her thumb touching his thumb, returning her fingers and thumb to the base of his hand. She repeated this motion several times.

"That feels good. Don't stop." Jack breathed out in a low, husky voice.

Ana smiled and continued the motion with her hand. "Be gentle and go slow with a woman. A tender touch is your first lesson."

"Is this school?" Jack whispered, leaning closer to her. "What is my next lesson?"

Ana released Jack's palm, softly reaching up, putting her hands on both sides of his head. She tilted him toward her, moving her right hand, touching his lips lightly with her fingers.

"Feel how soft I am touching you. You need to kiss that way. Soft and light at first. Gain a woman's trust. Do you like this feeling?"

Jack, looking directly into Ana's eyes, nodded.

Ana moved her right hand to his left cheek, gently brushing her lips to his, lingering for a time.

"Don't move," she whispered. "Let me show you how I want to be made love to."

Jack, thoroughly aroused, was speechless. He didn't move.

* * *

Ana thought back on that afternoon. What had she started? Why had she started it? It was her choice. Had she done it to spite Rib, fulfill her promise to Peggy, or had a connection been made with Jack? It was a combination of anger and commitment, but fondness for Jack stirred in her body.

Ana continued to spend weekends at Jack's. Friday and Saturday nights were spent making love. During the weekdays, Ana worked at the courthouse. Saturday and Sunday daylight hours were spent working, repairing machinery, cleaning shops, moving and feeding cows, and getting ready for calving season. Ana loved her new life.

To her delight, Rib arrived at Jack's to treat a sick cow on one of her weekends at the ranch, showing up in his fancy veterinarian truck. Ana made sure she was seen. As he worked over a downed heifer, she had casually strolled over to where Rib tended the sick animal.

"Is this what a vet does in his spare time?"

Never to be outdone, Rib, without looking up, retorted, "A good vet is hard to find, or is it a hard vet is good to find?"

Ana, not missing a beat and angry over his lack of remorse, hissed, "You SOB, you are screwing that schoolteacher, aren't you? Even after we had such an unforgettable Labor Day. What does it take to keep you happy?"

Rib tended to his animal without looking at Ana. "You sound like a wife to me." Standing up to face Ana, Rib tossed his head toward Jack. "Robbing the cradle, are you?"

Ana had a comeback about the frying pan calling the kettle black but sensed this conversation was a dead-end street. She remained silent, happy that she had riled Rib.

Ana turned, walking back to where Jack was unloading bales of hay. By the time she reached Jack, her eyes shone, matched by a smile as wide as the Missouri River.

Duke and Cobey, Jack's hired hands, were helping lift the hundred-pound bales.

Ana joined in with energy fueled by Rib's remarks. As she worked off her turmoil, she was conscious of Cobey scanning her body, which made her uncomfortable. It was a feeling of weirdness only sensed by a woman. She had the same feeling once before in a much different setting. A politician had shaken her hand but had placed his other hand on her forearm in a too-tight grasp. Now, those alarm antennae sharpened, warning her. Bad chills ran through her body as she looked into Cobey's leering eyes.

After finishing their chores, Ana and Jack returned to the farmhouse.

"What do you know about your man, Cobey?"

"Not much," Jack admitted. "He is from the Havre area and has a wife and two children. They live down on the old Pearson place, a couple of miles south of the school. He had been working in Idaho but wanted to get back to Montana."

"Is he a good worker? A good husband. A good father? Or do you hire these people without knowing them?"

"Cobey is as good as you might find for farm labor. He shows up on time, works reasonably hard, quits when the work is done, and heads for home. He brags about himself too much for my taste." Jack paused, thinking he didn't know much about Cobey.

"What work does he do for you?" Ana persisted. "Is he only involved in the cattle operation?"

Jack tilted his head to his right, considering. "He does all the jobs. In the wintertime, he works with the cows, and in the spring and summer, he adds on tractor driving when Swede is off on a bender. He fixes irrigation systems, helps with the harvest and haying, and generally keeps the place looking nice. Why do you ask?"

"Just a creepy feeling when he stares at me. He calls you 'boss man.' Ex-cons use boss as a derogatory word. Has he been in prison?"

"I don't know," said Jack, shrugging his shoulders "He gets his work done and that is all that matters to me."

"I get the willies when he looks at me like I'm a non-person."

"Don't worry about him. Cobey is harmless."

"I'm not so sure about that," argued Ana. "I don't get good vibes when he is around. Of course, I had the same feeling about you at the VFW hall." Then she smiled, casting a sideways glance at Jack. "Just kidding. I could see you were a diamond in the rough. And besides, I promised your mother I would look after you."

Jack gave her a scowl but didn't say anything.

Ana, backing away from this touchy topic again, reverted to her best smile. "How about we have a bite to eat before we cuddle up in bed?"

Jack's eyes shone at the thought of another night with Ana, and he forgot all about his mother.

* * *

Ana enjoyed her new role as mentor and lover to Jack. She had power in the relationship, and Jack had become a tender, lovemaking machine. At one point, he told her, "I had no idea that making love could be so..." He couldn't find the words to describe it.

Ana finished the sentence for him, "Sensual and satisfying, especially when you have slow hands." Jack stammered and shuffled his feet, nodding in agreement.

Ana, she thought, *you are a long way from perfect, but you have done a miraculous job with Jack.*

Ana's weekends were now being spent at Jack's place. She was developing a genuine passion for him and cherished taking care of the cattle. The days filled her need for being grounded and the nights for being physical. She had loved before but it was different with Jack. There was an intensity between them that she cherished, but still, Ana didn't feel the electricity in her body like she did with Rib.

Ana puttered around Jack's house content with herself. She had fulfilled her promise to Peggy, and Jack would come out of Ana's teachings a force to be reckoned with for any woman. The unexpected was the tenderness and affection she felt for Jack.

Jack had confided to Ana that he still had his heart set on Mariah, but there had been rumors that Mariah had taken up with Rib Torgerson, the veterinarian. Jack admitted he had seen Rib's pickup at his old barn where Mariah kept her horse.

"What does Mariah see in that old man?" he grumbled.

"What do we see in each other?" Ana replied. "Another lesson to learn: Where the heart is concerned, there is very little logic. How many times have you seen a couple and wondered how they ever got together." Ana hesitated, not sure how far into this subject she should go. "And another thing: It is usually the woman who makes a choice about whom she is going to allow to get close to her."

"You made a choice with us, didn't you?" asked Jack with a nod.

"Yes, I did."

She thought about the reasons she had taken up with Jack and couldn't explain why. *Damn, didn't I just tell Jack there is no logic where the heart is concerned?*

Ana turned her attention back to Jack, seeing an opportunity to discuss the next steps with him. "Is Mariah still your main squeeze?"

Jack looked at Ana, putting his right hand to his lips. "You never let me get comfortable, do you? Yes, Mariah is still my squeeze if that means what I think. There are times when you and I make love that I pretend it's her." Jack paused before asking, "Does that upset you?"

"No," said Ana. "I expect that happens between couples." Ana crossed her arms with a faraway look in her eyes and continued, "I might have been thinking of someone else myself. But that is neither here nor there. The question is, what are our next steps?"

Jack leaned his arms on the kitchen table. "I'm so damn mad at Mariah.

I could kill her before I let someone else have her. She is spending a lot of time with the old horse doctor. I have driven by the teacherage, and his truck is parked over by my barn! He is spending too much time on a cured horse. I'll talk with him."

"I wouldn't," cautioned Ana. "It's true that Mariah has taken up with Rib. I can't tell you how I know that. I just do. Think about it. What is going to be Rib's reaction, and even more importantly, what would Mariah do? She would never talk to you again. No, your best bet is to keep your powder dry and play the long game. Rib has a reputation for loving and leaving his women." As Jack considered Ana's advice, she asked him, "Can you handle that possibility?"

"I've heard that about him," said Jack. "He is my vet and does a damn good job. He knows what he is doing with cattle." Jack hesitated, his fists now clenched. "What the hell is he doing with Mariah? I can't believe she would fall for someone like him."

"Temper, temper," soothed Ana. "We've talked about staying in control. Sometimes, you scare me with what you say. You can't honestly want to kill Mariah."

"There are times I think I could kill her," admitted Jack. "But I never would. I get so mad and want to change her mind. Can't she see I would take care of her?"

"You love Mariah, but it takes two to make it work. Mariah is not ready for you, but if you play your cards right, there is a chance it could happen. Your plan to win over Mariah means you and I stay together. It sounds strange, but you have to lose before you can win."

"I'm not in a hurry to change my life with you," said Jack. "You have been good for me. I don't want us to end, but I know my heart is with Mariah. With you, Ana, I go day by day."

"Did you just say I'm only important in the moment?" Ana asked.

Oh my God, she thought. *Why do I find men who can't think long-term? What is wrong with me?*

"I talk too much," Jack admitted. "I don't mean I would kill her. I wouldn't do it under any circumstances. Do you see what I mean?"

"Sometimes you scare me," repeated Ana. "But I believe you are not a person who could kill someone you love. I've seen your gentle side, and it touches me."

Ana gave Jack a hug, then pulled away without a kiss. "You are such a surprise because I thought you to be arrogant and full of yourself." Ana smiled. "Which, of course, you are, but there is a sweet side too. You have a special place in my heart, for now and for always. I can't explain it, but we have today and tonight. For how long after, who knows? But right now, what we are doing is good for both of us."

Jack gently pulled Ana into his arms. "You've taught me that sometimes a woman needs a tender hug with no thought of sex. You make things simple when the whole world seems like it is coming down on me."

As an afterthought, Jack whispered, "I could make Mariah happy."

Ana ignored his whisper.

"Are you free this afternoon?" she asked. "We shouldn't pass up any opportunity."

PART TWO

THE SEARCH

CHAPTER 19

SATURDAY, JANUARY 3, 1976

It was the Saturday after Peggy's New Year's Eve party. A January snowstorm followed by blizzard winds had left drifts of snow around Fort Collins. The town was nearly deserted with only a few snow-covered cars parked on the streets. The clock on Peggy's wall neared high noon.

Ana sat in the recliner in Peggy's lair. Ana had spent the last two nights with Jack but had brought sandwiches and soda into Fort Collins for Peggy. A gin and tonic didn't strike her fancy this early in the day.

Peggy came back to join her as the store traffic had stopped. The locals were nursing hangovers, and bar owners had already arrived to replenish the cases of alcohol consumed during the New Year's celebration. Ana had her eyes closed, nearly asleep, and Peggy walked with a slow gait.

Ana, hearing Peggy say hello, opened her eyes. "Nice New Year's," she commented. "Your party at Busty's took it out of everyone, but what a good time! Jack and I ended up at the VFW dancing. God, he can dance."

"Dancing? Is that all you can talk about? I want to hear the juicy stuff," said Peggy, yawning. "On second thought, don't tell me a thing. I don't have the energy to hear about your wickedness with my son." Peggy popped open her can of soda as she sat in her recliner with her sandwich within easy reach. "Has he been treating you right?"

"Your pride and joy is a new man," reported Ana, stretching her arms out. "But not much has changed. Jack still has his sights set on Mariah, and I miss Rib."

Both women nibbled on their sandwiches, basking in their respective chairs.

"Full confession: I am going to see Rib next weekend," Ana whispered. "He called me yesterday. I can't say no to him."

Peggy remained silent.

Ana changed the subject. "Where has the time gone? First Halloween, then Thanksgiving, Christmas, and the New Year. I'm tired. I want off this merry-go-round."

"So do I," said Peggy. "I can't take one more night of booze."

"We need to talk," stated Ana.

"Can't it wait?"

"No. Jack and I are near the end of our rope."

Peggy didn't stir.

"We are starting to act like a married couple camped out in front of the TV."

Peggy knew to hold her tongue as she took another sip from her soda.

"Where does the spark go, or am I losing my touch? Or maybe it's just that calving season is coming on, and Jack has cows on his mind. Do I look like a cow? What do you think?"

"You don't look like a cow, only a stressed-out woman."

"Thanks for nothing," grumbled Ana.

"Calving is stressful," said Peggy. "The days and nights run together. It gets old, getting up in the middle of the night to check on a calf coming. I don't miss those days."

"Give me an answer. I deserve one because you got me into this crazy relationship with your son." Ana's eyes shone with budding tears.

"Don't get too down on yourself," cautioned Peggy. "A man thinks the world revolves around him, but what he doesn't know is his woman is the center of his universe. A woman has to hold things together, and that's where you are now. You have your job, your children, your misguided love for Rib, and now a good time with Jack. None of those things can last forever, so relax and enjoy the moment. Oops, sorry, I am starting to sound like Rib."

Ana became quiet, digesting Peggy's words. She wiped her eyes dry.

"Besides, this is the New Year, which means there's more than one way to have a hangover," said Peggy. "Call it the postpartum Christmas blues. We get rushed and buy presents, have family over, drink too much, and then it's over, and we get drunk on New Year's Eve. Put that into your cake and bake it. Get over it and get ready for spring."

The two women shared blank, tired stares. Peggy continued. "I get depressed too, at least for a week or so, and then I look forward to the coming year. Think about what the new year will bring. You might even find your man. God forbid it would be Rib, or even Jack, for that matter."

"I'm not looking for a man," said Ana. "Rib is my soulmate, but he has made me so angry these past months. Yet when he called me yesterday, my knees went weak, my heart fluttered, and I said, 'Yes, I will meet you in Great Falls!' My mind said no, but my heart took over. Am I weak, or what? I meant to teach him a lesson he wouldn't forget, and then I became a schoolgirl hungering for his touch. I don't feel like the center of anything."

"No, you aren't weak, only human and a woman to boot," said Peggy.

Ana took several seconds to reply. "I can't be involved with two lovers at the same time. Men seem to be able to do it and count it as a badge of honor, but not me."

Ana got up and paced to the back door as Peggy remained in her chair. Ana turned, walking back to Peggy. "I have to admit that I have a strong attraction to Jack, but I am older, and he wants marriage with children.

That's impossible for me. I don't love Jack, but I care for him. Does that make any sense to you?"

"Yes," said Peggy, sighing. "You have taken Jack under your wing and given him a chance. I could not have wished for more."

"Ending it with Jack will not be easy," concluded Ana.

"But Jack has changed, and for the better," Peggy added. "Can you believe he gave me a kiss and a hug the other night? I nearly filled my pink panties. I like what he is becoming. How did you do it?"

"But I can't give Jack what he really needs," said Ana between breaths. "His heart is set on Mariah, but it's hopeless as far as I can see, even if Rib disappeared from the scene. Maybe I could match Jack with someone?"

"You are not a matchmaker. Forget about trying to make that choice for him. But don't make any decision until you spend time with Rib." Peggy chose her next words carefully. "He might be getting tired of his fling with Mariah. You won't know until you see him. So, against my better judgment, my advice is to drive to Great Falls, spend your time with Rib, and clear the air. But be careful; keep your cards close to those stylish boobs of yours."

"You are right. Tonight is not the right time to get dramatic with Jack," agreed Ana. "I'll play it by ear."

Ana considered her next question for Peggy.

"What do you think Rib's intentions are in calling me out of the blue when we have not seen each other since Labor Day?"

"Same as they always are," answered Peggy. "I told you he'd come back to you. You give him more than your body. You give him stability, grounding him in a way no one else does." Peggy hesitated, not knowing if she should continue. Finally she blurted out, "Rib is jealous of your relationship with Jack."

Ana sat up straighter, nearly spilling her soda, with questions in her eyes

"Is he jealous, or something else? I don't feel any different, and I can't see Rib changing. He is set in his ways. There must be something else on his mind, although he has a knack for being focused on keeping his lifestyle."

Peggy couldn't argue with Ana but shifted her attention back to Jack. "Be smart with Jack, and like I said, don't be in a hurry to end it with him. Give Jack a dose of studied neglect."

"Studied neglect? What does that mean?"

"You realize you have a problem, so you study it and study it some more, and finally, you neglect it and don't do anything."

"Hmm. Studied neglect! I like it. I am going to live in a world of studied neglect, solving all my problems." Ana lowered her head, muttering, "I can't see how my life could be more complicated."

Ana rose from her chair, put on her winter coat, ski hat, and fur gloves, and then slowly walked to the back entrance. "Jack and I will need food for tonight and a bottle of good wine. I'll see you next week."

CHAPTER 20

FRIDAY, JANUARY 9, 1976

On the Friday evening of January 9, as Mariah sat in her teacherage waiting for Rib, Ana tapped on the bridal suite door at the O'Haire Manor in Great Falls seventy-five miles south of the younger woman.

Rib opened the door.

"Goddamn you, Rib Torgerson," Ana began without preamble. "You call and expect me to come running, and damn me for not telling you to go to hell."

Ana carried her overnight bag in her left hand, her purse draped over her right shoulder. Her black dress buttoned to her neckline projected the same seriousness she put on display when going before a jury.

She rushed past Rib and stormed into the room, putting down her night case and purse.

"I could spit on you, but I'm as angry at myself for being here in this... this...oh, this shit hole motel! You make me feel so cheap."

Ana had her hands on her hips as she turned to face Rib. Rib stood with his arms crossed, remaining silent.

"Aren't you going to say anything?" Ana asked. Rib shook his head.

"Let's have it out in the open. You are seeing Mariah, you ignored me, and you can't even defend yourself, can you?"

"No, I can't," said Rib. "I'm not even going to try."

"But I'm in the mood for a come-to-Jesus meeting with you. You are such a butt."

"I've been called a lot of things," said Rib with a smirk, "but never a butt. Do you want to explain?"

"I'm not the one to have to explain anything," snapped Ana. "Stop trying to change the subject. I am at a complete loss as to where we stand. I put up with you being married for reasons I don't understand, but for you to start up with a woman twenty-five years younger is going too far."

"You are right," agreed Rib. "I can't stay faithful to any woman, but Mariah gave me the go-ahead, and now my time with her has run its course. I always come back to you."

"I can't go on like this sneaking off for a weekend. What am I doing here with you? You use me!"

"No, that isn't true," Rib argued. "I'm using Mariah, and I will stop seeing her. She left a message asking to meet her tonight. I never called her back."

"That is so cruel," exclaimed Ana. "Mariah deserves better, and I'm mad because I am your excuse. I keep running back to you when I should demand more than this." Ana threw her right hand in the air.

"There isn't much for you to demand," Rib countered. "You can be as mad as a hornet, but not much will be different between you and me."

Ana and Rib stared at each other. Ana determined she would not be the first to speak. Rib broke the silence.

"How many times have I told you I love you, only in a different way? You've been part of me for twenty-five years or more, and that isn't going to change. We are bound together forever."

"That pisses me off," said Ana. "I hate you for being a constant reminder." Silence held between them for several seconds. Then, Ana continued, "What a crappy way to live."

"Jack Moser is in your life. What kind of game are you playing with him? How is it any different with me and Mariah than it is with you and Jack?"

Ana smugly realized Rib was jealous of Jack, but still gave him a dead-eye stare. Rib continued, "You can't answer, can you?" Silence measured the distance between them, neither of them caring to speak.

Ana turned to pick up her suitcase and purse, then headed toward the bedroom, calling back over her shoulder, "We aren't done with this conversation. Pour me a glass of wine. I need room service. I'm hungry and want food for this fight." A warm sensation passed through her body as she thought she was winning this battle with Rib.

Rib nodded, moving to the wet bar to open a Chardonnay bottle in the wine cooler. He filled a measure of wine into a long-stemmed glass. Then, grabbing his own empty drink, he poured two fingers of Black Velvet whiskey, added a splash of water, and sat down to await Ana's return.

Ana and I have had these wars before, he thought. He wondered how this one would end. On a Memorial Day two years ago, Ana had stormed out of the Two Medicine mountain cabin and jumped in her car, throwing gravel the entire length of the cabin's driveway. Rib shook his head with a slight grin at the memory of rocks crashing against his cabin porch.

"Ana, you are a work of art," he playfully declared to the empty room.

Ana, emerging from the bedroom in her terrycloth bathrobe, asked, "What did you say about me?"

"Something about how you are a cantankerous old woman who doesn't know enough to keep her mouth shut," answered Rib with a twinkle in his eye. "You do have a way of expressing your opinion with no filter."

"Don't try and change the conversation with those cutesy comments," warned Ana. "I am damn mad at you, and you aren't going to sweet-talk your way out."

"Merely trying to make nice," assured Rib. "I know better than to make you too mad. I remember you tearing out of the driveway at the cabin one time. I didn't see you for weeks."

"If I had any brains at all, I'd leave you right now and never come back," sighed Ana, then she paused, turning serious. "The horrible truth is I wanted you to fly my kite years ago and still do. God, if I had only seen the future, I'd have saved myself a lot of pain and heartache."

"Yes, you could have avoided some hurt, but look at what you would have missed," Rib said. "Our times together count more than any pain, so concede that whatever holds us together runs deep."

"But there are times I want more," lamented Ana. "Our last time together at your cabin felt perfect. I wanted that glow forever. Why can't it be permanent with us? Is it too much to ask to have sharing and solitude at the same time? You give me both, then take them from me."

"We have each other tonight," Rib offered.

"Big deal. I have no hold on you. I'm jealous that you might have that special something with Mariah too. These weekends when you sneak away from your wife, and now from Mariah...they are all I have. Where do I fit?"

"You are worried about what happened yesterday or what will happen tomorrow," concluded Rib. "Why think about those things? We are here tonight. Isn't that what matters? You insist on something permanent, but I can guarantee that kind of thing doesn't come with a marriage license. How many divorces have you done?"

"A woman doesn't think like that," Ana snapped. "I've seen lots of broken marriages, but some stay together for whatever reason. You and Connie are the perfect pair. I worry about us. I worry about me. In ten years, will I still be meeting you at the O'Haire? I don't think so."

"You want to cling to something from yesterday," realized Rib. "And at the same time, you want a guarantee that whatever yesterday brought will be there tomorrow or ten years from now. To me, that is not realistic. Look what happened to your husband. Cancer took him too early. Were you living in the moment with him, enjoying the benefits of marriage?"

Ana, thinking back on the days before the cancer diagnosis, couldn't argue Rib's point. She and Richard had been at odds over his late nights, drinking, and chasing after that other woman.

Ana, with her glass of Chardonnay half full, walked around the room, ignoring Rib. Standing next to the bedroom door, she sipped the wine.

Spinning to face Rib, who still sat, watching her with his whiskey in his hand, Ana folded her arms and retorted, "Is bringing up the past the best you can do? Richard and I had our issues, but we would have worked them out. I didn't love him the same way all the time, but it worked. I liked the stability that Richard and I had. He would always come home to me. We slept in the same bed and raised our children. There was a rhythm to our life that I loved. The words 'safe' and 'comfortable' come to mind."

"What do we have?" Rib asked.

"It's not safe or comfortable. It might have been exciting at one time, but we are older. Yet here I am at the O'Haire. What is wrong with me?"

"Nothing's wrong with you," Rib soothed. "It's called living in the moment. You want structure but only in a certain way. You are clinging to some weekend in the mountains or dreading some event in the future. This is the here and now. I love you. I accept you. Can you accept me as I am?"

Ana walked back to Rib and put her half-full glass of wine on the table, not answering the question. She sat next to Rib silently, hands in her lap, and looked straight into his eyes, not touching him. No one spoke for several minutes.

Finally, Ana sighed deeply, keeping her gaze locked onto Rib's face. "Let's order room service. I'm hungry, and this conversation is going nowhere." She stood up to retrieve the menu, looking through it even though she knew she would order her usual Caesars salad. Rib had not moved as she handed him the menu.

"Look who is changing the subject," Rib commented. "I asked you a question, and you have not answered. Will you accept me as I am?"

"I'll tell you when I'm good and ready to," answered Ana. "Right now, I want food. Pour me more wine too."

"You are the damnedest woman I have ever met," Rib said as he rose to get the wine bottle. "Just as we were getting to the meat of our little talk, you change the subject, get me to fill your glass, and demand room service." Rib had a slight smile on his face.

"Wipe that smirk off your face. This evening has just started. You are not getting off easy demanding a commitment for your benefit with none of the burdens. You haven't earned the right since you are tricking some sweet young thing. Don't forget your age. My daughter is only a couple of years younger than Mariah, and I would kill you if you took a run at one of my own."

"Do you hear what you are saying?" Rib asked. "How did your daughter get into this mix?"

Ana ignored the question, her mind forming her response. "Mariah has a family who cares for her. Don't be surprised if her dad shows up on your doorstep," she stammered.

"I'm breaking it off with Mariah. I told you that. What more do you want? The past four months are water under the bridge. The time I spent with Mariah isn't up to your standards, but it can't be changed. The real question is how we spend this weekend. Tonight is real."

"I still want a Caesars salad," said Ana. "And, I want to be in bed with you, but only if you will hold me and not touch me. Do you understand what I mean?"

"Holding you without touching you is not possible. But I get what you want. You are angry with me. I can't say I blame you. You know me, and I will respect your wishes, but having my arms around you seems like touching."

"You are one perceptive turd, aren't you?" Ana allowed a small smile to creep across her face. "You have promised me there will be no messing around, but I think you have something in mind for tomorrow morning.

You can forget that too. My holding without touching rule is in place for twenty-four hours. Let's get through the night and tomorrow morning and see what Saturday brings."

"As you have demanded," obeyed Rib, putting his hands together in front of him and bowing slightly.

His inner voice told him to enjoy this moment. However, a more profound inner voice realized that Ana could cast a spell on him like no one else. *Enjoy, but you are not in Ana's league.* Rib went to the telephone to call room service.

* * *

Ana awoke the following day shortly before seven, hearing Rib in the shower. She stretched, thinking the previous evening had gone as she had planned. Rib had lived up to his promise to hold her but not touch. Ana smiled at his gentleness. Rib had gone to sleep almost immediately, which ticked Ana off because she had lingered in the closeness with Rib touching her bare back comfortably to his chest with his right arm around her waist and his left arm tucked under her pillow. Ana felt secure in his arms, finally falling asleep.

She had not heard Rib leave the bed at six.

Ana arose, put on the terrycloth bathrobe, walked to the bathroom door, knocked on it, and asked, "Do you need someone to wash your back?"

Ana could hear the water stop running.

"No, I am done. Do you need the shower?" Rib asked.

"I need a hug more than a shower," said Ana. "Can I come in? Or is that too much to ask of a shy cowboy? You have no clothes on and are still on twenty-four-hour probation, so how strong is your willpower?"

"No, you can't come in," Rib shouted through the closed door. "I respect your rules, but the sight of you might be too much for me to resist. I'll wrap a towel around me. Then I can give you a hug without giving myself away."

"Your intentions are obvious. You only have one," said Ana. "My probations are still in place, but I do want a hug."

"Forever at your service," said Rib through the closed door. "But you do have me compromised with no clothes on and just a towel for protection. Could you at least find me a bathrobe so I can keep some dignity?"

"You don't have much to bargain with, do you?" said Ana. "I'll find you a robe only if you promise me a hug."

"Yes, I promise," agreed Rib. "Damn, you make the craziest demands. Why do I put up with you?"

"Because you love me, and I call you on your misguided ways. I'll be back in a second. Promise you won't make a dash to escape."

Ana got the robe, handing it to Rib through a crack in the door. Rib emerged with a smile and gave Ana her required hug. As she walked away, Rib playfully slapped his towel at her behind, missing but causing Ana to turn to him and smile.

"See what fun we have together?" noted Ana. "Can't you picture us teasing each other, day after day? Or do you think we would lose the magic of the moment?"

"Christ almighty," grumbled Rib. "You get on a subject and don't let go. It's no wonder you are the finest lawyer in Fort Collins."

"Flattery gets you nowhere with me," retorted Ana. "I'm still beyond angry with you over this Mariah thing. Are you honestly promising to end it?"

"Yes, I am going to end it," said Rib. "But first, I have to make meetings today and tomorrow with the Stockgrowers Association. Showing up at these events is ninety percent of my job."

"Then get your cute little butt dressed and get out of my way," ordered Ana. "I intend to have a leisurely morning, a cup of coffee, and shop. Then I am coming back here and having a long, hot bath."

Ana danced around Rib, his eyes following her moves. She flicked her hand under his chin. "I'll have some wine too. When will you be back?"

"Around five," said Rib. "I'm on a panel at two today and have another session tomorrow at eleven." Rib reached over to Ana, giving her another hug.

"Will we have time tonight to discuss my probation?"

"Don't count on it," she said, giving Rib the evil eye. "I'm not sure where I fit into your life, but I want an answer."

* * *

After Rib left the room, Ana decided to drive to the 10th Avenue Mall for the day. The Great Harvest Wheat Company had tasty cinnamon rolls that she knew would fit nicely with a hot cup of coffee.

Ana dressed warmly, picking from the options in her overnight bag a blue turtleneck layered under a white sweater to go along with her jeans and winter boots. After putting on her powder blue ski coat, a matching blue ski hat, and gloves, she placed the "Please Make Up the Room" sign on the doorknob, then walked down the back stairs to her car, avoiding the main lobby. A brisk northern wind caused her to lower her head against the cold. The car's windshields were frozen, but the engine turned over, starting the process of warming the motor so Ana could defrost the windows. Ana decided to stay in the car, even though the cold pierced the warmth of her body. The windshield slowly gave up its frosted coat, allowing Ana to drive to the mall.

Ana ordered her cinnamon roll heated while sipping her coffee from a paper cup, planning her day. Her concern focused on the evening with Rib if he decided to come back to the motel. *He damn well better show up*, she thought.

After finishing her roll and coffee, Ana strolled past the many stores in the mall corridor, window shopping. The bookstore drew her in. Peggy had made her promise to pick up the latest *Time* magazine featuring the Person of the Year, which happened to be twelve American women, accompanied by an article showcasing the National Organization of Women movement.

Peggy had embraced the feminism it represented, the changing roles, and the diversity of American women.

Ana felt her plate too full to join some new group; besides, she didn't fully embrace this growing movement's ideals, though she considered herself an independent woman. Life had forced her to be strong-minded, get her law degree, and survive in the male-dominated legal world.

Ana returned to the motel, ran a hot bath, poured a glass of wine, and plotted her evening. She had to give Rib credit for holding but not touching her last night, and the back and forth this morning was the highlight of her weekend. After her bath, she picked up the *Time* magazine, along with the glass of wine, and settled into the couch, anticipating Rib's return.

* * *

Rib had left Ana in the room that morning as he made his way to the motel's restaurant. After a breakfast of steak and eggs with hash browns and coffee, he drove to the Western Livestock Auction Yard ten miles west of Great Falls.

The Stockgrowers' meeting wouldn't start until nine, but Rib wanted an opportunity to greet the general manager, keeping up good relations with the man who bought Rib's cattle. At one point, he thought he might stop by and see the office manager, Susan Gollahan, but then shook his head, thinking that even he couldn't be that dumb, with Ana waiting for him to come back to the room. Rib silently cursed himself.

Ana didn't put up with any crap from him. *And what was this whole probation thing all about?* he wondered. Usually, their first night together after long absences boiled down to deep passion.

Ana didn't hesitate to challenge him about his relationship with Mariah. He never let himself be caught talking about marriage. For sure, Ana held a spell over him, but that could be changed this evening. *I'll talk about marriage and see how that scares her.* On second thought, he would steer away from talk of tying the rope as Ana could make greater demands on him. Women were fascinating to him; he couldn't understand their way of thinking, but why bother trying? He never quite knew which way they would jump, so he went with the flow. Rib loved the challenge; he loved women.

* * *

Rib arrived back at the motel at five-thirty. Ana lounged on the couch with a glass of wine, waiting for him. She wore the terrycloth bathrobe.

Rib, forgetting his decision, kicked off the conversation. "What if I said yes to marriage? You were hinting the whole night about it. It might be something I would consider."

"You are so full of it, your blue eyes have turned brown. You have no intention of divorcing Connie to marry me or any other woman. Remember, I know you. You broke my heart once a long time ago, and that isn't going to happen again."

"That's a harsh assessment," said Rib. "Why don't we talk about marriage?"

"Ha. You need me more than I need you. You have a certain attraction, but a wedding isn't your style. Think about the uproar in the community. We're not fooling anyone with what we are doing, but we are discreet about it. If Connie can put up with you, then I will enjoy our time together. But make no mistake, we are not the marrying kind, at least with each other."

"I thought talking about marriage was what you wanted," Rib pointed out. "Now, marriage is the furthest from your mind."

Ana crooked her finger at him. "I might find the right man to marry, but it won't be you. I'm still looking, but you don't have a chance in hell of changing your ways."

"What kind of person do you think I am? I could marry you. We're good together, like you said before. You challenge me, and I challenge you. Don't deny it. I know that much."

Ana, seeing him defensive, kept up her attack. "The only thing good about us is our lovemaking. No one else gives me goosebumps like you do. You have a slow hand, a tender heart, and I love you for it. But, we have no future as a husband and wife, only as lovers. How could we build a marriage on lonely nights when you are out doing what you do? We'd last a month, at best." Ana smiled, showing a bare shoulder, enjoying her upper hand in their conversation.

Rib reached to touch it, but Ana pushed his hand away.

"I miss being with you, but I haven't seen you since Labor Day," Ana reminded him without a smile. "The mountain air of the Two Medicine is what I remember most. Surely, it wasn't the lovemaking in the meadow at sunset or at dawn in that creaky old bed." Ana made a face of disgust.

Rib smiled at the memory of that weekend. "Three days living in the moment. Wish I could put that in a bottle and keep it."

Ana poked him in the ribs. "Are you comparing me to a bottle of booze or a tiny wooden ship? Don't I mean more to you than that?"

"What kind of booze are you talking about? You know my weakness for Black Velvet."

"That isn't your only weakness," said Ana, keeping Rib off balance. She moved closer to Rib, allowing him to take her into his arms. Ana reached up and kissed Rib on the lips, a light, lingering moment between them.

"Must be a woman thing when I am around you," she observed. "Can't we be forever? You laugh at me walking around naked. You don't make any judgments and understand how important that is. Every day going to work, I have my guard up. Am I dressed properly? Is my hair messed? Is my makeup on right? What sort of games will be played today by the commissioners? Will I have to outwit the sheriff? Yes, to all those questions. But, with you, I can be me."

"That's giving me a lot more credit than I'm due," replied Rib. "Look at me, here with you, and I don't have guilt. What kind of man acts like that? We haven't judged each other, except this weekend when you are waving a *tsk tsk* finger." Rib tilted his head to the right, grinning.

"You might want to give me the other finger sometimes, but you never do."

Ana smirked. "But you have this thing for a twenty-five-year-old woman, and she doesn't have a clue what kind of man you are. Now, you talk about ending that relationship with her, expecting me to fall directly in your lap as though nothing has happened. And here I am, cuddling with you."

Ana kissed him again, then pulled away. "Don't kid yourself. This weekend has a different feel."

"It is still you and me," said Rib. "Can we talk about my probation?"

"Give me your hand," said Ana, placing his right hand in her left hand. She gently circled his palm with her right hand, then gently traced Rib's lips.

CHAPTER 21

WEDNESDAY, JANUARY 14, 1976

Ana walked into the Collins County commissioner's meeting room at precisely nine in the morning on Wednesday, the 14th of January, 1976. Neither fuming nor smiling, she greeted the three male commissioners and their secretary sitting at the oblong table.

"Good morning, everyone." Ana took her seat. "It would be a better use of time if legal questions were put in writing before the meeting so I could research them to give you an in-depth opinion."

The commissioners' meetings followed a pattern: The first hour consisted of catching up with each other, having their secretary, Jody Myers, bring in coffee and rolls. The commission chair, George Daniels, would eventually call the meeting to order with a bang of his antique gavel.

Ana was intent on making sure that didn't happen this morning as she needed to get back to her office to work on the past weekend's events, which included a missing person, a fatal car wreck on Interstate 15, a drug bust, an assault, and a rustling complaint; wasting her time at a social hour with the commissioners could not happen today.

Ana knew the commissioners had tricky business; they had to grapple with the upcoming hospital upgrade project and deal with a Hutterite woman's demand that the county pay for her cancer treatment. Both issues would demand plenty of attention.

Commissioner Sam "Jesus" Johnson, fired back at her, "You are the county attorney! It's your job to advise. Start earning your damn salary by being at our meetings."

Jesus Johnson did not frighten Ana. "Commissioner Johnson [she almost said Jesus but caught herself], this weekend, we had a missing schoolteacher, a fatality in a car wreck, an assault that sent Swede Davidson to the Great Falls Hospital, a drug bust, and a cattle rustling complaint."

The commissioners looked at each other.

"That's quite a weekend for our county," remarked Chairman Daniels.

"Yes, it is most unusual," agreed Ana. "I'm most concerned about the missing schoolteacher. The sheriff has his deputies searching the area for her as he is convinced she has been kidnapped, or worse."

"Get that lazy sheriff to solve those problems," retorted Commissioner Johnson. "We are dealing with millions of dollars getting a new hospital built before the nuns close down the old one. Get your priorities straight," he snarled. "Stay right where you are."

Ana tilted her head to the side and squinted her eyes, thinking, *Jesus Johnson, you are a complete ass without any idea of what I do*. She realized, though, that nothing she could say would make him any more competent.

She smiled as she sat, pulling from her briefcase a yellow legal pad and her black and red pens, rubber-banded together—red on one side, black on the other. She determined that Jesus Johnson's contributions would be in red.

Ana's opening strategy had worked as Chairman Daniels immediately gaveled the meeting to order, breaking the tension. Secretary Myers gave Ana a discreet nod and smile; no coffee or rolls served.

Ana winked back at her. Such subtle acts on Ana's part cultivated a kinship among the female staff in the courthouse offices. Ana knew that more than anything else, internal politics determined success or failure. Ana wanted to keep her job, and the coming election would decide if she stayed.

The meeting had progressed to a discussion on the massive amount of federal money for the new county hospital when Ana's secretary, Elaine Haleck, burst into the room.

Elaine, perky and petite, had worked for several county attorneys in Collins County. She was an institution not only in the courthouse, but in the city and county. Elaine's perfectly coiffed gray hair accented her position of assumed authority. If Ana ever wanted information, she relied on Elaine's contacts and her experienced advice.

Ana had given Elaine specific instructions not to disturb the meeting, but Elaine honed in on Ana, waving a memo pad, and stated powerfully, "The sheriff needs you right away."

Ana responded with a shake of her head and a wry grin. Elaine was rarely wrong regarding her grasp of critical events. If the sheriff needed her, Ana felt it imperative that she find a way to leave this meeting ASAP.

Ana couldn't be angry at Elaine. After all, the woman had absolved her of any need to sit there and listen to the commissioners for who knew how long; God had answered her prayer. Ana stood and acknowledged the four curious heads at the table with a simple shrug. *What's a county attorney to do?*

Commissioner Daniels, who had the best head on his shoulders, smiled and waved Ana away. "Duty calls for your services. I hope it is not as crucial as Elaine thinks."

As Ana left the meeting, she called back over her shoulder, "Keep me up to date with the hospital. If there are legal questions, put them in writing for Elaine. I'll get back to you as soon as possible with answers, and I will keep you apprised of what the sheriff has on his mind."

"Get back here as fast as you can," demanded Jesus Johnson.

Ana ignored him and smiled her best smile, leaving the meeting.

Before heading toward the sheriff's basement office, Ana walked Elaine back to her office to see what the woman knew about the sheriff's message.

Elaine filled her in on the call from the teacherage and the sheriff's investigation and his upbeat mood, noting it meant that the sheriff had a crime to solve.

Two days before, the sheriff had told Ana about Mariah and the stained gravel along with the watch. Ana guessed the sheriff had the analysis report back from the Greats Falls lab or information on the wristwatch found on the road.

Ana descended two floors to the basement level where the sheriff's office was located—its unique smell stung her nose. She hated coming to see him. The odor from the jailhouse cells attached to the back of the office combined with a strong disinfectant cleaner made Ana imagine sterilized urine.

The sheriff emerged from his office to meet her. He got as far as the counter that stood between them and waited behind it, not offering to take her back to his inner office. The outer office consisted of a chest-high counter separating the visitors from the staff. Five desks were crowded together in that basement room, all of which were covered with papers. Only a secretary was present. The room was painted in a light brown with a large clock on the north wall, and bulletin boards with papers thumbtacked on them on the other walls.

"Thank you for reaching out," Ana began. "What do you have?"

Ana thought how life would be simpler if she didn't have to deal with male egos, and those of Jesus Johnson and the sheriff topped her list.

The sheriff confirmed Ana's guess. "Deputy Severtson has the results from the gravel sample, and it shows human blood—Type O."

"Have you told her parents yet?" Ana asked.

"No, but I called them on Monday, and they are here in Fort Collins staying with the Morgans south of town. This news won't make them feel better, particularly after they told me Mariah's blood type is O."

"Will you call them, or should I?" Ana asked. "On second thought, you call them because they know you."

"Mariah's mother confirmed the wristwatch is a Christmas gift she gave her daughter," continued the sheriff. "I have more than a missing person. I have a murder to solve!"

"We may have a crime, but let's not give up hope yet," Ana replied, shaking her head in disbelief at the sheriff's declaration. "You need to find Mariah, and then we can decide what to do. Be extra careful in gathering evidence. Follow the law when obtaining your search warrants and talking to witnesses. Document everything in writing, turn over every stone, and keep me informed. Do you understand?"

"Don't tell me how to run an investigation," snapped the sheriff. "I've had FBI training."

"Spare me the details," retorted Ana. "Don't screw up this investigation. Do you have any suspects?"

"None that I'm telling you. When I think you should know something, I will be in touch."

"That doesn't cut it with me," Ana shot back. "Who are your suspects?"

"I don't have any right now. My deputies are talking to neighbors, and Deputy Severtson has been searching the backroads near the school. We will find something."

"Do you have any theories?" Ana pressed. "Are you looking for a body? Tell me what you are doing!"

"I told you what my deputies are doing. We haven't found anything yet."

"Promise me you will contact me immediately!"

The sheriff didn't speak, but his jaw tightened, his lips pinched together, and he squinted his eyes. She noticed his hands had clasped the edge of the counter.

"Sheriff, you don't like me. I understand that," Ana said. "But Mariah is missing, so get over whatever your personal opinion is and cooperate. Finding her is our priority, and your job is to keep me in the loop. Do you understand?"

The sheriff remained still, not speaking, with undisguised disgust evident, his lip slightly curled.

Ana turned and bound up the stairs two at a time to her office.

CHAPTER 22

THURSDAY, JANUARY 15, 1976

Chief Deputy Sheriff Jerry Severtson scowled. Since Tuesday, he had been scouring backroads, canyons, and farmhouses looking for a possible missing female schoolteacher. Jerry kept his police vehicle running for warmth, but when he had to leave the car to inspect buildings or terrain, his hands quickly froze despite his gloves. The wind burned his face, and his toes were in danger of frostbite. The days were short, with a wind chill in the low teens.

There had to be more important things to do, and the cold didn't suit him.

The sheriff was always on the rampage, looking for the next drug deal to bust. The deputy thought his search for the missing teacher had all the earmarks of a goose chase.

Jerry recalled his training. The mantra he had learned from that experience came down to: hurry up and wait or just be glad you are not in a courtroom being grilled by some attorney putting words in your mouth. God, he hated testifying.

It could be worse, he decided, but he *was* freezing, so he turned his thoughts toward his coming retirement. Sunny beaches danced in his head; if he could just hold on for another ten months, he would have his pension, his wife, and his freedom from working with his sheriff.

He turned his attention back to the job at hand. His police car warmed him up, and he started his search thinking about what was known.

Damn, what had he and the sheriff discovered after the call? His mind turned. *There isn't much evidence*, he thought.

Mariah's failure to show up for school on Monday was a little strange, and the disarray of the house might have been the result of a struggle. Then again, she may have run off with a friend or lover or just gotten tired of living out in the country and had shimmied off to Great Falls. There were slight signs of a struggle in the living quarters but no bloodstains except the one on the road. Besides, who knew what went on in the mind of a woman?

He would keep looking and driving those graveled and dirt backroads, though. Maybe something would turn up.

"Mungo, looks like another wasted day," he said as he scratched his dog's head. Mungo was a blue heeler named for its mottled blue look caused by dark and white hair mixed together. The dog had black markings around its eyes, giving a mask look to its face with a silver streak running from his muzzle to the top of his head. "It's a good thing you are here to keep me company. Now all you need to do is round up this missing person."

On Tuesday and Wednesday, he had searched east of the schoolhouse and found evidence of beer parties and discarded trash, but nothing pointed toward her disappearance. Of course, that area stretched clear to the North Dakota border, and he was a mere dot on the prairie.

He patted Mungo again. "We will endeavor to persevere, won't we, Mungo?" He mimicked a line he had heard in the movie *Little Big Man*.

He always silently mouthed those words when the sheriff assigned cases to him.

Today, he decided to go west of the schoolhouse and toward Interstate 15. At least his search would be limited by the highway and its fences. He took in the view of the Rockies, topped with snow-capped peaks and a slight haze, giving them a smokey look. He could see Chief Mountain to the northwest and Ear Mountain to the southwest.

Some days, the mountains looked so close and other days so distant. Today, they were mysterious and majestic at the same time, looking more intimate than they actually were. He ignored the stark beauty of the prairies and indulged himself in the mountain finery. Damn, he would like to go skiing at Teton Pass. He could feel the powder rushing past his boots and into his goggles.

Jerry had been instructed to start his search on Tuesday at the farmstead across Yoakum Road where Swede Davidson lived, and he recounted the first day of his hunt. Jerry knew that Swede now resided in a Great Falls hospital and wouldn't be home, but orders were orders. He had checked up on the horse in the barn, seeing that someone had been watering and feeding the animal. He wondered who would have an interest in the horse and made a mental note to find out who would take the time to care for Tucker.

Jerry didn't have a search warrant, but he walked about the property, confident that no one would challenge him, looking into the other buildings. There was an old chicken house and what looked to be a one-time ice house or a Finnish sauna, but both were empty. He walked about the trailer and peered into its windows, cupping his hands over the sides of his eyes to block out the glare. The door was locked. He made no attempt to enter the home. Nothing out of sorts there, so he started what turned out to be a two-day search in an easterly direction from the house that would ultimately turn up no trace of the missing Mariah. He searched as far east as Tiber Reservoir, always keeping the Knees' landmark to his right.

On Thursday, with Mungo sitting in the passenger side of his police car, he set about on his search west of the school toward Interstate 15. That past fall, he had hunted for pheasants in this area, walking the irrigation ditches in the hopes of flaring up a rooster. Hunting weather in October was far more pleasant than this ten-degree, wind-chilled January day. God, the aching in his bones from the cold hurt him to his toes.

After searching all morning on several dirt roads paralleling irrigation ditches, he turned west on another road bordering a harvested grain field; noontime loomed, but he would check one more irrigation ditch before he opened his lunch pail. A circular irrigation system lay to his right, tied down with fence posts to keep it from blowing away. The road itself had parallel tracks worn down by vehicle use with a linear tuft of grass in the middle. He didn't think he would become high-centered in his police car, so he wove his way down the road following the ditch's contours.

He drove slowly, still about a half-mile from the interstate, where he could see the cars and trucks streaming down the highway. Between his vehicle and the interstate were two metal grain bins looking like oversized thimbles perched on the ground next to a set of John Deere grain drills. As he got closer to the implement, the hairs on his neck started to tingle.

"Holy shit! Oh, my God, there is a body on the hitch," he yelled to his dog. He was still a hundred yards from the implement, but he could clearly see that its hitch cradled what looked like the body of a naked woman.

He grabbed his binoculars for a better look.

"Jesus H. Christ," he muttered.

The body was lying on the triangle section of the hitch, the head partially concealed by the supporting angle iron and a support tire. The woman's blouse and sweater had been pushed up above her breasts, and her right arm was splayed out, touching the ground. Her left leg was propped up high on a drill crossbeam, and the right leg was spread out on the other side, exposing the most intimate part of her body. There were red stains near her head on the surrounding patches of snow. A pile of clothes lay between her legs.

One red tennis shoe lay on a small snowdrift.

His thoughts raced. *How could anyone do this to a woman?* His stomach roiled.

Control your emotions and call the sheriff, he told himself. He reached for his mic and radioed home base.

His voice was cracking when he got the sheriff on the line. "You are not going to believe what has happened to the schoolteacher. At least, I think it's her. I am looking through my binocs and can identify a woman's body spread out on grain drills. You need to get out here as quickly as possible and bring the county coroner and forensics with you. I can't describe how bad it is. You need to see it for yourself!"

The sheriff asked his location, to which Jerry replied, "Meet me on the gravel road about a mile north of Jack's Moser's ranch house, just past the main irrigation canal."

The sheriff didn't need further directions and warned him not to contaminate the scene.

Jesus, what did the sheriff think him to be, a dunce? Jerry did not consider getting any closer.

Jerry gulped. "You have to see it yourself," he repeated.

"I'll be there in twenty minutes." The radio went silent.

Jerry took another look with his binoculars, staring in disbelief at the image that seemed so nearby in the glasses. He turned his vehicle around and headed back to the gravel road to wait for the sheriff. He did not want to think about the day ahead as securing the crime scene and searching for evidence was likely to be a long process. Meanwhile, the body would remain in place.

The prospect of hours of waiting in the presence of that woman spread-eagled on those drills sickened him.

CHAPTER 23

THURSDAY, JANUARY 15, 1976

Ana had instructed the sheriff to call her immediately with news of Mariah's disappearance.

That call came on Thursday, a short time before noon.

"Mariah's body has been found a mile north of Jack Moser's ranch house," the sheriff's voice reported into Ana's ear. "Deputy Severtson is at the scene now. I am driving out there as soon as I get off the phone. I recommend you wait here in town until we have more information as the investigation might take a long time."

Ana's heart sank. Her worst horror regarding how this search might end had just become real; she slumped back into her office chair. *This can't be happening*, she thought. Bile rose in her throat as she fought back the tears. *Be strong*, she told herself. Thoughts tumbled through her head...

"I'll call you when I have more info," added the sheriff, breaking through Ana's grief.

"No," Ana shouted. "Where is Mariah? I need to see her."

"You won't like what you see. It's pretty bad. Stay here in town and let us handle it."

"I need to be at the scene," argued Ana. "I will follow you out in my car and stay out of the way. It's important to see what happened. I know you will take pictures, but being there in person is crucial."

"The body is on grain drills," said the sheriff. "You know, the ones that put the wheat seed in the ground. Mariah has been severely beaten and is naked. Besides, it is damn cold out there. The wind must be blowing at twenty miles an hour. You should stay away."

"I'm dressed for the cold," said Ana, perplexed by the sheriff's continued attempts to distance her from the case.

"I can meet you at the back of the courthouse in five minutes," Ana finally offered. "Can you wait that long?"

The sheriff hesitated before answering. "Yes, I can wait, but hurry up."

Ana had anticipated finding Mariah every day since Monday and had dressed each morning in outdoor clothes. This morning, Ana had put on her winter ski jacket over her turtleneck, layered over a heavy sweater. She wore pantyhose and wool slacks along with ski gloves, a tassel hat, and warm boots. *I'll be warm enough*, she thought and dashed to the basement back door to meet the sheriff at his office, cursing him with every step.

She followed him out of the building to her car. The sheriff turned on his siren and overhead panel lights as the caravan motored down Fort Collins' main street to the interstate.

Ana shook her head. This was definitely serious business, but the sheriff was putting on an unnecessary show. People would realize what the emergency was. Ana would have preferred a more subdued exit from Fort Collins.

Ana followed the sheriff, turning off the paved highway onto the gravel roads, passing by Jack's ranch house on the way. *Jack will hear the siren. Hell, the whole county will*, she thought. How would she tell Jack? What would his reaction be? Shocked? Sad? Angry? Ana couldn't guess, but telling him would not be easy. She promised herself to stop at the ranch on her way back into town when she had more information.

The sheriff crossed an irrigation culvert a half-mile north of Jack's house, then made an immediate left turn onto the irrigation road, meeting with Deputy Severtson. After a brief conversation, the sheriff led the three cars, following the winding dirt path parallel to the irrigation ditch.

Interstate 15 could be seen in the distance. The trees of a distant farm's windbreak broke the horizon; there were no sounds of birds and no animals in sight. The Rocky Mountains stood silent, watching the little band of law enforcement officers and Ana reach the scene.

The sheriff parked his vehicle fifty yards from the drills on the dirt path in a spot where he could see the body on the grain drill. The dirt road curved in an "S" pattern, following the contours of the irrigation ditch. The bunch grass on the uncultivated land between the path and the ditch rose up between windblown patches of snow. The grass, peaking above the icy drifts, swayed with the force of the wind from the north. Patches of ice from melting snow had refrozen on parts of the path, but tire tracks indicating that a vehicle had turned around near the drills were still visible.

A small snowdrift had been formed on the drills' leeward side, where Mariah's body lay with her head touching the ground and her body spread-eagled on the left front hitch. Ana could see Mariah's left leg propped up on the machine's crossbeam and her right leg resting on the frozen ground.

Ana put her hand to her mouth, tears welling up in her eyes. "Oh, no," she cried out. "That poor girl."

The sheriff had left his vehicle, binoculars in his hand. He scanned the scene, shaking his head. "Goddamn, this is ugly. Don't anyone try to get any closer. There may be evidence we need."

As he spoke, Jack Moser's pickup raced up behind them, coming to a stop behind Ana's car. Jack jumped out of the vehicle, leaving it running and the door wide open. Jack was dressed only in his work shirt and jeans without his hat or his sunglasses.

Jack started toward the drills, but the sheriff and Deputy Severtson restrained him.

"You can't go down there." The sheriff looped his arm through Jack's. "It's a horrible scene, and we need to preserve any evidence we can find. Do you understand?"

"Let me go!" yelled Jack. "I can help Mariah."

"It's too late," the sheriff told him. "Mariah is dead, likely murdered from what I can see."

Jack's legs buckled beneath him, and the man collapsed, crying out Mariah's name.

Ana rushed to his side, holding him. "I'm so sorry you had to see this." She kissed his bare head gently.

The sheriff took note of her actions, turning to the deputy and making a writing motion. Deputy Severtson turned his head, putting his pen to the evidence book to record the pair's encounter.

Moments passed as the sheriff gathered his thoughts, surveying the scene. He pointed to his deputy. "Radio the coroner. Tell him we have a homicide. Contact the office and the highway patrol. We need pictures and evidence bags. Keep Jack here. I am going to take a closer look. I don't want anyone driving or walking any closer."

Pointing his finger at Jack, the sheriff added, "Stay where you are and don't get in my way!"

Jack bowed farther toward the ground, still on his knees, not appearing to hear. Ana had knelt down to his level and had her left arm around his shoulder.

The sheriff took a circular path toward the drills, avoiding the dirt road. He moved carefully, inspecting the ground with each step. He stopped twenty feet short of Mariah's body, studied the scene, and retreated to his police car, watching Ana and Jack kneeling on the frozen ground.

Ana hugged Jack, feeling him shiver. "You don't have a coat on—you must be freezing to death. Come with me and sit in my car until the sheriff finishes his work. There is nothing we can do at this point."

Tears streamed down Jack's cheeks. "I don't believe that," he cried. "I saw her last Friday afternoon. I wanted her to have dinner with me, but she refused, saying she had other plans. Oh, God. I can't believe this is happening. Tell me I'm dreaming!"

Ana helped Jack stand and put her right arm around him as they walked back to her car.

"Do you want me to turn off your pickup?" Ana asked as Jack staggered to the hood of her car.

Jack nodded, and Ana walked to the Chevy pickup, turned the engine off, took the keys, and shut the door. She turned back to her vehicle and saw Jack, head down, hands on the hood, shaking his head. Ana led him to the passenger side of her car, opening the door and getting him seated.

Fifteen minutes later, Montana Highway Patrolman Sam Loftus arrived, followed by two deputies from the sheriff's office carrying cameras and plastic evidence bags. Fifteen minutes later, the coroner in his hearse drove up behind Jack's pickup.

Coroner Pat Crawford took his time surveying the scene in front of him from his black hearse, making no attempt to leave the comfort of his warm seat.

The sheriff came to his car door and leaned his head close to the driver's side window. "It took you long enough to get here. What kept you?"

Crawford held up his left hand. "You are not going to let me close to that body until you get your work done, are you? So, do what you have to do. I suppose you will want me to take the body to Great Falls for an autopsy, but tell me what you think happened."

As coroner, Pat had the authority to take charge of the investigation but preferred to allow the sheriff to do the work. In the end, Pat would authorize an autopsy and issue a death certificate.

"I don't know what happened," admitted the sheriff. "The victim has a deep head wound, and she is positioned in a way that indicates a sexual assault. She is naked with her left leg on the drill and her right leg on the ground." The sheriff hesitated, then added, "You are right about taking our time and getting this right."

"If you need me, wake me up," said the coroner. "You know I am here to help, and I can officially pronounce the woman dead and order an autopsy once you're finished—I think we need to have Doctor McPhillips in Great Falls do that work."

The sheriff nodded, then walked back to the grain drills.

The deputies had been instructed to start their investigation and gathering of evidence. A deputy stood on top of the middle drill with his camera pointed down at the body. His face had lost its color, and he slapped his free hand against his leg to stop it from shaking.

Deputy Severtson called the sheriff over to the dirt roadway closest to the body and the drills.

Tire tracks were clearly visible between the ice and snow remnants.

"Try and get imprints from those tracks," ordered the sheriff. "And gather up that broken piece of bronze in the center of the road, but be damn careful where you step."

The deputy slowly walked to the bronze piece and with gloved hands placed it into a plastic evidence bag, taking his time labeling the date and time.

"Looks like this might have been dragged from a vehicle," ventured the deputy. "What do you think?"

"Yeah, you might be right," the sheriff agreed. "Hang on to the evidence bag and make sure you record the facts, then sign and seal it."

The sheriff turned his attention to his other deputies, who continued to search for other items.

After another fifteen minutes sitting in Ana's idling car, Jack had stopped crying and finally broke the silence.

"I want to go back to the ranch."

Ana, still holding his hand and giving Jack an occasional hug, nodded. "Can you drive your pickup, or do you want me to take you?"

"I can drive, but I can't stay here any longer. Goddamn this world," he shouted.

"I'll stop by on my way in, but I don't know how long that will be," said Ana. "Are you sure you will be okay?"

"I don't know," replied Jack. "What are they doing down there?" He banged his fists on the dashboard. "Cover her up, or something!" he shouted at the window as the tears began to flow again.

Ana held her silence, giving Jack a squeeze with her hand. *Jack should go home*, she thought.

Sitting here would only make matters worse for him.

"Let me drive you home," offered Ana. "One of the deputies can drive your pickup when they finish. I have your keys and will give them to Deputy Severtson."

Jack gave her a blank stare that Ana took for approval.

After delivering Jack's keys, Ana put her car in gear, turned around, and drove parallel to the hearse. As she passed the driver's side of the black vehicle, she rolled her window down, got Pat's attention, and then told him what her plans were.

"I don't know if I will come back," she said to the coroner.

She turned onto the gravel road leading back to the ranch house.

No words were spoken; Ana couldn't think of any way to console Jack except to be with him.

CHAPTER 24

THURSDAY, JANUARY 15, 1976

Ana drove slowly back to Jack's ranch, trying to process what she had seen. Mariah's nearly naked body on the grain drills was etched into her mind. Ana had not walked closer to where Mariah's body lay because of the description given to her by the sheriff and the warning to not contaminate the scene. Ana could only see Mariah's legs and a portion of her body up to where the sweater and bra had been pushed.

Ana turned to Jack, who sat in the passenger seat with his head bowed, tears in his eyes.

Ana, processing the reality of their situation, broke the silence. "I feel so helpless. I can't tell you that everything is going to be all right because it isn't right. I want to help you to get through this, but I don't know where to start, and you will have to help me too."

Ana paused, waiting for a response.

"Talk to me," she pleaded.

Jack grunted but said nothing.

"I'll stay with you as long as you want. I can't leave you alone. I will call Peggy when we get to your ranch. She'll help too."

Getting no response from Jack, Ana sighed, looking at the vast countryside as she made her way to Jack's. Her gaze could find nothing green, only empty Montana prairie with drifts of snow set off by bare ground. The seeded winter wheat, yellow from the freezing weather, lay curled over and dormant in its furrows; no birds were singing, no sounds other than the noise from her car on the gravel road. Ana had loved the wide-open spaces, but today, those sweeping views only brought sadness and a sense of doom.

My God, thought Ana. I don't know how I'm going to get through this, let alone what Jack might do.

I need to talk to Rib, she thought. *How will he take the news?* She wanted to see him and have him take her in his arms, but she shook her head. *That is not a good idea.*

Think straight, she kept telling herself, but the image of Mariah on the drills, coupled with Jack's reaction, weighed Ana down. Ana couldn't decide on her next move as she turned into the entrance to Jack's ranch.

Arriving at the house, Ana walked around her car to help Jack out of the passenger side. Jack slumped over as he stood up, grabbing the open car door. Ana rushed to his right side, giving him support as they walked up the back doorsteps. Ana led Jack to the kitchen table, where he sagged into the chair.

"I'll make some coffee for us," Ana announced. As she busied herself, Jack sat silently. He no longer cried but held his head in his hands, elbows on the table. Ana grabbed a bottle of Canadian Club Whiskey, spiking Jack's coffee and giving her own cup a splashed dose.

"Talk to me," pleaded Ana again. "I can't read your mind. You are hurting. I am too. Talk to me, please. Here, drink this coffee—I've added a kick to it so don't be surprised."

Jack lifted his head out of his hands. "I can't believe Mariah is dead. I talked with her last Friday afternoon, asking her to dinner," he repeated. "I thought she might accept, but she didn't; she had plans." Jack took a deep breath, exhaling out slowly. "Mariah didn't throw me out or tell me she didn't want to see me again so I thought I had made progress with her. Now she is dead. I'll never see her again."

Jack took the cup of coffee, holding it between his hands. His head slumped between his elbows.

Ana walked behind Jack's chair, giving him a hug. She had difficulty maintaining such an awkward stance, but she couldn't leave him so she held on tight.

"Let's go do something," Ana suggested. "Even if it's wrong. What do you do at this time of the day? Feed your cattle?"

Jack tilted his head over his left shoulder, anger on his face. "How can you talk about doing something when Mariah is laying out there in the cold? I need to go back out there and help."

Ana kept her arms around him. "You can't go back out there. Mariah is beyond our help, but we can't sit here all day. Tell me what you would be doing! I don't like this any better than you do, but I can't sit here any longer. Please, let's do something!"

Silence.

"I'm sorry," said Jack. "I shouldn't yell at you." He broke away from her and stood, supporting himself with both arms on the table. "I can't believe Mariah is dead," he whispered. "I thought she would always be here. Even if she wouldn't spend time with me, I could be near her, and now she is gone."

Jack walked to the kitchen window, looking out at the barn and corrals. "I'm out with the cattle around this time, but since Mariah came up missing, I have been taking care of her horse in the afternoons."

"Is the horse here on the ranch?"

"No, it's across from the schoolhouse where Swede lived." His voice had dropped to a whisper again. "There is an old barn there with stalls. Mariah and I had an agreement so she could have her horse close to her."

"Come on, I will drive you over there," offered Ana. "One of the deputies promised to drive your pickup back here. He has the keys. Let him drive it home, but we need to do something, so it's 'feed the horse time.' Can you make it?"

"I saw death during Nam, but this is different. Who would do something like that? I thought of her as the perfect woman. I loved her like no one else. Why did this happen?"

"I don't have an answer for you," said Ana, jarred into thinking that her job as the county prosecutor had suddenly and dramatically changed into that of finding a killer. *Clear your mind*, she told herself. *You have a job to do.*

Going to Jack, she grabbed him by the elbow and started for the door. "Mariah's horse needs to be fed, and you need to move. We can't change Mariah's death, but we can work to find who did this to her. If you have a better idea, tell me what it is, and we will do it."

Jack, unsteady on his feet, caught his balance on the kitchen sink. They left the kitchen and walked to Ana's car.

Ana drove out of the ranch driveway, then turned left on the gravel road that would lead them past where Mariah's body had been found. As they approached the irrigation ditch, Ana could see another vehicle at the scene parked behind the black hearse. The outlines of a man and a woman standing next to the sheriff's car led Ana to guess they were Mariah's parents.

The sheriff's sirens leaving town must have tipped somebody off to the crime, as Jack had guessed the news when the sheriff had driven by with lights and sounds; news traveled fast in Fort Collins. Ana cursed beneath her breath at the siren show leaving the courthouse.

She should have stayed and talked to those people. It would have been difficult, but the sheriff could handle it. Still, Ana felt guilty.

Ana turned her attention to Jack as she drove. "Tell me everything you know about Friday afternoon. Did Swede show up? Or anyone else?"

"No," answered Jack. "Swede didn't show." Jack turned away from Ana. "I don't want to talk about it."

"You have to talk about it," pressed Ana. "You might have been the last one to see Mariah before the murder." The lawyer in Ana came out as the notion crossed her mind that Jack could be the killer. *No,* she thought, *Jack is not a killer type. He has a big ego, but he couldn't have killed Mariah.* Yet, the possibility had reared its ugly head.

"At what time were you talking to her on Friday? Give me the details."

"All the kids were gone, so it had to be after school," recalled Jack. "Mariah had on winter clothes and told me her horse needed some attention. She pretty much brushed me off, but I did ask for her to join me for dinner that night. She refused with a smile. She reached over and touched my arm."

"How did Mariah's mood strike you?" asked Ana.

"Happy, playful, upbeat," said Jack, still whispering. "God, I loved that about her. I thought I still had a chance. I was disappointed and tore out of the parking lot."

"Were you angry?"

"Yes. Why couldn't she have gone to dinner with me?" Jack's voice raised.

"What did you talk about?"

"She headed for the barn, saying she wanted to take her horse for a ride," said Jack. "I asked her if she wanted help saddling up, but she refused. She gave me one of her smiles that melted me down."

"What did you do then?"

"I went straight back to the ranch to help with feeding the cattle. We had an hour of daylight left, and Duke and Cobey were already at the haystack. I joined them, and we finished putting the hay out."

"Where did you spend the evening?"

"I stayed home," said Jack. "Alone." He looked at Ana. "Remember, we had been spending weekends together."

Ana blushed thinking of her weekend with Rib.

"I ate leftovers and watched a movie. I had a couple of whiskeys, then went to bed around eleven right after the first half-hour of Johnny Carson."

"Did anyone see you with Mariah?" asked Ana. "Swede or one of the students or their parents?"

"No one. Absolutely no one. I'm sure of it."

Ana passed the schoolhouse, immediately turned right at the tee, and drove into the homestead, pulling up in front of the barn. Tucker whinnied for them, anticipating hay and attention. Ana and Jack spent an hour feeding and grooming Tucker, mostly remaining silent and thinking of Mariah. The two took turns with the curry comb, slowly brushing Tucker.

Jack spoke first. "Taking care of Tucker is right for me. How about you?" Ana could only nod in agreement.

"I feel a closeness to Mariah," continued Jack. "Mariah spent hours out here. It seemed every time I came to see her, this horse had her full attention. At first, I thought Mariah used Tucker as an excuse, but I came to realize that she loved this horse more than anything. Mariah chose Tucker over me."

Ana didn't respond, realizing that Jack had entered a state of shock. She remembered her reactions after Richard had died, where she forgot all the hurtful things and put Richard on a pedestal. Jack was following the same pattern, saying something that might not be entirely true. Ana guessed the process was necessary as she had heard it many times from grieving families; the departed became a saint upon death.

"I'm going to move in with you," said Ana. "Don't get the wrong idea, but we need each other to deal with Mariah's death. I could help with Tucker and around the house or the ranch. This will be hard on both of us, and being alone isn't an option. How do you feel about that?"

"I don't know. I can't think about it now. I can only think of Mariah. She was an angel."

"Then it's decided," concluded Ana. "I will stay at the ranch and take care of Tucker. It's the least we can do for Mariah, but if we could move the horse over to your place, I'd feel much safer. The school and this barn give me the heebie-jeebies."

"Yeah," said Jack, "whatever you say."

"It's time for us to go back," decided Ana. "I'll fix us a meal, and we could both use a shower. Tomorrow afternoon, I can ride Tucker back to your ranch if you want to keep looking after him.... Do you have a place for him?"

Still grooming Tucker, Jack didn't respond right away. "What did you say? I wasn't listening."

A worried Ana took a moment to decide her next step. *Jack is in another world*, she thought, *and I've got to get him right.*

"Come on, let's go," said Ana. "You close up the stall and barn, and I'll warm my car. Daylight will be gone soon. We need to go back to your place."

Jack took care of Tucker and returned to Ana's car. Ana drove slowly onto the county road, still deciding on her next move with Jack, who stared vacantly out the side window. Ana decided to go back the way they came, passing the murder site. She could have taken a longer route and should have, knowing Jack's condition, but not being too sure of the exact turnoffs, she wanted to be safe.

As they drove by the dirt road leading to the grain drills and Mariah's body, Ana could see the sheriff's vehicles but not the hearse, nor the Morgans' car. *Mariah's body must be on its way to Great Falls*, she realized. An autopsy had to be performed.

"Let's stop. Maybe we can help," Jack pleaded.

"Mariah has been taken to Great Falls," Ana said. "We can't help her now. We must take care of ourselves first so we can find who killed her."

"Mariah is dead, isn't she?" cried Jack.

"Yes, Mariah is dead. She is not coming back, but you and I must move forward. We owe it to her memory."

Ana desperately tried to find the right words to comfort Jack but concluded nothing she said could wipe away Jack's grief. Ana wondered if time would help.

Ana cooked a meal for both of them at Jack's place, but Jack only toyed with his food. They showered individually and went to bed. Ana held Jack until he fell asleep, his emotions spent. Ana tossed and turned until she dozed off.

Upon arising in the morning, Ana dressed in her same winter clothes, awakening Jack as she closed the bedroom door on her way to make breakfast.

Jack stumbled out of bed, trying to remember if yesterday had been a bad dream. *Mariah couldn't be dead*, he thought, but the sight of her body splayed out on his grain drills was forever burned into his mind. Tears came to his eyes as he heard noises in his kitchen.

"Who's there?" he called out.

Ana came rushing back into the bedroom. "It's only me. I've been with you all night and am going to cook us breakfast. Is that okay?"

Jack nodded. "Yeah, but I'm not hungry."

"Get dressed and come to breakfast. You hardly ate anything last night."

The stillness between them as they ate breakfast did not come from the aftermath of tranquility from a lovers' evening. Both sat, enveloped in their memories, tense moments spent reliving Mariah's death keeping them stiff and anxious.

"Did you stay the night?" asked Jack. "I remember we fed Mariah's horse but not much after that."

"Yes, I stayed the night. You are in a state of shock. I'm worried about leaving you alone, but I have to go to my office today. Do you want me to call your mother?"

"No. What good would she do? Besides, I have cattle to look after. Duke and Cobey should be out feeding by now. I'll go help them."

Work would give Jack a purpose today, Ana figured. She wondered how long it would take for him to deal with his grief. Ana still grieved over her husband, and that death had happened years ago.

"I'll come back out this afternoon and ride Tucker back here to the ranch if you have a place for him. Do you have room in your barn?"

Jack didn't answer, still staring out the kitchen window.

"Answer me," demanded Ana.

"What did you ask? I didn't hear you," replied Jack, turning back to face Ana.

"Don't you think it would be the right thing to do to bring Mariah's horse here to your ranch? Someone is going to have to look after Tucker. I can help you because I intend to move out here to be with you."

"I guess that is okay," decided Jack. "Bringing the horse here works for me. There is room in the barn to make up a stall for him. It's the least I can do. I'll go out and get it ready."

"Good," said Ana. "I'll drive to town, check with the sheriff and commissioners, and figure out our next moves. Peggy may want to come out too so I'll stop by and keep her up to date."

Ana walked with Jack to where Duke and Cobey were working. Ana couldn't be sure if either of them knew Mariah had been murdered.

"Have you two heard the news about the schoolteacher?" Ana asked.

Duke indicated he knew, but Cobey had no reaction. Ana thought it strange as word traveled fast in this tight-knit community.

She couldn't think about it now; Ana had to make sure Duke and Cobey looked after Jack while she was at her office.

"Look after Jack, would you, please?" Ana pleaded to the two men. "Mariah had a special place in Jack's world so make sure he is doing okay. I'll be back this afternoon to bring Mariah's horse here to the ranch. Any questions?"

Neither of the men spoke.

Ana hugged Jack and went to her car, soon on her way back to Fort Collins.

CHAPTER 25

WEDNESDAY MORNING, JANUARY 21, 1976

Ana arrived late for work in the courthouse, having come from Jack's ranch rather than her own home. The commissioners would be enjoying their social hour so Ana did not worry about them, but she did not expect Elaine's greeting.

"Get ahold of the sheriff as soon as possible," bid Elaine as Ana entered her office. "He has something you need to see. It sounded important."

"Everything is important to that man," replied Ana. "I hate going to his office. Can you get him on the phone?"

Ana walked into her inner office, closed the door behind her, and then waited for Elaine to buzz the call through. Lifting the phone to her ear, Ana listened as the sheriff told her of the autopsy report for Mariah. They argued about which of their offices should be the meeting place this time around and finally agreed to meet on the first floor, not in any office but in the hallway, halfway between both of their offices.

Ana opened her door and walked down one flight of stairs into the hall, thinking they shouldn't discuss the case in the middle of a public building where the walls have ears.

"Here it is," said the sheriff as soon as he saw her. "It's not pretty, and you will be surprised. The autopsy pictures are included. They show a violent death."

"A surprise, in what way?" Ana asked.

"Just read it and look at the photos if you have the stomach for it. I've got a suspect in my mind, but you are going to have to form your own opinion."

"Is that all you have to say? If we are going to solve this murder, you need to include me in whatever direction you are going. The important thing is to find Mariah's killer. Can't you see that?"

"I can see lots of things," retorted the sheriff. "When I have something concrete, I will let you know. Until then, stay out of my way. You won't find the answer in your law books. I will solve this case by doing work on the ground."

"Where is that coming from? How many times do I have to tell you we need to work together to make an airtight case? Who do you think did this? You just said you have a suspect."

She looked around the hall, wondering how many people had overheard their conversation. The sheriff turned and left for his office without saying a word. Ana stared after him, the heat rising in her forehead.

"I'll find out what you are doing," Ana whispered to his backside as the sheriff disappeared down the staircase.

Ana climbed the stairs to her office, commanding Elaine to follow her into her office. Elaine grabbed a pen and her steno pad and shut the inner office door behind her.

"Here's my problem," Ana declared as she paced her office floor while Elaine sat at the front of Ana's desk. "The sheriff won't cooperate, and I need to know what is going on in his office. Can you get me information about what he is doing? You know more about what is happening in this courthouse than anybody."

"Yes, I can help," replied Elaine. "I have FBI contacts. I'll find out what the sheriff has in mind."

"FBI contacts? There are no FBI offices in this courthouse. Is there something I don't know?"

"It stands for Feed Bag Information," Elaine explained. "You'd be surprised how coffee and donuts loosen tongues. The women in this building do the grunt work and know what is what. Any information in the sheriff's office won't stay secret for long."

"FBI at its finest," said Ana with a slight grin. "The sheriff brags about his FBI contacts and doesn't even know that the best information network exists under his short, stubby nose."

"Is there anything else I can help with?" Elaine asked.

"Give me a chance to read this autopsy," Ana requested. "I'll skim through it first, so sit tight."

Ana read the first page of the nine-page report while Elaine quietly waited. Ana abruptly stopped reading and scratched her head.

"I don't understand some of the medical jargon. Can you tell me what *avulsed* means? Or where the superior-posterior parietal region is? Or what is a basilar fracture? I don't have a clue, but I need to know more about this case than anybody, including the sheriff."

"I'll look them up," Elaine assured Ana, reaching for her pen and pad and writing down the instructions.

"I'm going to rely on your feedback," Ana said. "You are my sounding board so don't be bashful with any theories. Also, I need a rundown on how the community is reacting. We have a killer at large."

"Is that all?" Elaine asked with a puzzled look.

"No." Ana had a glint in her eye. "Solve this case for me! Who had the motive and the opportunity?"

"Right away," replied Elaine, pausing. "You're kidding me, aren't you? My last boss wouldn't ask me to do those things."

"I'm not kidding. What I am serious about is your opinion. I need someone to bounce ideas off of. It should be the sheriff, but he is an ass and thinks he can solve this case on its own."

"Just from what you have told me," Elaine mused, "I can't imagine anyone around here who would commit such a crime. I know bad actors but not depraved monsters. Maybe it's an outsider."

Both women looked at each other as Elaine's last words sunk in.

"Damn," said Ana. "I never considered that possibility! You've helped me already."

"Anything else to add to the list?" Elaine asked.

"Find someone to connect to the crime." Ana settled back into her chair. "We have work to do, and I need to read this autopsy."

Elaine scurried out of the room, excited to be included in the serious business of finding a killer.

Ana turned to the autopsy. Minutes passed as she read the report, cursing silently under her breath at the medical terms and graphic details. Her eyes narrowed as she read what came after Roman numeral IV on the paper, not believing what the pathologist had written.

The quiet stillness of both the front office and Ana's inner office ended abruptly with a loud crash from Ana's office inner wall. Elaine jumped from her chair and rushed into Ana's inner office.

"Goddamn that sorry son of a bitch!" Ana cried as Elaine came into the room. "How could he do such a thing?"

Tears flowed down her cheeks; her shoulders sagged as she stood with her arms supporting her on her desk. The bouquet of plastic posies that once sat on her desk lay scattered among the broken pieces of the vase on the floor.

"What is it? Who did what?" Elaine asked.

Ana collected herself before answering, not wanting to reveal her anger at Rib. She wiped the tears from her face.

"This case is getting uglier and uglier. Not only was Mariah horribly murdered, but guess what else?"

"What?"

"Mariah was two months pregnant at the time of her death."

No words came from either Ana or Elaine, as they stared at each other, weighing the implications of this news. Elaine had put her open palm to her mouth.

But Ana's mind whirled at lightning speed. *Rib is the father*, she thought, and that shit-shed sheriff has fingered him as his chief suspect.

"Oh, God, what a mess," Ana sighed out loud.

"What does it mean?" Elaine asked. Ana shook her head, not wanting to answer.

Ana considered the possibilities. *Rib is the likely father*, she thought. *Damn him to hell. And I am his alibi for the weekend of the murder, except I don't know where he went on Saturday from breakfast to dinner or what he did late Sunday.*

Ana flipped back the autopsy's pages to read the report's page showing the date and time of death, seeing a question mark between *January* and *1976*; no day of the month.

Sighing and casting her eyes to her feet, she turned to Elaine. "The autopsy doesn't show an exact day of death, although Mariah was last seen on that Friday. I'm assuming that is when the murder happened, but it could have been anytime during that weekend. Copy this autopsy, and read it closely."

Elaine took the report to copy it.

Ana retreated to her chair and her thoughts. She pounded the desktop with both fists, pushed her chair back, and stood to retrieve her coat from the closet.

"I'm going out," she said to Elaine on her way out of the office.

"When will you be back?" Elaine asked. "The commissioners want you in their meeting as soon as possible."

"Tell them to put the questions in writing, and I'll get back to them." Ana started for the stairs. "And tell them to stuff it too!"

As Ana entered the hallway, Commissioner Jesus Johnson stepped out of his meeting room, demanding that she follow him as he blocked her path.

"Sorry, I have a murder to solve," said Ana, sidestepping him, wanting to tell Jesus Johnson to mind his own damn business. "Mariah's autopsy just came back. I'm checking on its findings." Ana rushed past the commissioner, who then called after her, "The county needs a lawyer who knows what he is doing."

Ana continued walking, wanting to slap Jesus Johnson. "I know what I am doing," she called over her shoulder.

The commissioner hollered back at Ana's backside. "If you want to solve Mariah's murder, you need to step aside and let us hire a man capable of solving it."

Ana turned around to face the commissioner. Several replies came to her mind, as well as the thought of showing him her special finger. Instead, she raised her right hand, flashing a five-finger salute, and left without saying a word.

Once outside, Ana walked toward her home but didn't stop as she passed it with long strides. She walked another half-mile to the city limits, turned around, and retraced her footsteps to her house. The half-run, half-walk in the cold wind sharpened her mind like a pencil. Inside, Ana collected her thoughts and her emotions, which were flying in many directions; she was saddened by the death of Mariah, angered at Rib's involvement in the pregnancy, and frustrated working with the sheriff and the commissioners.

Ana sat at the kitchen table with her head in her hands, sighing, but no tears wet her cheeks. Finally, she arose from her chair, intent on marching back to her office.

"Get it together," she said to the stillness of her kitchen. "Mariah can't be brought back, but solve her murder. That is your job."

* * *

"Bring that autopsy and the pictures with you," she commanded Elaine as she entered her office. "And some writing material. Let's analyze this case."

"Those pictures are awful, but I can't stop looking at them," admitted Elaine.

"Yes, they are awful," said Ana. "We have to find clues, so keep at it."

The women sat in Ana's office.

"The sheriff has a suspect, but he won't tell me who it is so I need to know what he is doing." Ana paused. "Our priority is finding who his suspects are, and I am trusting you to get that information. But first, I want to talk about the possibilities from what we know. Do you have any ideas?"

"Not yet," replied Elaine.

"Write this down, will you?" asked Ana.

Elaine took her pad and pen in hand.

"Mariah was last seen on Friday the 9th. On Thursday the 15th, her body was found. The autopsy was delivered to us on Wednesday the 21st. Death was caused by a vicious blow to the head, causing severe blood loss. A rope was tied around her neck; there was evidence of sexual assault, and Mariah's body was found on grain drills in sub-freezing weather far from any busy road..."

"And she was two months pregnant," Elaine volunteered.

"Yes, there is that, isn't there?" Ana gritted her teeth. "Does the pregnancy create motive? If so, how do we determine the father? With all his FBI training, the sheriff must think he has found a suspect, but from what I know of proving paternity, it is never 100-percent foolproof. Proving who fathered a child is not exact; maybe it will be someday, but not now."

"Did you tell me Jack Moser saw Mariah on Friday?" Elaine asked, cocking her head as she studied the far wall for an answer. "Or was it someone else? I can't remember."

"I might have told you, but I think the sheriff has someone in mind." Ana hesitated to tell Elaine about Rib and Mariah. "Have you heard anything about Mariah? Any boyfriends? Anything?"

Elaine shook her head.

"What else?" Ana asked, glad to skip the subject of the pregnancy. "The one red tennis shoe found on the floor in Mariah's bedroom matched one found near her body. Mariah bled heavily; the first sign of blood came on the gravel road, along with her watch, and there was lots of blood on the ground around the grain drills, and..."

"Slow down," said Elaine. "You're going too fast for me to write."

"Sorry. I'm trying to picture what happened." Ana collected her thoughts before speaking as Elaine finished writing.

"Let's assume Mariah is attacked in her bedroom because one tennis shoe is found on the floor. Does that mean she knew the person or persons and invited them into her bedroom? That doesn't sound like Mariah...."

"Don't forget the rope around her neck," interrupted Elaine. "I think an intruder forced his way in and strangled her."

"That could be, but the sheriff found the door ajar but not forced open. Do you think Mariah opened the door and let someone in?"

"I don't know," admitted Elaine. "I'm going to have to think about it."

"Me too. Read over the autopsy, and we'll talk tomorrow. Right now, I've got to reread this report. Leave me a copy of what you have written down."

Ana settled into reading as Elaine left the inner office. Elaine came back into the office with a copy of their notes, which she left on Ana's desk before silently exiting.

An hour later, Ana stood up from her office chair and started pacing the room. She had questions that needed answers. Ana buzzed Elaine on the intercom, asking her to set up a meeting with the sheriff tomorrow morning.

Ana reached for her desk telephone.

CHAPTER 26

THURSDAY MORNING, JANUARY 22, 1976

Ana, arriving for work, called Elaine into her office. "What did you find out?" she asked as soon as Elaine closed Ana's door behind her.

"I had coffee with Rosalind. She's in the sheriff's office. You were right. He has three suspects. Rib Torgerson is the main one. Jack Moser and Swede Davidson are the others. The sheriff suspected those Air Force guys checking on the missile sites, but they aren't his focus now."

"Why is Rib the main suspect?" asked Ana.

"As best as Rosalind could tell, Rib's pickup had been seen parked by Mariah's car out at the school late at night on most Fridays since last October. Several of the neighbors verified it. The sheriff's theory is that Rib, as a married man, had an affair with Mariah. She gets pregnant, then Rib kills her. Cut and dried, according to the sheriff."

"That's too simple," argued Ana. "Besides, I know that Rib can account for himself on that weekend."

Elaine looked at Ana with a questioning eye.

"Don't ask me how I know. I just do. However, the sheriff is right about Rib and Mariah, and Rib is likely the father of the unborn child." Ana leaned forward. "This is confidential, you understand?"

Elaine rested the back of her hand on her chin, then slowly ducked her head so her index finger and thumb pinched her lips tight.

"Good. Your trust is essential. I called the pathologist yesterday. He tells me that Mariah's head wound would have cast significant blood in a spray-like pattern from the force of the blow, yet the blood on the road is showing a circular drip pattern. How does that make sense?"

"It doesn't," said Elaine. "I shudder when I think about it. I can't imagine hitting someone like that."

"That brings up your point about the killer being an outsider," mentioned Ana. "But who would know the lay of the land well enough to know where the grain drill was? Answer that for me."

"I can't, but are you sure Rib has an alibi? I can see a married man hiding a pregnancy."

"Mariah had been planning on meeting someone, and it might have been Rib...." Ana postulated.

"How do you figure that?" Elaine asked.

Ana remembered that Rib was to meet Mariah that Friday night. Ana decided to not put that fact in writing and save it for another day.

"Because Jack admitted as much," Ana dodged the question. "He asked Mariah to join him for dinner, and she refused, telling him she had other plans."

"But we don't have any idea who that person is," Elaine pressed.

"No," Ana hedged. "We don't know, but the autopsy indicated that Mariah had freshly shaved legs. A woman expecting to meet someone special would make sure she had covered her bases."

"That's right," agreed Elaine. "A man would never think about it, but a woman would. Did the autopsy really report shaved legs?"

"God, yes, and more. An autopsy strips you naked in every way, even checking under fingernails. The other interesting thing is a small door spring found in Mariah's hair. It had a broken end. If the other piece could be located, we could figure out where Mariah had been." Ana threw her arms in the air and shrugged. "It's a long shot, but we don't have many clues."

"I read the report last night," added Elaine. "It doesn't really offer any insight as to who killed Mariah."

"No, it doesn't," Ana agreed, "but it does give us an idea of what Mariah had planned. Write this down."

Elaine took her pen and notepad, ready to write.

"Mariah had a date for Friday night, so we can conclude she opened the door willingly, but we don't know if the visitor turned out to be the one she expected. If we assume a different visitor, who comes to mind besides Rib? The sheriff has Jack Moser and Swede Davidson as possibilities in addition to the Air Force guys. I discount the Air Force theory, but it is a possibility, so leave it in. Let's think about an outsider. Do you have anyone in mind?"

"No," said Elaine. "I just can't think of anyone I know who could kill like this."

"Also, we have a remoteness problem because whoever did this had to know the area. Who would know Mariah, her schedule, and then be bold enough to knock on her door? Jack and Swede fit that description, but I can't see either one of them killing Mariah. Jack loved her, and Swede is a harmless drunk."

"Both of them would know the area," said Elaine. "Who knows what goes on in a man's mind? Someone driven by sex or money—or jealousy, which would point to Jack. Swede might be harmless, but who knows?"

"I agree. It's got to be sex because the autopsy shows the assault. Who do we know depraved enough to force himself on a woman?"

"I still think it is an outsider," insisted Elaine. "However, the sheriff's theory about Rib is one I could believe."

"But who?" asked Ana, ignoring Rib's involvement. "That area is so off the beaten path, it had to be somebody who lives or works there."

"That limits the possibilities," deduced Elaine. "Rib works for ranchers in that area."

"Who else?" Ana was determined to steer the conversation away from Rib.

"Ranchers and farmers in the area, and the men who work for them?" suggested Elaine. "Hunters or repairmen come to mind. But how to limit it to someone specific, I can't figure that out. Where do we go from here?"

"We keep digging. When is my meeting with the sheriff?"

"At eleven. Also, the commissioners are in today, and they want you to stop by."

"I know what they want," Ana grumbled. "Good old boy Jesus Johnson suggested I take myself off this case and hire an experienced lawyer—a man, he said. I don't need them to complicate finding who the killer is. If they continue to call, ask them to put their questions in writing. It annoys them to death."

"I don't envy you," said Elaine.

Ana sat quietly, thinking over the possibilities. Finally, she asked Elaine, "What is your impression of the sheriff?"

"Like pulling teeth," said Elaine. "At first he didn't want to meet you, but then he became all excited about some idea he had. Who knows what goes on in that man's mind?"

"Power," answered Ana. "Power drives the sheriff, and that leads to bad decisions. Pulling teeth is a perfect description of where we are right now in this case."

* * *

The sheriff arrived at Ana's office ten minutes after eleven.

"What do you want? My time is important," he growled without preamble.

"Solving Mariah's murder is more important than your time. We have to work together. Do you have any suspects?"

"I can't give you that information, but what I do need from you is a John Doe search warrant."

"You have to be kidding me. A John Doe warrant?! It might be possible in a special set of circumstances, but you have not given me anything concrete. Where is your evidence?"

"You'll have to trust me," said the sheriff.

"Like I did in Gus's marijuana case? I thought you had learned your lesson."

"Trust me because I know who killed Mariah. I just need more proof."

Ana's shoulders slumped, and she drew a deep breath before speaking. "You know about the Fourth Amendment, searches and seizures, probable cause, and the concept of innocent until proven guilty, right? Who is your suspect?"

"You don't need to know," answered the sheriff. "At least not now. Get me the search warrant, and I will solve this murder."

"I'm not going to a judge without evidence. Give me a name and something tying that person to the scene. I did mention probable cause, didn't I?"

The sheriff ignored her question, still standing with his arms crossed.

"It's deliberate homicide, not murder," corrected Ana. "I can't go to a judge on your word alone. Get me more facts, and I will help you."

The sheriff sat down, glaring at Ana. Ana glared back, waiting for him to speak.

"All right, my main suspect is Rib Torgerson. He had an affair with Mariah and probably got her pregnant. I need a saliva test to determine blood type proving he is the father—that gives him motive. Is that enough for you?"

Ana bit her inside cheek, thinking she was dealing with an idiot.

"No. Just because you think someone committed the murder isn't grounds for a warrant. Can you tie Rib to the scene of the killing? What if he has an alibi? A judge will laugh me right out of the courtroom."

"You aren't helping," grumbled the sheriff. "Rib has motive if he is the father of the unborn child. She demands he marry her. He refuses and kills her. That's what you call motive."

"I call it speculation," argued Ana. "It's a possibility, but you need more facts, and you can't go on a fishing trip with a search warrant unless you tie him to the scene. Can you put him at Mariah's on the weekend she went missing?"

"No, but I can prove it if you get me a search warrant."

"Tie him to the scene, and you get your search warrant."

Ana sighed, struggling to keep her temper under control.

"I didn't write the law on search and seizure. It's a judgment call to determine probable cause, and the judge makes the final decision. Facts are what I need. Give me solid ones."

The sheriff sat up and moved from his chair, ready to leave. Ana commanded him to stop.

"You don't need to ignore me. Include me in your investigation. What do you think happened?"

The sheriff used the back of a chair to lean on as he answered. "The crime was committed by someone who knew Mariah. Her door was not forced. She let someone in, and the situation deteriorated. One tennis shoe was found near her bed, the other at the drills where we found her. The killer had to have known Mariah and the area."

"I agree with you," said Ana, surprising the sheriff.

"Then why can't you get me a search warrant?"

"Because you can't tie Rib to the crime on that particular weekend. You may have motive, but opportunity is the other part of the equation."

Their eyes locked, neither smiling nor speaking. The sheriff blinked first, turning and leaving the room.

Ana sat down, rubbing her forehead with her two hands, thinking about the sheriff's inflexibility. What a waste of time, she thought. Why can't I have a decent conversation with that man?

"Elaine, come in here," she called. "We need to talk."

CHAPTER 27

FRIDAY, JANUARY 23, 1976

Sheriff Wendell Wagner drove west into the afternoon sun, heading toward Rib's ranch. He had the gravel road all to himself, with time to think through his plan to prove that Rib was Mariah's killer. The Rockies covered his horizon, the north wind blowing steadily cold. However, the sheriff glowed inside, anticipating his interview with his main suspect in Mariah's death. *Rib being the father of the unborn child is the key,* he thought. A saliva sample would do the trick. Even though he had no warrant, the sheriff believed he could get what he wanted from Rib.

Motive and opportunity... He pondered those two concepts, the two keys to cracking this case open. Rib's pickup had been seen often at Mariah's but not on the Friday night Mariah disappeared. That worried him some, but if he could prove Rib was the father of Mariah's child, that proved motive, and all that would be needed was to place him at the scene.

"Damn that woman lawyer, making this hard. All she needs to do is issue that search warrant," he said to the interior of the car.

Rib's white pickup, with the veterinarian toolbox covering the entire bed of the vehicle, made identification easy. The sheriff needed someone to verify the vehicle had been at the teacherage on the weekend that Mariah disappeared.

Swede came to mind as a potential witness, but Swede had been comatose since the attack. Neighbors had seen Rib's recognizable truck at Mariah's on previous weekends but not on the weekend of the murder.

One thing at a time, he reminded himself as his mind raced with the possibilities.

The evidence consisted of Mariah's blood type and that of her unborn child. He would appeal to Rib's sense of fair play. If Rib was innocent, why would he refuse? He would promise that Rib would be eliminated as a suspect. No, he couldn't use the word *suspect*. He would use Rib's standing in the community and mention that taking the test would prove him to be 100 percent innocent.

He would worry about proving opportunity when the time came.

Wagner didn't like Rib. They were the same age and had been competing all their lives, although there had been a time when they were friends, way back in grade school. In junior high, the competition between them had grown more robust, with Rib always seeming to gain the upper hand. And Rib had married Connie, even though the sheriff had asked her first.

Rib's ranch came into view.

Sheriff Wagner wheeled into the immense compound of Rib's home and ranch buildings. The house was surrounded by a lawn, now frozen brown and covered with patches of snow, framed in by a circular concrete driveway. Wagner glanced at the home entrance, shadowed by the tiled roof overhang above it. A stamped concrete porch that extended along the length of the house was so large Rib could have offered ample enough seating on it to fill a restaurant. The house had two stories with bay windows breaking up the brick frontage. Two red-bricked chimneys puffed out clouds of smoke from the warm fires within the ranch's wide walls.

Someone was home; the sheriff longed to see Connie, he realized as he lifted the horseshoe knocker on the front door three times. A flicker of disappointment shot through him as Rib appeared.

Rib did not invite him in; instead, he blocked the doorway. "What the hell is the sheriff of Collins County doing at my front door? You're the worst excuse for law enforcement in Montana."

Iceberg silence settled between the two as their eyes narrowed to slits and their fists clenched; had it not been for circumstances and the cold wind, a fight might have broken out between them on the porch.

The sheriff broke the tension. "Why am I here? Just doing my job, trying to find Mariah Morgan's killer. You *do* know who I am talking about?"

"Am I under arrest? Do you have a warrant? Or is this a fishing trip? You know I'm not going to answer any questions."

Wagner regained his bearings, forgetting all about his interest in seeing Connie. "I've got a murder to solve, so I won't beat around the bush. Your pickup truck—you know, the one with the veterinarian toolbox that makes it easy to recognize—has been seen at Mariah's schoolhouse several times during the past few months. They were nighttime visits. Were you tending to some animal, or to something else? Neighbors can place you at her house, and you know how nosy neighbors are, particularly the women."

"So? What has that have to do with the murder?" Rib asked.

"I need you to give me a spit sample," replied the sheriff, forgetting his strategy. "If you had nothing to do with her killing, you don't have anything to worry about. You're a big dog in this community, always lecturing people about doing the right thing. Well, this is how you can walk the talk. What do you say?"

Rib laughed. "Am I under arrest?"

"No, but you're damn well a suspect," blurted out the sheriff, forgetting his strategy. "This is a chance for you to clear your name. Where were you the weekend Mariah went missing?"

Rib changed the subject. "A fishing trip is what you are on, isn't it? You don't have a clue how to solve this killing. Having fantasies lately about a certain woman, is that it? You would love to have me out of the way so you could pursue my woman. Jesus, Sheriff, get a life."

When Wagner didn't respond, Rib continued, "I've got a damn good mind to run you off this place. The only reason I'm not is that you are the sheriff, and I respect the law. But you are barking up the wrong tree trying to catch this mountain lion. I had nothing to do with Mariah's death, and I have an alibi. Not that I'm going to tell you what it is, but you're on notice that I have one."

The sheriff noted the regular use of Mariah's name by Rib. Clearly, he had known her intimately.

"If you have an alibi, you better tell me right now and save yourself a lot of trouble down the line. Or better yet, give me a mouth swab, and we can end this right now. I've got a kit in my car."

Rib walked past the sheriff to the edge of the porch, hawked up a lump from his throat, and sent it sailing ten feet onto the snow-covered lawn.

"That's the only spit you will get from me. It's time for you to mosey on back to where you came from. Don't be showing up here without a warrant."

The sheriff eyed the wet blob on the frozen ground, knowing there was no way to retrieve it. "You are a damn fool. We could end this right now if you were half the man you think you are."

"Calling me names isn't getting you off my property any faster. Go, Sheriff, before this gets out of hand."

The sheriff reluctantly nodded. "Yeah, I'll go, but you better hope I don't come back with a warrant." Wagner smirked at his own remark, thinking he had gotten the last word.

Rib waved the sheriff off with his right hand.

On his drive back to his office, the sheriff focused on Rib's use of Mariah's name. Rib had not denied knowing her or stopping by her place, and he was too quick to admit he had an airtight alibi. The sheriff scratched behind his left ear. Rib was still in his crosshairs.

Rib stood on the porch, making sure the sheriff had left. Once the sheriff's car had disappeared over the hillside, Rib turned back into the house, slamming the door behind him.

CHAPTER 28

FRIDAY, JANUARY 23, 1976

Deputy Sheriff Jerry Severtson left the courthouse after lunch. He did not call Jack Moser to let him know he was coming, thinking a surprise visit would unnerve the rancher and potentially lead to more information. Jerry was concerned over the sheriff's focus on the three suspects, particularly Wagner's conclusion that Rib was the killer.

Jerry didn't have a search warrant.

Jerry petted his dog, continuing his custom of discussing his thoughts out loud with the blue heeler. "Mungo," he said, "this trip out to Jack's could be a goose chase. I don't even know if he is home, but I want to surprise him. Sometimes it works to show up without warning. Guess we'll find out how he reacts. What do you think?"

The dog lay on the front seat, casting a quizzical eye to the deputy.

"This murder makes no sense, does it?" he said to Mungo. "Everything happened in one of the county's most rural areas, so you would think it would be someone local." Yet, Jerry decided none of those suspected by the sheriff were killers. He drove on, lost in his theories.

Deputy Severtson took the Valier exit off Interstate 15, turning to his right and coming to the county road leading to Jack's ranch, where he turned left. His thoughts were still on the three suspects.

"Rib is an outstanding citizen," he said to his dog. "Jack, while younger, is an up-and-comer. Swede is Swede, harmless, wanting to be left alone. No, none of those three killed the schoolteacher. But who else knows the backroads out there? The woman was pregnant with no known boyfriends. What's that all about? Too many questions. People in town are nervous and want an arrest. How do we lock someone up if we don't have clues?"

Silence filled the rest of the drive. Upon arriving at Jack's ranch, Jerry took in the scene. Three men were bundled up against the wind, currently unloading a semi-truck of baled hay. Cows were bawling in the corrals waiting for their dinner, and smack dab in the middle was Fat Jack Moser, with Duke and Cobey.

Fat Jack worked right along with his men. Deputy Severtson knew him to have returned from Vietnam a party hound, but Jack was fit enough to sling hundred-pound bales of hay as if they were made of foam plastic.

Jerry pulled in near the men and rolled down his window.

He called to Jack, "Hey, you got a few minutes?"

Jack glanced his way, scowled, and then pulled off his gloves.

"What do you want? We are busy here trying to beat the wind blowing up a snowstorm."

The deputy didn't move, and Jack shrugged.

"Okay, let's get out of the cold and have some coffee," he finally offered the deputy.

Jerry agreed, as he got out of his car while telling Mungo to stay.

He hesitated regarding whether to come right out and tell Jack the sheriff's suspicions or make this friendly. The latter was his choice. Neither Jerry nor the sheriff had enough evidence to accuse anyone. *Get some facts*, he told himself, *and build a foundation*.

The two men walked to Jack's kitchen door where Jack reheated coffee left over from the morning breakfast. He poured a cup for Jerry, and filled one for himself, as they sat at the kitchen table across from each other.

Jerry decided to be honest.

"Jack, I'm here about the schoolteacher; we have very few leads on the killing. The body was found on your land. Death was by a heavy blow to the head. There was no sign of blood in the schoolhouse, and we don't have any concrete evidence or suspects. We know you had an interest in the woman. What can you tell me about her?"

Jack went quiet, instantly on the alert, suspecting a deeper motive.

"I can't tell you much," said a suspicious Jack. "Mariah was younger than me and only wanted to be friends. I wanted more and gave it my best Montana try, but it didn't fly. I hadn't seen her except at church. Wait a second—I did stop by to see Mariah that Friday afternoon."

"Why did you stop by?" asked the deputy.

"I asked her if she wanted to have dinner with me, but evidently, she had other plans because she refused my invitation."

Jerry wanted to ask where Jack ended up that night but decided that was too obvious. Since Jerry had batted blind, he couldn't tip his hand. The question should be asked, but not at this time. He had gathered the fact that Jack had seen Mariah on the Friday she disappeared.

Jack was ahead of him.

"Why don't you ask me where I was on that night? We could spend all day circling your purpose here, but I've got a storm to beat with hungry cattle."

"The sheriff sent me out here to get information," said the deputy. "I'm doing my job."

"I watched *Run, Rabbit, Run* on television by myself," Jack said. "And Johnny Carson at ten-thirty before going to bed...alone."

"Thanks, I was wondering how to get around to that question," admitted Jerry. "That doesn't mean I think you did it, but checking out any leads is what I do. You made it easy on me. Do you have any ideas about who killed Mariah?"

"I didn't do it," Jack said. "I loved her and wanted to marry her. I don't have any idea who killed her, but whoever did should be hung from the tallest tree. And you are barking up the wrong one if you think I had anything to do with it."

"I didn't say you had anything to do with the murder."

The two men stared at each other.

"Finish your coffee. I've got work to do," said Jack.

The deputy gulped the last of his coffee, then walked ahead of Jack and stepped out the door. He couldn't rule Jack out as a suspect because of his lack of an alibi, and jealously could be a motive. *Oh, hell,* he thought, *Jack isn't capable of killing a woman he loved.*

On second thought, it could have been a rejected lover killing—and Jack had claimed his innocence all too quickly, even before any accusations had been lobbed against him.

He wondered how the sheriff had made out questioning Rib.

CHAPTER 29

MONDAY, JANUARY 26, 1976

After work, Ana and Peggy met in the back of the liquor store.

Ana paced back and forth, the Fort Collins newspaper in hand. "Damn that editor! He comes off like some expert on crime, but basically, he's a drunk. It's obvious where he is getting his information: our tough-on-crime sheriff! Who, by the way, doesn't have an original thought in his head either."

Peggy was listening with a sympathetic ear but added nothing to the tirade. She sat quietly, enjoying her straight gin, relaxing in the recliner.

Ana lowered the newspaper so she could see Peggy's reaction. Peggy shrugged her shoulders.

Ana raised the paper to her eyes as she stopped pacing, and continued reading.

"The death of Mariah Morgan is a stain on our local county attorney. This killing was a hideous act of rape, torture, and murder. The person responsible is still in our community and, like the rabid dog he is, needs to be captured and shot on the spot. His continued freedom shows the futility of the current county attorney. Justice must be swift and certain.

However, there has been no arrest nor much progress toward one. Our sheriff has several suspects, but he has not been able to obtain a search warrant to further his investigations because our county attorney refuses to go before a judge to obtain one..."

Ana took a deep breath. "It goes on and on, but you get the point. This has the fingerprints of the sheriff all over it. Can you believe the editor refers to Wendall as 'our sheriff' and hangs me out to dry as though I am impeding the investigation? I should go over to the publisher's office and tell that poor excuse of an editor that I was sleeping with the main suspect on the night of the murder. Though I doubt that would help my case much."

Ana crumpled the newspaper in her hand and threw it at the wastebasket. "Damn it."

"Yep, the sheriff has dumped a pile of crap on you. What are you going to do?"

Ana raised her hands in the air. "I don't know. And that's not all. In the mail today, I got a letter addressed to the county attorney from Ella Laughlin. Do you know her?"

Peggy shook her head.

Ana walked to her purse, took the letter out, unfolded it, and shook it at Peggy.

"I don't know her either. Anyway, this do-gooder starts out with 'Dear sir...' Hell, she doesn't even know I'm a woman. Do you want to hear what she said?"

"Absolutely. I need some entertainment while I finish my drink. And, honey, you are on a roll."

Ana ignored the jab holding the letter in her left hand and began reciting.

"'Dear sir, I am writing to you to let you know I am concerned about the crime that has been committed in our county. Mariah was a very dear person and a credit to our society. How anyone could commit such a brutal act is beyond me. I hope you will do everything in your power to see that justice is done. So many crimes have been committed and left unsolved. Let us get these criminals and put justice to work for the victims. God be with you in your work for justice. Sincerely yours. Ella Laughlin.'"

Ana, frustrated, waved the letter in the air.

"What kind of person writes a letter like this? Justice for whom? Mariah has no justice. She is dead. The editor wants justice too, and a shooting, and so does this woman, whoever she is. Are you sure you don't know her? I think this is all part of a coordinated attack. A newspaper editorial and a personal letter on the same weekend with the same message. Too much of a coincidence for me."

"You are absolutely right," Peggy agreed. "Now, do you want to hear about my weekend with Rod?"

"Hell, no." Ana sighed. "You have to help me figure this out." Ana paused, waiting for a reaction from Peggy. Seeing none, she announced, "I've got a theory about Mariah's killing!"

Peggy shrugged. Ana continued, "It's more of a feeling, or dare I say it, a woman's intuition. The sheriff is right about this crime being committed by someone who knew the lay of the land. I'm sure Mariah was attacked at the school, then driven to the grain drills by someone who knew exactly how to get there. That narrows it down to the owner of the land, his help, or his neighbors. You following this?"

"Are you accusing my son of this murder?" Peggy stood up, ready to fight. "Watch your step. You know I get real mean when somebody attacks my family."

Ana, sensitive to Peggy's mother-bear protectiveness regarding her son, assured her that Fat Jack was not the prime suspect.

"Your son is not a killer. He is a kind and gentle soul with an outsized ego. Oh, he can be difficult, but he isn't a killer."

"Thank God you have come to that conclusion. You are smarter than you look."

"Thanks for the vote of confidence," retorted Ana. "Listen to me, I had the weirdest set of goosebumps when Jack and I were helping unload hay for the cattle. One of his hired men gave me such a look, it scared me to death, giving me the willies because he looked at me like a piece of meat. Have you ever had that reaction around a man?"

Peggy became more serious. "Yes, the sensation is not describable, but it's real. A woman has the power to read people. You can call it intuition, but it is something more. It's a fear of not being in control or dealing with a situation where you could get hurt. I don't think men recognize it."

Ana nodded knowingly. "It's only a hunch, but I don't have anything else. This hired man is my only possibility right now. I don't know where else to look."

Ana left the liquor store, dreading the coming time at Jack's.

CHAPTER 30

WEDNESDAY, JANUARY 28, 1976

Ana had been staying at Jack's since Mariah's death. The two weeks had passed slowly, but Jack's willingness to return to his rancher personality became stronger as each day passed. Ana brewed coffee, scrambled eggs, and sizzled up bacon and hash browns every morning. Today, Jack intended to drive a load of cattle to the Western Livestock Auction west of Great Falls, a trip he had put off for the last two Wednesdays. High winds were ongoing but with sunny skies and temperatures in the mid-twenties.

"You are hurting," said Ana. "And so am I, but life is for the living, and we must go on. Mariah is not coming back. You have to accept it and move forward."

"Yeah, I know," said Jack. "It's hard right now. Maybe this trip to Great Falls will be good for me. There are times I want to give it all up. My dad had the right idea, leaving this ranch for sunnier days in Hawaii. Maybe I should join him."

"You can't run away from this," said Ana. "You are getting better every day. I'll be here for you. You are strong, so you must look ahead. You've got a ranch to run."

Jack could only nod his head in agreement.

"I need your help too," Ana murmured when he didn't answer, her eyes steady on his. "Mariah's death has been hard." Jack kept nodding. They sat in silence.

Finally, Jack sighed and lifted his cup of coffee to his lips. "I forget you are hurting too. Has the sheriff come up with any suspects?"

"Yes, he has," said Ana. "You are one of them as you know from the deputy's visit. I can't tell you the others. But the sheriff's theory is that the killer knew the area well enough to leave Mariah on those grain drills, and I agree with him. You own the land and the grain drills, and you've been placed with Mariah on the afternoon she disappeared. Plus, you don't have an alibi for that evening. Jealousy might be a motive, but we have no real evidence placing you at the scene. However, you are on the sheriff's list."

"I didn't kill Mariah. I wanted to marry her," he said as he had so many times in the past.

"But the sheriff has a theory, and he can be a bulldog," Ana reminded him. "He considers everyone capable of committing a crime. If he can tie you into the scene, he will come after you with an arrest warrant. However, I follow the law and make the decision of who goes to court. Keep in mind, though, you will most certainly be arrested if the sheriff can connect you to the crime."

"But you don't think I killed Mariah, do you?" Jack asked with a hurt look.

"Did you?"

Jack's face twisted in disbelief. "How could you ask that question?"

"I'm thinking like the sheriff and not leaving any stone unturned. Did you kill Mariah? You are going to be asked that question time and again."

"Damn it, no, I did not kill Mariah!" Jack's face turned red with anger.

"I don't think you did, but I agree with the sheriff that it had to be someone who knew the area. But the horrible way Mariah died… Nobody I know is capable of something like that. Including you. You are a suspect in the sheriff's mind because of where you live. He can't discard any suspects at this point. Even Swede, in a coma, is a suspect."

"How do I get taken off his list?" Jack asked.

"You don't, not until the sheriff finds more evidence. Right now, all we have is Mariah's autopsy, a small, broken latch spring found in her hair, and the semen samples. Also, a broken copper flange had been found on the roadway next to the drills. No one saw any different activity around the school, and a couple of days passed before Mariah was reported missing. We don't have a lot to go on right now, so be patient."

Ana chose her next words carefully. "I suggest you talk to a lawyer, someone besides me if you have any worries. I would have a conflict of interest, giving you advice. Remember, if anyone asks you about our relationship, tell them I have advised you to see another lawyer." Ana paused, gathering her thoughts. "Hell, tell them nothing. It's none of their business."

"Okay," said Jack, finally smiling. "I can tell people to take a flying leap off a cliff."

Silence reclaimed them, and Jack finished his breakfast and coffee, then slowly stood up from the kitchen table, putting on his sunglasses. He went to the coat rack, retrieving his coat and hat, then pulling out his work gloves.

"Duke and I will load up those cattle and drive to Great Falls. Cobey will stay here to keep an eye on the rest of the cattle." As he opened the door, Jack looked back at Ana. "Are you sure you don't want to come with us? You need a break too."

"No," said Ana. "I need time alone right now to figure out what to do about finding this killer. I will take Tucker for a ride this morning over to the schoolhouse. Thanks to the editor of our local paper and the sheriff, the community is upset over the fact that the murder is not yet solved and no one has been shot vigilante-style over it. The sheriff is being tight-lipped about his investigation. I'm pretty much on my own with this case."

"Will you be here when I get back from Great Falls?" Jack asked. "You are the only person keeping me upright. I need you."

"Yes, I am here for you. I'll be back by five after I ride Tucker this morning and go to my office this afternoon. Would a good steak and baked potatoes do for dinner? I will stop by the grocery store on the way home."

Ana walked to Jack and gave him a hug. "What time do you expect to get back here?"

"We'll see how busy the stockyard is, unload the cattle, have lunch, and watch some of the sales. We should be home around five." Jack hesitated, then returned Ana's hug.

"You are becoming my savior," he said. "I don't think I could have survived the last two weeks without you. Anything you cook is fine. I can't tell you how much it has meant to me to have you close."

Ana smiled. "You mean a lot to me too," she said. "I can't detach myself from the loss of Mariah. I don't think I will ever get over her body stretched out on those drills."

"I don't want to think about it," said Jack. "I feel so empty."

"Duke is going with you to Great Falls?"

Jack nodded.

"Where is Cobey?"

"He'll be out riding herd with his pickup up in the north pasture. I doubt you will see him. Are you concerned?"

"No," lied Ana. "I just want to know where your hired hands are."

"Why would you want to know that?" asked Jack, cocking his head to the right.

"Just curious," Ana replied. "I don't know Duke all that well, and I don't trust Cobey. I'm jumpy and will be until we find Mariah's killer."

Jack didn't respond. His shoulders slumped at Mariah's name, and his head ducked downward as he walked out the door. Ana cleaned up the breakfast table, then followed Jack out to the barn where Tucker had his own stall.

After saddling up, Ana led Tucker outside, waving to Jack and Duke, and they loaded fifteen head of cattle into the semi. They waved back.

Ana eased onto the saddle. She reined the horse toward the gravel county road. The ride would be three miles each way, time for Ana to clear her head and plan her next moves with the investigation and regarding her future with Jack. She had not talked with Rib since their weekend at the O'Haire but longed to see him.

Oh, God, I'm a mess, she thought as she rode Tucker to the schoolhouse, passing first by the irrigation ditch where Mariah's body had been found.

Ana wanted to look at the schoolhouse and visualize what might have happened that night with Mariah. The thought of Maria's death sickened her.

She would keep her obligation to Jack. The past two weeks had made their relationship more like that of a parent and child than of lovers; she wondered which role she played. Ana tried to anticipate how to proceed with Jack, finally deciding to take it one step at a time. Before Ana had time to make any decisions, the schoolhouse loomed in front of her.

Wow, she thought, *that ride didn't take long.*

* * *

Ana arrived at the school's front entrance, bringing Tucker to a stop. She soothed him with gentle words and a soft pat on his shoulder before dismounting, which he seemed not to mind one bit. Ana led Tucker by his reins as she peered out over the grounds, picturing an evening ending in murder.

Ana assessed the facts known to her. But they didn't identify a killer, she concluded.

Ana led Tucker around to the building's west side and looked north to the gravel road, where the stain and watch were found. Ana closed her eyes, imagining Mariah being dragged from the building, tossed over the fence, and then what? Was she placed on the road or in a vehicle? The circular designs of blood on the road stumped her. To Ana, that meant the fatal blow to the head had been struck on the road, but the blood splatter would have to be in a fan-like pattern. The rope around Mariah's neck indicated she had been rendered helpless, most likely while inside the building. *But that is a guess too*, she thought.

A picture slowly formed in Ana's mind.

Yes, the first attack occurred in the building, but no broken lock or door, indicating Mariah had let her killer in. Ana remembered Rib telling her that Mariah wanted to see him the night Mariah disappeared. Would Mariah have opened the door expecting Rib?

Why had Mariah been dragged out of the building, her body taken to another location? Ana shook her head, thinking; there were so many unknowns. Only the person who did this could give her the answer.

Mariah's body had been driven west from the school building. What type of vehicle could she have been transported in? Ana didn't have an answer, nor did she know which direction it had come from. *If only someone had been here*, she lamented.

Looking at the closed schoolhouse only added to her despair and sadness. Tears came to her eyes as she thought of the young, vibrant woman now dead. Ana mounted Tucker and turned to head back to Jack's ranch. As she did, her resolve stiffened as she said to the Montana countryside, "I'll find that son of a bitch if it's the last thing I do."

* * *

Ana looked at her watch as she rode back into Jack's ranch, no closer to solving the case than when she had started. Her focus had been on the murder, not Jack or Rib.

The sun had reached its high point of the day in the southerly sky. She ignored the hunger pangs in her stomach. She would eat when she returned to Fort Collins. Peggy might need a break, and Ana needed someone to talk to.

A few months ago, Ana had thought that her life couldn't have gotten any more complicated, but since Mariah's death, she had been buffeted by new challenges. She had a murder on her hands and very few clues as to who had committed the crime. Her relationship with Jack, Rib's affair, and even the constant frustrations of her county attorney job paled in comparison. Ana wanted to shout her frustration out loud.

"Shit!" was all that came out.

As Ana approached the barn, riding tall in Tucker's saddle, she winced as she saw Cobey working on the old Dodge pickup right in front of the barn door. He had not been there when she'd started her ride. The Dodge's hood, lifted up, concealed Cobey completely as he had his head deep into the motor well.

Ana thought she could ride by him, and he would not notice until she had passed by the vehicle. The Dodge's tailgate hung down, opened to expose the pickup's bed; the bold letters on the end gate on the vehicle were inverted, as though looking in a mirror.

Nearing the vehicle's backend, Ana's eyes caught different black shades on the rear right-hand metal side and the wooden planks of the pickup's bed. The area's darkest black looked fresh; Ana guessed spray paint. A large piece of cardboard and a wooden toolbox that sat in the middle of the pickup bed also had splashes of new black color on them in an irregular pattern.

Ana could see a sizable, two-inch copper valve for an irrigation pipe with a broken rim and an eighteen-inch-long, heavy engine manifold, freshly painted black, along with various broken or discarded metal objects.

The pickup bed's wooden planks seemed out of place to her; she thought all truck beds were basically one piece of metal.

Ana, from her perch atop Tucker, could see right into the bed of the pickup, which was comprised of strips of eight-inch-wide wooden planks fastened together by three-quarter-inch strips of metal nailed into the wood. Oddly colored stains of black and red on the wooden bed met the pickup's metal sides. Ana immediately saw other distinct reddish colors showing on the edges of the fresh paint, extending from the crack caused by wood and metal joined at a ninety-degree angle. Those stains crossed the first board next to the metal side, then covered over the first metal strip and the second board beside it.

Ana had not thought of the possibility of a wooden floor in the back of a pickup. She pictured Mariah lying unconscious, her head pouring blood onto the wood, which had then seeped down through a crack where the wood met the metal side at that ninety-degree angle and on to a graveled road in a circular pattern. Ana needed to look under the bed of the pickup.

Ana climbed off Tucker, walking to the right rear of the Dodge. She bent down, looking at the tires and beyond them to the heavy-duty leaf springs right under the wooden planks of the pickup's floor bed.

"Oh, my God," she blurted out with her right hand to her mouth.

Between the tire and the pickup frame, red stains covered the ends of the springs. Tucker whinnied, and Cobey peeked his head out from the hood.

"I didn't hear you come up," said Cobey. "What are you looking at?"

Ana froze. *Mariah's body had lain in this vehicle*, she thought, *driven by this man*.

"Nothing, really," Ana said as casually as possible. "I had never seen a pickup with a wooden bed. How is it attached?"

Both were silent.

"Aren't pickups these days all metal?" Ana pressed.

"This one ain't new," answered Cobey. "It's a 1948 model. That's how they built them in those days. What are you looking at back there?"

"Nothing," hastily replied Ana. She hurried to Tucker's side. "I've got to take care of Tucker and then go into Fort Collins. Do you need anything from town?"

Cobey gave her a suspicious look. "Is that all? You shouldn't be poking your nose where it's none of your business. You've come out to this ranch asking a lot of questions about that schoolteacher. I heard that Jack is the main suspect. Is that right?"

"No," said Ana as she led Tucker to his stall. "We have very little evidence and really no suspects."

Cobey grabbed Tucker's reins and Ana's arm in one quick movement, spinning her around to face him. "Don't be getting any ideas about that murder. No one out here is involved—unless it's Jack. Before you came along, Jack had the hots for that woman. My guess is she turned him down, and he couldn't stand it and killed her." Cobey's eyes had narrowed and the veins stood out on his neck. "What do you think?"

Ana, her arm hurting from the firm grasp, tried to pull it away from Cobey's grip, but his hold kept it in place. Ana ignored the question.

"If you just let me go, I can take care of Tucker," Ana hissed out, pain searing through her arm, frightened by the ugly look in Cobey's eyes. "Please take your arm away. Can't you see this horse needs to cool down? Look at the sweat underneath his saddle blanket."

Cobey sneered. "Don't try and evade the question. I asked you who you thought killed that woman."

"I don't know who killed Mariah. But there will be evidence turning up, I'm sure of it. And then the killer will be arrested. Right now, there is very little for us to go on, much less make an arrest. The sheriff will catch a break and solve this case. It works that way every time."

Cobey released Ana's arm with a sudden twist of Ana's wrist. She winced, dropping Tucker's reins.

"I don't believe you when you say you have no clues," he sneered.

Ana picked up the reins and hurried Tucker toward his stall, calling back to Cobey, "It's true. The sheriff has no clue." She entered the barn. "But I do," she added under her breath.

Her mind raced. *I've got to get to town for a search warrant before Cobey catches on that I've got probable cause to search his pickup.*

Cobey walked to the back of his pickup where Ana had been standing. He bent down, inspecting the space between the tires and the undercarriage. His eyes narrowed. He closed the endgate of the pickup and turned toward the barn.

Ana couldn't rush out of the stall until she had taken care of Tucker. As she removed the saddle and blanket, she felt the presence of Cobey behind her.

Ana ducked under Tucker's neck to get to the other side of the horse, now facing Cobey across Tucker's back. He reached under Tucker's neck, grabbing for her, but he missed. Tucker nipped at him, catching the man's right ear. Cobey threw his fist at the horse, delivering a glancing blow to his head. Tucker reared up with his front hooves and came down hard on Cobey's right boot. Cobey swore at the horse.

Ana slipped away to Tucker's rear, thinking she could reach a pitchfork, but Cobey, though limping, ducked around Tucker and grabbed Ana's arms from behind, twisting her shoulder sockets painfully. Tucker reared up, then slammed his back hooves down onto the floor of his stall, trying to break away from his tied-up halter.

The pain from Cobey's grasp tore at Ana, but she couldn't move.

God, she thought, *this man is strong.*

Cobey pulled her back into his chest. He spat the words into her ear: "You know, don't you? You know I killed that dumb schoolteacher. She asked for it, being so high and mighty. She's just like all schoolteachers, giving out punishment, acting like gods. Well, she needed a sex lesson, and I gave her one, plus a little extra."

Ana tried to break free, but Cobey turned her around to face him. His eyes shone with cold hatred.

"Let me go, you animal!" she cried. "Why? Why would you kill her?"

"Did you ever have a teacher hit you? Well, I have when I was too young to do anything about it. Here is what it feels like."

Cobey released his grip on Ana's elbows and slapped her with his right hand. Ana tumbled to the ground, her head ringing, shoulders still aching. She still thought she had a chance, thought she could fight back. But before Ana could react, Cobey had stood her up and backhanded her, sending Ana into the wall of the stall. Ana heard Cobey's voice through the fog in her head.

"I killed her and left her lying in the school. If my damn pickup had started, I would have walked away, and no one would have known. But, damn my luck, I had to get Swede to jump-start the pickup. He could place me at the scene, so I had to eliminate him, which I did the next night by busting a pool cue over his head. I didn't think he would survive, but he is a tough old nut."

Ana could not speak; her mind told her she wouldn't survive this.

Cobey lifted her up again with an animal look in his eyes. "You are going to take a ride in my Dodge pickup, just like that schoolteacher, right after I give you a sex lesson."

Ana felt his fist slam into her face at full force, heard her nose crack before she fell unconscious to the floor near Tucker's rear hooves. Cobey kicked her head and body repeatedly, cursing in pain from the injury Tucker had caused to his right foot.

Cobey grabbed Ana's heels, dragging her to the stall's wall, pinning her body against it. He apprised his unconscious prey. "We'll have our lesson, and then you get to take your last ride," laughed Cobey. "But first, I'm going to teach that goddamned horse a thing or two for stepping on me."

PART THREE
THE AFTERMATH

CHAPTER 31

MEMORIAL DAY WEEKEND, MAY 29, 1976

Four months later on the Saturday morning of the 1976 Memorial Day weekend in Montana's Northern Rockies, the dawn broke with clear, blue skies and a soft wind from the east. Spring had come to the Two Medicine in its most delicate splendor. The meadows lush with green grass, the mountain air crisp, and squirrels and chipmunks chattering through the pine trees all tried to calm Ana's sense of turmoil on what she knew would be a watershed day.

Ana had driven to Rib's cabin on Saturday morning, declining an offer to spend Friday night with him. She planned to spend the late morning and afternoon riding, with a picnic lunch she had packed, then return to Fort Collins the same day. Rib had saddled a horse for her.

They rode in silence with Rib leading, Ana wincing in pain with each step of her horse.

"It seems like only yesterday we were last here," said Ana. "Do you suppose this mountain has a spirit looking down on us in wonder at the great and stupid things we do?"

Rib rode straight ahead.

"You believe in Blackfoot medicine, don't you?" Ana asked, trying to make conversation.

When Rib didn't answer, Ana continued, "So much has happened since last Labor Day. That time is dreamlike. I sometimes have to pinch myself to remember this is reality."

Ana paused again, waiting for a response, but Rib remained silent, pushing his horse straight up the trail.

"The aches and pains in my head...and jaw...and ribs...and basically my entire body keep reminding me that I'm not yet fully recovered from Cobey's beating."

"I'd thank my stars that I was still alive, if it were me," Rib finally said. "Have you pieced together what happened that afternoon?"

"No. Guesses are all we have."

"This is our first chance to be together since you got out of the hospital," Rib reminded her. "Do you want to talk about it?"

Ana hesitated, collecting herself. "It's hard for me because I thought I would die."

"You don't have to say anything," replied Rib. "I understand."

Ana rode forward until she was even with Rib.

"No, I need to tell you about it. But it can wait until lunch."

They continued their ride without speaking until they came to an open meadow, where they dismounted from their horses. Ana's climb down from her saddle sent jabs of pain through the left side of her body. She nearly fell from the agony coursing through her legs and hips as she put full weight on the ground. Rib rushed to her side for support.

"I'm okay," she grimaced a smile as the torment in her lower body subsided. "I need a little time to rest. Ridding a horse is not my long suit."

Rib spread a blanket for them on the green mountain grass. He brought out the picnic lunch as Ana slowly settled onto the blanket. Silently, he reached for the bottle of wine Ana had brought and poured her a glass and one for himself. He waited for her to speak.

Ana sat, looking at the blue sky, framed by the majesty of the Rockies, listening to the sounds of the forest.

"Some of it I remember," she said hesitantly, trying to find a comfortable spot.

"Jack and Duke came back to the ranch after five o'clock. They found me unconscious on one side of the stall floor and Cobey lying dead partway inside the barn's center aisle. The last thing I remember is Cobey laying into me with his fists, calling me all sorts of names. I couldn't fight him. He was too strong."

"Yeah, I can believe that," said Rib, sitting down beside her and holding her hand. "From what I had seen of Cobey, he could handle himself."

"He had chased me around Tucker," said Ana, reliving the moment with tears in her eyes. "I ducked and turned, trying to find something to fight him with. I tried to run to the haystack, where I'd seen a pitchfork, but he grabbed me from behind and nearly pulled my shoulders out of their sockets."

Ana stopped and looked off to the mountains, drying her eyes.

"Then he slapped me twice, and the last I remember is seeing him ball up his fist and his knuckles sailing toward me. The doc said I had marks on my body where he kicked me. A broken nose, a concussion, five broken ribs, and bruises all up and down my left side."

"You didn't see anything else?" Rib asked. "How did Cobey end up stone-dead in the center of the barn?"

"That's where the guessing part comes in," explained Ana. "The autopsy showed he died of blunt force wounds to the head, the conclusion being that Tucker had kicked Cobey full-force with his hind legs. The pathologist who did the autopsy said a horse's kick is like being hit by a car going twenty-five miles an hour."

"Yeah, I've been kicked a few times," admitted Rib. "Fortunately, all glancing blows, but they still hurt like hell, particularly when the horse had been shod. Those steel horseshoes pack a wallop. I did know a rancher up by Cut Bank that got kicked in the head, killing him right on the spot."

"I thought I wouldn't make it either," murmured Ana. "The look in Cobey's eyes nearly paralyzed me. I tried to run. I desperately wanted to do something, anything...but he caught me. I couldn't fight him off. He was just so determined to hurt me. He was enjoying himself. That is what haunts me most. I remember him saying that I would enjoy the lesson and my ride in his pickup."

"You aren't built to fight with your fists," said Rib. "You are better with words."

"Scared doesn't describe how I felt," recalled Ana. "Cobey would have killed me without thinking twice. I know it...and I couldn't have done a thing to stop him. Being helpless is the worst feeling in the world. Thank God for Tucker."

Chief Mountain could be seen to the north and Ear Mountain to the south; Half Dome Crag loomed above them.

"I remember he spat in my ear and told me he killed Mariah." Ana's voice trailed off. "That's all until I woke up in the hospital."

Ana took a sip of wine, the smooth taste calming her. Rib nursed his drink as they sat looking at each other.

"I'm going to miss you in these mountains," sighed Ana. "My best times have been right here. It's hard to let go, but I've got to move away."

"Well," Rib began, surprised at Ana's announcement. He took his time to answer. "You don't have to go. Stay in Fort Collins, and we can be together like this."

"No, although it is tempting. It's time for us to call it quits. You aren't going to change, and I need something more from you than occasional weekends. Mariah's murder, my time with Jack, and nearly getting myself killed have changed how I look at us. Our time together was all fun and games before this happened, but it seems so small now. We are hurting people, and I can't go on. I'm feeling hopeless, and that is as bad as feeling helpless. At least now I can move on to something else besides waiting for you."

Rib didn't respond right away. Ana had more to say but waited for Rib.

"I don't look at it that way," Rib finally offered. "But I haven't gone through the downsides you have. I would like to think you could work your way through all the crap of the past year, but if you can't, you can't. You have to do what you have to do."

"Yes, I do." Ana sat up, angered at Rib's words. "I'm resigning from my job as the county attorney. I don't have a passion for the job any longer. I've got to do something different."

"That doesn't sound like you," argued Rib. "You enjoy being the only woman prosecutor in the state. You were going to run for reelection! Why stop now?"

"I've lost my zip for everything around me, including you," Ana admitted. "You will be the same old Rib, and the campaign would be too much to handle. Politicians are like salamanders who change colors as needed. I want to shout back at the world—I want to tell the truth. I don't want to go through fake promises, either with you or to win an election."

Ana took her time before continuing. "Collins County is Republican to its core, and the only reason I won before is the two idiotic attorneys running against me fought amongst themselves, forgetting I would get a fair amount of the votes. The competition this fall would be Daniel Jacobson, who is younger and won't have an opponent in the primary. I doubt I could beat him in the general election."

Their eyes met before Ana confessed.

"And I hadn't yet recovered from the beating when the filing deadline came so I missed it. I was relieved; not filing lifted a load off my mind. I realized it's time to change my life."

A sunny spot beckoned to them as an outcropping of rock met the grassy field. Rib helped Ana get up, with Ana clenching her teeth from the hurt of the movement. They walked in silence until Ana admitted she didn't want to go any farther. They turned around, still searching for more to talk about, but to no avail.

Upon returning to the blanket, Rib poured another glass of wine for both of them. She lifted her cup to his.

"Here's to our love for each other."

Rib smiled and brushed his cup against hers.

"It doesn't have to end," he offered gently.

"Yes, it does. I'm sad thinking about not seeing you. I'm moving to Helena. I have job offers; it's a question of wanting to stay in government or go with a private firm."

"A big change for you," commented Rib. "I still don't see why you want to leave Fort Collins. Your life has been built around everyone you know here."

Ana shook her head. "But, it's time to make a change. Can't you see that?"

"No," Rib disagreed. "The grass is always greener. I don't think you will like Helena. It's the state capital, which means a lot of insincerity and meetings and boring stuff will be part of the package. It's not you. I've spent way too much time in front of those do-gooder committees and political types who all think they have the answer on how you and I should live. Hell, politicians make it worse for you and me."

"You might be right," agreed Ana. "But I won't know unless I try. It's time for me to move on, even though you are my soulmate. The hardest part will be getting over you, but we can't go on like this. I can't imagine us, five years from now, meeting here at your cabin or spending the weekend in some motel like we have been doing for so long."

Rib took a new tact. "Helena is only a couple hundred miles away. I could come and see you...if you want?"

"I know I would want that, but we have to make a clean break. I've my life to live. Not seeing you will break my heart, but we have to stop."

Ana slowly and painfully stood up, throwing the remaining wine in her cup onto the grass meadow. She hovered over Rib.

"Divorce Connie and marry me!" she blurted out abruptly.

Silence engulfed both of them, neither party willing to speak. Rib stood up with his hands laced together on his chin. Ana looked away, knowing what would come next. An eagle glided above them, the wind blew gently down the mountainside, and the horses were content to munch on the mountain grass.

"Awkward, isn't it? I have no right to ask you to divorce your wife, but the thought popped into my mind, and I had to try. I'm taking your silence as a no. It won't happen. Am I right?"

"Yes." Rib broke his silence. "I'd be an unfaithful husband to you. Connie accepts me, so I will save you more heartache by being honest. You would demand more of me, which would mean fighting about every little thing. You are a lawyer and like conflict, but I would just walk out and leave you talking to four walls. Marriage is not for us. It's what you say you want, but the truth is that no matter how hard you tried to keep me faithful, it wouldn't happen."

"True," said Ana wistfully. "Don't you see I have to leave? Living in our small town, so close to you, would be too much if you weren't by my side."

"I hope this doesn't kill the tree," said Ana as she turned and poured the remaining wine left from the bottle onto a tiny sapling. Rib finished his drink, and they mounted their horses in silence.

The ride back to the cabin seemed to take an eternity.

Ana started to pack her car with the remains of the lunch. Rib unsaddled the horses. Neither spoke until they had their respective chores done. Then they met at the rear of Ana's car.

"Silence is not golden," said Ana. "At least not today. I'm devastated, and you are stubborn. I still love you and always will, but I am a survivor, and I can go on without you. I might find another lawyer to marry and live happily ever after. What do you think of that?"

"Being married to a lawyer would worry me too," said Rib with a slight smile. "If I married you, I would be married to a lawyer."

Ana laughed.

"Damn it. Do you see why I love you so much? You have a way of flipping my words upside down." Tears glistened in Ana's eyes. "We would be so good together."

Ana, brushing away the tears, grabbed Rib's hand and looked up into that square-jawed, blue-eyed, handsome face. "You good-looking son of a bitch, I'd still like to take a run at you."

Rib, with a growing smile, shook his head. "I thought you would start crying and make me feel guilty, but no, you are flirting with me. Or are you making fun of me?"

"A little of both," Ana replied. "You are getting older and more desperate. You had to take up with Mariah because her age gave you hope that you could go on being who you think you want to be. Pretty soon, a good-looking young gal will come along, call you Pops, and tell you that you remind her of her grandfather. Time always wins."

Rib's smile left his face. "Serious talk again? I go day by day. We'll see what happens."

"It's time for me to get back home," concluded Ana. "I don't want to burst your bubble. I've said what I wanted to, and I can live with your decision. I don't like it, but it is what it is. I suppose a brighter day will come for both of us. In fact, I'm going to seek it out."

Ana fell into Rib's arms for one last hug.

"You'll always have a place in my heart," she murmured. "And maybe, just maybe, when you are eighty years old and finally grown up, there might be a future for us. Would you promise me to give that some thought?"

Rib's slight smile returned. "Yes, by the time I'm eighty, I could take a run at you...you good-looking son of a bitch."

Ana reached up and kissed Rib lightly on the lips. "I'm going to hold you to that promise!"

Ana limped to her car door, with tears in her eyes, waved at Rib, started the engine, and roared down the driveway, the gravel thrown from her rear tires nearly reaching Rib.

Rib took his hat off and waved it at the disappearing vehicle. With a giant smile, he said to the mountains: "I'll see that woman again before I turn eighty."

ABOUT THE AUTHOR

DAVID HENRY NELSON's lifetime of experiences as a lawyer, a wheat farmer, and an Oregon State Senator have given him innumerable highs with as many lows. He earned a Juris Doctorate from the University of Montana Law School in Missoula, Montana. He considers his 16 years (1997-2013) in the Oregon State Senate as his most rewarding, and cherishes his days as a Montana lawyer (1967-1981) as his most educational.

As Senator Nelson, David served as Majority leader in 2001, chaired the 1999 Business Committee that produced an Oregon state-wide broadband system, and chaired the Capital Construction Committee as a minority member.

After his retirement from politics in 2013, he began writing fiction and chaired the Board of Trustees for Eastern Oregon University from 2015 through 2020. He received the university's Distinguished Service Award and delivered the 2021 Commencement address.

David's first novel, *Mariah is Missing*, is a fictionalized drama of an actual event in 1974 while he served as the county attorney in Pondera County, Montana. He realized years later that the disappearance of a young school teacher had a long-lived ripple effect on many people, which inspired him to write this book to honor her.

He lives with his wife, Alice, and Boo, a Bolognese dog, in Pendleton, Oregon, home of the world famous Pendleton Round-Up and an amazing whiskey. To learn more about the author and this book, please visit www.davidhenrynelson.com.

CPSIA information can be obtained
at www.ICGtesting.com
Printed in the USA
FSHW010505091121
86078FS

9 781737 717409